Midnight Sea

Other Books by Colleen Coble

Fire Dancer

Alaska Twilight

Aloha Reef series
Distant Echoes
Black Sands
Dangerous Depths

Rock Harbor series
Without a Trace
Beyond a Doubt
Into the Deep

visit colleencoble.com

Midnight Sea

COLLEEN COBLE

THOMAS NELSON
Since 1798

NASHVILLE   DALLAS   MEXICO CITY   RIO DE JANEIRO   BEIJING

Published in Nashville, Tennessee, by Thomas Nelson, Inc.

Thomas Nelson, Inc. titles may be purchased in bulk for educational, business, fund-raising, or sales promotional use. For information, please e-mail SpecialMarkets@ThomasNelson.com.

Scripture quotation is from the New King James Version®, copyright 1979, 1980, 1982 by Thomas Nelson, Inc., Publishers.

Publisher's Note: This novel is a work of fiction. Names, characters, places, and incidents are either products of the author's imagination or used fictitiously. All characters are fictional, and any similarity to people living or dead is purely coincidental.

Library of Congress Cataloging-in-Publication Data

Coble, Colleen.
    Midnight sea / Colleen Coble.
      p. cm.
    ISBN-13: 978-1-59554-140-6 (pbk.)
    ISBN-10: 1-59554-140-3
    I. Title.
PS3553.O2285M54 2007
813'.6--dc22

2006036308

Printed in the United States of America

07 08 09 10 11 RRD 6 5 4

For my agent, Karen Solem—
you are more than a great agent; you are a friend
who tells me the truth.

Words Used in this Book

aloha (ah-LOW-hah): "hello" as used in this book. Aloha is a wonderful word. It's a blessing of love, mercy, and compassion bestowed on the receiver.

fa'e: Tongan for "mother"

honu (HO-new): sea turtle

imu (EE-moo): fire pit for cooking luau pig

kaina (KY-nuh): cousin

keiki (KAY-kee): child

kiu' (KEE-oo): Tongan for "egret"

mahalo (mah-HAH-low): thanks

mahalo nui loa (mah-HAH-low NEW-ee LOW-ah): thank you very much

'ophihi (oh-FEE-hee): a tasty delicacy of limpet

pa'anga: Tongan money

pipipi (pi-PIP-ee): black marine snail

pupus (POO-poose): appetizers

slippers: flip-flop sandals

tamai: Tongan for "father"

vog: smog created from volcanic gases

Hippie Slang

beat feet: leave in a hurry

blitzed: drunk

boogie: cut out

bookin': going fast

bread: money

bug out: leave the premises

bummed: depressed

chick: a woman

choice: really cool

chrome dome: a bald man

climb it, Tarzan: an expression of defiance, usually said while giving someone "the bird"

copacetic: very good, all right

don't sweat it: don't worry about it

far out: excellent, cool

fuzz: the police

golden: cherry

groovy: nice, cool, or neat

hook: steal

kipe: steal

meat: a term for a man

outta sight: fantastic, awesome

righteous: extremely fine or beautiful

shake it, don't break it: said to a girl with a wiggle in her walk

Taylor Camp, Kaua'i, 1973

Thresh tossed a cigarette into the water. "Absolute power corrupts absolutely." The roar of the waves nearly drowned out his words. The six of them were seated Indian style around a campfire on the beach. Thresh glanced around the circle: Blossom, Ash, Goob, Angel, and Reefer. Not their real names, of course. No one here went by real names.

Blossom had her gaze on Ash, and Thresh shuffled on his rock. He knew one way to get her attention. She hated the president. "Nixon is the Antichrist," he said loudly. "Someone should take him out."

"Who cares?" Ash lay back with his head propped on a lava rock.

Thresh slumped when Blossom continued to stare at Ash and didn't even remark on his comment. The sweet scent of roasting marshmallows mingled with the salty breeze. The blue sky was a curtain above their heads. He tried to think of some other way to capture her attention.

"I still haven't seen Elizabeth Taylor," Blossom said, clasping her arms around her legs as she sat on the sand. "Her cousin owns this place. You'd think she'd come visit sometime. She's so fab."

Thresh smiled at her. "No one is more fab than you, Blossom." As fragile as an orchid, she could sit on her black hair. Dressed in a

1

bikini with a ginger blossom in her hair, she looked a little like Annette Funicello. Thresh watched as she fingered the pearl peace symbol on her necklace.

Taylor Camp had been their home for three months. They had inherited the tree house above his head from a couple of residents who got busted for growing weed. The tree house had real glass windows and doors. It looked right up the Na Pali Coast. The camp used to be on the beach, but the winter rains kept washing it out, so the residents took to the trees. About a hundred residents wandered in and out of camp on a regular basis. Thresh never wanted to leave here.

Ash stood. "I'm bored. Let's go for a swim."

Thresh glanced around. The others were all too stoned to move, but a swim sounded good. "I'll go. Want to come, Blossom?"

She shook her head. "I'm going to take some clothes to the stream and wash them. Have fun."

Her dark eyes seemed illuminated from within. He watched her sashay across the sand, stepping lightly from one black rock to another.

"Shake it, don't break it," Ash called after her.

She turned and blew Ash a kiss. Ash grabbed at the air as if he'd caught it, and Thresh wanted to puke. Was something going on between them? "You going to stand there staring all day?" Thresh snapped.

Ash flipped Thresh the bird. "Climb it, Tarzan," he said. He stalked toward the ocean.

If Thresh weren't so angry, he wouldn't brave the surf, but he plunged after Ash, anger giving him power against the waves. The blue-green water enveloped them, and they kicked out in long strokes to get past the breakers. In the next moment, a riptide grabbed hold, and the waves tugged Thresh down. His lungs burned, and he fought the panic that had him in an even tighter grip. The rocky bottom rushed past in a kaleidoscope of brightly colored coral, golden sand, and black lava rock.

The next instant, the churning waves slammed his body onto the bottom. Rocks battered Thresh's chest, and streaks of red ran through the water. Which way was up? He was too dazed to even watch the bubbles rise as they hissed from his lips. He had to breathe! His lungs burned with a nearly unbearable desire to draw in oxygen, but it was impossible to break the undertow. Swimming parallel to the beach, Thresh quit fighting and let the riptide have its way. Ash tumbled past, his eyes wide, and a silent scream opened his mouth. The two collided in the churning current and grabbed instinctively at each other. The tide tumbled them around, then just as suddenly, it released them.

Thresh bobbed to the top like a seal. He took a huge lungful of the best air in the world and stared up into the blue sky. He floated there a moment and tried to collect his thoughts, but he felt another tug, and before he could react, the current took hold again. He managed one gulp of air before the riptide took him under again. Fish rushed past, or rather, he rushed past them. He had a vague impression of parrot fish.

His lungs began to burn again. The current propelled him toward a rocky finger that jutted into the water. If the water rammed him against the rocks, he'd die. Thresh dove deep, trying to break the current's grip. The riptide seemed to weaken, then it took a stronger grip and hurled him toward the rocks, then down along the bottom. He realized Ash was on the same course he was. They rushed through a narrow tunnel so dark they couldn't see anything, adding to the sense of impending doom.

Then the grip of the undertow relaxed. Feeling as though his lungs were about to explode, Thresh kicked up and up, past glowing plankton on the walls, past a colony of shrimp, until his starving lungs could take no more. He inhaled water just as his head broke into the air. The shock of salt water in his lungs made him gag and sputter, but he managed to keep from vomiting.

Ash bobbed up beside him and flailed in the still water. "Where are we?"

"Some kind of cave." The ceiling hovered only about five feet overhead. The water was as clear as a goldfish bowl, and plankton lit the area enough for Thresh to make out Ash's face. Thresh glanced around. "Hey, look at the coral. I've never seen anything like it."

"Far out!" Ash dove to the bottom and grabbed a piece of the lapis lazuli–colored coral.

Thresh knew enough about coral to realize they were looking at some of the rarest and most valuable coral on the planet. Aware his mouth was gaping, he closed it.

Ash bobbed to the surface with a piece held up in his hand like a trophy. "Blossom will dig this."

Thresh's heart clenched at the mention of her name. "I thought you were gone over Angel."

Ash shook his head. "I already plucked that flower, man. And she's knocked up. Can you dig it?"

He was always on the make. Blossom would be his next victim. Unless Thresh stopped him. Blossom deserved better. "Hey, dude, do me a favor and lay off her," he said.

Ash widened his eyes. "Jealous, Thresh?"

Ash's smirk sent a white-hot wave of anger over him. Thresh launched toward him, his hands digging into Ash's throat. Gulping in a lungful of air, the hated face went under the water against the coral reef on the bottom. After the ride on the current, Ash struggled very little, and it was over quickly.

Thresh stared at the body floating in the water. He backed away as Ash's body bobbed closer. Then the sea foamed, and dorsal fins emerged from the water. He gasped and flailed back as three tiger sharks zoomed around the enclosure. They were easily twenty feet in length, and he saw a flash of teeth from the closest one. He expected to feel those sharp teeth at any moment as they circled, but the scent of fresh blood pulled them away. They homed in on Ash's body. It was tugged around in the water, then disappeared under the surface. In moments, the sea boiled blood red.

Thresh knew the sharks would not be satisfied with Ash's body for long. They would destroy him next. He slammed his eyes shut and waited to feel the first shark's teeth tear into his leg. His heart thundered in his ears, and he prayed to Kanaloa, the god of the sea. Time stretched out until he thought he would howl. Then the sound of churning bodies in the water faded, and he opened one cautious eye. Then the other.

What was that he heard? Whispers of voices seemed to radiate from the walls, but the sharks were gone. It was a sign. Kanaloa, Hawaiian god of the ocean, must have intervened. Thresh answered the voices: "I hear, Kanaloa. I hear and serve."

one

*L*ife had a way of offering up morsels of pleasure when she least expected it. Leilani Tagama held on to the rail of the old truck as it bounced along the perimeter of the coffee grove. The neat rows of trees resembled laurel with their glossy leaves. The sun shone as usual from a blue bowl overhead, with light rain expected this afternoon, again the usual. The slope of Mauna Loa on the Big Island of Hawai'i boasted a perfect climate for the sweet coffee cherries ripening on the trees.

Her aunt Rina stopped the truck and hopped out. Josie Oliver got out on the other side. Both women still wore the trappings of their glory days—long hair, sandals, and an attitude that could stop an attacking shark. Strands of white streaked Rina's black hair, plaited into a braid that reached her waist. She wore a wild shirt in hot pink and green with a long, flowing pink skirt. Well-worn Birkenstocks let her toes, covered with hot-pink polish, peek out. A beaded headband stretched around her head.

"You get the Sonic Bloom started, Lani. I want to beat feet today and take the afternoon off." Rina opened the back of the truck.

Josie stepped in front of Rina. A big-boned woman with hair more gray than blond, she wore a red aloha shirt and matching bottoms that made her look as if she still had on pajamas. The Birks she wore were the same style as Rina's.

"Let me get that, Rina," she scolded. "That thing will squash you like a gecko."

"I'm a big girl," Rina protested. She moved out of the way. "You spoil me, Josie."

Lani smiled as she watched the two women. They put her in mind of Laverne and Shirley from the old TV show. Josie hauled out the equipment, then Lani went to flip it on. A high-pitched sound similar to birds chirping began to broadcast. Her aunt strapped a tank to her back and began to spray fertilizer on the coffee trees.

"If I didn't see this with my own eyes, I wouldn't believe it," Lani said. The sound made by the Sonic Bloom caused the stomata in the leaves to open up and take in more nutrients. The coffee beans coming off these trees were huge, fancy grade with a wonderful sweet flavor. In the year Lani had been here, she'd seen the growth first-hand. The yield since Rina had started using the system had doubled.

"We hate pesticides," Rina said. "We were willing to look at anything organic." She gave Lani a glance. "I don't know what I would have done without you, Lani."

"I'm thankful for the job." Lani grabbed another tank and joined her aunt and Josie.

"You've got a righteous green thumb. The coffee trees love your touch as much as your orchids do."

This kind of praise soothed Lani's soul like cool aloe vera on a burn. She'd done so few things right in the last few years. "Thanks, Aunt Rina. I made a big sale yesterday. I've been commissioned to design an orchid display for the Home and Garden Show in Kona next year."

Josie clapped her hands. "That's wonderful, Lani! You deserve the recognition that will bring." Her warm glance of approval washed over Lani's face before Josie turned and went back to mixing more natural fertilizer.

"Do you need to cut back on your hours?" Rina asked. A worried frown crouched between her eyes.

Lani's smile faded. Her aunt needed her. "I'll be fine." She clutched her arms. "I'll work on the design in the evenings."

Josie shot a quick glance at Rina. "You'll do no such thing. We can spare you in the mornings. Work on your designs while you're fresh."

Rina nodded, but the frown remained. "Josie is right. We'll manage. You've always wanted to get into landscape design. We won't stand in your way."

Lani shuffled her feet and looked down. Their reassurances only made her feel worse.

Her aunt gave a slow smile. "Joey asked me about you yesterday."

Lani's cheeks flooded with heat. "You don't have to get me wrapped up in an entanglement. I'm not going anywhere."

Rina's frown returned. "Lani, you're being stupid. God doesn't expect you to swear off men."

"Men have been my weakness in the past. I'm trying to start a new life." Her hand crept to her stomach. Men were the least of her sins.

"Such silliness," her aunt huffed. "I believe in God, but your ideas are extreme. You can still have fun."

"Fun is what got me into trouble a year ago," Lani said.

She saw a car approaching fast, dust billowing from the tires. "Looks like Willie."

"I was expecting him," her aunt said in a grim tone. She straightened and put one hand on the small of her back.

The car stopped, and a man with graying hair got out. The grass stains on his khakis matched his green aloha shirt. Lani always thought he looked a bit like a grizzled monk seal—all hanging jowls and wrinkled skin. He strode with purpose across the green lawn.

His scowl darkened when he saw Rina. "You've done it now, Rina. What right do you think you have to keep me from growing what I want on my own property?"

"Maybe I should get the gun," Josie whispered.

Gun? Lani grabbed Josie's arm, latching onto it with tight fingers. "Call the police if he's dangerous," she said softly. "Don't get a gun."

Though the man towered over her tiny form, Rina didn't back down. "If you had your way, there would be no natural coffee trees left on the island. Only those freaks of nature you want to plant."

Willie's sigh eased out, almost too soft to hear, and his gravelly voice softened. So did his gaze. "It's progress, Rina. Look, I don't want to be your enemy. You know how I feel about you—how I've always felt about you. I've tried to explain it to you. I'd think you'd be in favor of trees that produce decaffeinated beans. No chemicals will be needed for that process anymore."

"And how are you going to stop them from cross-pollinating with my trees?" Rina asked. "Look, Willie, I don't have time to argue over this. I'm not pulling the injunction, if that's why you're here. All you care about is making the most bread. You don't care about what's right for the island."

"Bread," he scoffed. "Grow up, Rina, and use today's language. We're not in Taylor Camp anymore."

"You sold out, Willie. You're just like our parents used to be— all hep on seeing how much you can hook from the other guy. No regard for the environment, the natural order of things. I'm disappointed in you."

He flicked a finger toward her feet. "At least I'm not still wearing psychedelic clothing and sandals. I get my water from the tap and not from a distillery."

The curl of his lip didn't seem to bother Rina. She stared him down until his face reddened and he looked away. "Why did I even bother trying to talk with you?" he muttered. "You've always been pigheaded." He stomped back to his car and drove away, gunning the engine hard enough to spit gravel.

"Do you think we can stop him?" Lani asked. "I assume you filed the injunction against him?"

Her aunt nodded. "My lawyer filed it yesterday afternoon. No way is Willie going to plant genetically altered coffee. Ten percent of coffee trees cross-pollinate. In no time, there would be no true Kona coffee left on the island—just some watered-down version without the full flavor of the bean."

"Is there really such a thing as growing beans that don't have caffeine in them?" Lani folded her arms over her chest.

"Unnatural, isn't it? Coffee is meant to have caffeine. I've worked too hard on Kona Kai's reputation as the best organic coffee in the world to let him ruin it."

"There seems to be history between you two, but you've never talked about it."

Rina nodded. "We were at Taylor Camp in the early seventies. He used to be my best friend." Her mouth drooped. "He parted ways with us a few years after the camp burned down."

"He's not good enough for you." Josie's voice pulsed with loyalty. "And he doesn't know you very well if he thought corrupting the natural order of things would be copacetic with you."

The "us" her aunt mentioned must be the others who had helped Rina get the coffee plantation going after her trees started bearing fruit. She and her Taylor Camp friends had reconnected at a reunion a little over a year ago, and Rina hired several of them. The rest were due to come for a vacation and to help with the harvest. It would be a time for them all to get to know each other again, and Lani looked forward to getting to know the people who knew her aunt when she was young.

"Your best friend?" Lani murmured. "Is that all?"

Rina looked away. "I thought he might ask me out when we found one another again. He's not married either. Divorced."

Lani studied her aunt's downcast face. She always seemed so self-sufficient. It had never occurred to Lani that Rina might be lonely. "Can he get around the injunction?" she asked.

"I doubt it. There's an uproar on the entire island about it. Most of the coffee growers are opposed to any kind of genetically engineered coffee trees. Some altered plants are said to be nematode resistant; others are supposed to ripen at the same time. It all sounds fab, but no one knows what the alterations will do to the taste. Kona coffee is the best coffee in the world. The changes may make it funky."

Josie smiled and patted Rina's hand. "Don't worry about it. It will all come together. Let's boogie and get this done."

Clouds obscured the blue sky by the time they finished and put away their equipment. The scent of rain freshened the air, and Lani felt the first drops begin to fall as she settled into the back of the truck for the ride back. Her aunt dropped her off at the Kona Kai Coffee Company building. She waved to the older women and went inside. A large shipment of extra-fancy beans needed to go out today. When she finished, she could call her sister, Annie.

The back room held the heavenly aroma of roasting coffee. Lani sniffed the heavy note. It smelled like one of the darker roasts, double French or espresso. Small bags of roasted coffee lined the shelves.

Fallen beans crunched underfoot, releasing even more aroma as she walked through the roasting room.

Pam Aberstrom waved at her from over near the coffee roaster. Lani stepped to the big roaster, a metal contraption that stretched an inch or two taller than her own height of five foot two. Pam moved out of the way, and Lani stopped at the drum. Glancing at the temperature gauges, she pulled on the small round cylinder to examine a sample of the roast. She smiled at the dark, rich brown color. "Double French?" she guessed. A typical roast took about twelve minutes, and the darker ones went a little longer and had to be watched. Inattention could ruin a batch in seconds.

Pam nodded. "It's almost done. I was getting ready to dump it." About fifty-five, she'd been with Rina since the beginning—another Taylor Camp friend. A bandana kept her curly red hair off her face, and she wore shorts and a T-shirt to stay cool in the hot roasting room.

Lani didn't know her well. Pam kept to herself, did her job, and went home. Lani thought the other woman resented her being hired as a supervisor when Pam had been there longer, though Pam had never been insubordinate. "Good job," Lani said, moving on to the packing room.

Several Filipinos filled burlap bags with the dark roast that had to go out today. Looking at the sacks piled by the shipping bay, Lani smiled. The order would be shipped out on time.

Joey, the shipping room supervisor, wiped his broad face with a bandana, then stuffed it back in his pocket. "It's finished," he said. "We're cutting out now."

Thanks to her aunt's remarks, Lani found it impossible to even look him in the face. "That was fast," she said. "I didn't think you'd be done till midday."

"Um, I was wondering if you'd want to go see a movie sometime," he asked.

What defect in her character made her flush with pleasure that he found her attractive? Something inside made her feel better about herself when men fell all over her. Maybe she would always have to fight the urge to seek male admiration.

"Sorry, Joey, I'm not ready for a relationship."

He sniffed. "I'm not talking about a relationship. From what I hear, you just like to have a good time."

Heat scorched her cheeks, but she felt cold inside. She could blame no one but herself for her poor reputation. "I'm a different person now. I'm a Christian."

He stiffened, giving her a long look before turning away. "Yeah, right."

She was sure her face was beet red. Would the shame never leave her? Maybe she should move away, go where people didn't know her. Her eyes burned, and she turned away from him and walked toward the shelves of coffee. As she left him behind, she gave a slow shake of her head. No, she wouldn't run. Someday everyone would see that she'd changed. She wasn't the good-time girl anymore. And she had a new future, one spent with the beauty of flowers.

Stepping to the stack of burlap sacks, she lifted a bag and inspected it. Fancy-grade beans, large and perfectly formed, were inside. Though she normally didn't inspect further than that, she couldn't resist digging her fingers into the rich, dark beans. The handful of beans she brought to the surface were complete perfection—

Blue? Intermingled with the perfect coffee beans lay a blue object larger than her hand. She glanced behind her, but the workers had dispersed. She walked to the window and examined the odd item. When the sun hit it, she realized she held a piece of blue coral, a richer color than she'd ever seen. Exquisitely beautiful—and illegal. Blue coral was rare, and trading it was forbidden.

Who would hide illegal coral in the beans? And why? Someone was taking advantage of Rina's trust. Maybe Pam or Joey.

"What are you doing?"

Lani whirled to see Pam standing in the doorway. "Do you know anything about this?" Lani asked, holding up the coral.

Pam moved to Lani's side and stared down at the coral in her hands. "Where did you find it?"

"In this bag of coffee. It's coral." Pam bit her lip and avoided Lani's gaze. "Who's behind this, Pam?"

Pam backed away. "Don't ask me. I need to get to work."

Lani's stomach muscles tightened. Pam knew something. "How could you betray my aunt like this?"

Pam opened her mouth, then her gaze shot over Lani's head, and her eyes widened. "No!" she shouted.

Lani jumped at the sound of a car backfiring. At least that's what she thought she heard until she saw Pam slump to the ground, a red stain flowering on her T-shirt. Something whizzed by Lani's head, and she realized bullets flew around her. She ducked and scrabbled for cover behind the stack of coffee bags. Peering over a bag, she saw a face over the top of a rifle. The eyes mesmerized her. They locked gazes, then something stung her head, and she fell into the pool of the eyes' darkness.

Blackness pressed in on Lani, pushing against her head, her throat. Why didn't someone turn on the light? A vicious pain pounded at her temple, and the back of her head ached. A scream built in her throat, filling her mouth and nearly suffocating her with the need to let it out. In spite of every attempt to hold it back, a whimper escaped her lips.

"Lani?"

A whisper of movement, the light breeze of someone nearby impressed itself on her senses. The voice seemed familiar. Lani touched her eyes and found them unbandaged. "Can you turn on the light?" She heard the squeak of shoes on the tile floor and the rattle of a tray. She rolled onto her side.

"You're awake. Good morning, Lani. I'm Dr. Cooper."

The man's deep voice penetrated the cocoon around her. "Where am I? Please turn on the light."

His cool hands, smelling faintly of antiseptic and soap, touched her face. "Can you tell me how many fingers I have up?"

She batted at his hand. "Turn on the light! No one can see anything. What time is it?" She tried to remember what had happened. Pam. She'd been there. "Where's Pam?"

"Calm down, Lani." Her aunt's voice came through the darkness. "You're going to be okay."

"Aunt Rina?" The scent of coffee blossoms—her aunt's signature perfume, a sweet fragrance that smelled much like jasmine—floated up her nose.

"Do you want to sit up?" Her aunt slipped a small hand behind Lani's back.

Lani struggled to a sitting position. "Why won't you turn on the lights?" Her questing hand touched her aunt's face. Rina caught it and pressed it to her cheek.

The doctor cleared his throat. "The lights are on, Lani. What happened?"

A blanket as suffocating as the darkness covered her memory. How did she end up here? The last thing she remembered was heading into the coffee building to check the shipment. "I don't remember," she said. She felt her aunt inhale sharply. And why were they lying to her?

Did they think she couldn't tell the lights were off? What was going on? "What happened?"

"Someone shot Pam, I'm afraid."

"She's going to be all right, isn't she?" The silence echoed around her. "She's okay, right? Aunt Rina?"

"I'm sorry, Lani, but someone killed Pam." Her aunt's voice sounded thick.

"Turn on the lights!" Lani screamed. She threw back the covers and swung her legs to the side of the bed. She opened her eyes fully, straining to see something, anything. It was as though she swam in a black sea that blocked out all light, all visual sensation. The darkness seemed impenetrable. She could almost touch it, thick and stifling. She reached for some kind of anchor, anything she could grasp, but felt only air.

"I can't see," she whispered. "I can't see!" Her shriek rose and echoed off the blackness.

She heard the sound of the door whooshing open, and a familiar voice spoke out of the darkness. "She's okay, isn't she?"

"Yoshi?" she whispered. She stretched a hand out toward her cousin. If only she could touch him, he'd be her anchor. He was a police detective, and she wondered vaguely if their aunt minded being around this particular cop, given Rina's antipathy to the police.

His warm fingers held hers in a tight grip. "I'm here, Lani. Did you see the shooter?"

"Shooter?" She rubbed her forehead. "I can't remember," she moaned. She clutched at her cousin's hand. Bile rose in her throat. "I'm going to throw up."

"Here." The doctor pressed something hard into her hand. "If you feel sick, use this."

Her fingers traced the perimeter of a small plastic bowl, kidney shaped. If she remembered right from her last stay in the hospital, it was pink. She clutched it to her chest, the hard edges reassuring. "Why can't I remember?"

"I'm Dr. Cooper," the doctor said. "Your memory loss is not unusual. With a trauma to the brain, the actual incident may be lost. Or it may come back when the swelling goes down."

"Can you remember anything?" her cousin asked. He kept hold of her hand, and he sounded grim.

"I don't know," she moaned. Pressing her hands to her temples, she tried to think, to remember. "I remember eyes. Dark ones."

"Describe them," Yoshi prodded.

She wrinkled her forehead, but nothing came. "I don't remember." She put her hand to her mouth to cover her sobs, the tears burning her cheeks.

"Hold still." The doctor's cool fingers held her chin and tipped her head up.

A trembling started inside her. *Don't say it.* If she didn't hear the words, it might be a nightmare. She dug her nails into the palms of her hands. *Wake up, wake up.* This couldn't be real.

The doctor released her chin. "Try not to worry, Lani. The bullet only grazed you, and I doubt you'll have much pain from it. The real problem came when you walloped your head against a metal bar. As the swelling in your brain goes down, we can tell better whether the blindness is temporary or permanent."

Blindness. She shook her head, whipping it in such a frenzy her hair slapped her cheeks. "It's not true. I can't be blind." *Permanent, permanent.* The word echoed in her head. She couldn't live like this the rest of her life. She couldn't be blind.

Someone shuffled into the room, then her aunt spoke. "I tried to get hold of Annie and your father, but there's been an eruption on Montserrat, and the phones weren't working over there. I left a message at the consulate. They were going to try to find them. I also left a message for Tomi with the consulate office in Iraq. They said it might be weeks before they could locate him, though."

Lani wanted Annie, longed for her sister's calm, take-charge attitude. "Try again," she said. "I need Annie." She stifled a moan.

A clatter came from behind her, then the doctor pressed her back into the bed. "Let's give it a couple of weeks. I'm going to discharge you in the morning if you're as alert as you are today."

Her pulse fluttered at the thought of going outside. People would stare. She would need someone to lead her around. "How can you discharge me when I can't see?" she asked. "You have to fix this. You have to!"

"It's going to take time," Dr. Cooper said. "You've had an IV of mannitol to reduce the swelling. That's all that can be done right now. I'll check you every week, but you must be patient. And I can assign a therapist to help you learn to cope with your blindness."

"I've got a friend who might do it," Yoshi said. "Let me check with him."

"What will I do?" Lani muttered. She ran her hand over her face. It felt the same, the angles and planes. She hadn't changed, but she felt such distance from everyone. The black bubble insulated her from her family in an unpleasant way.

"I'll take care of you, Lani," Rina said.

She was an adult—she shouldn't need taking care of. Lani dropped her hand and shuddered. "What day is it?"

"Wednesday," Rina said.

Metal clinked on metal again. The doctor must be putting his instruments away. The finality of it began to sink in. Hadn't it been Monday? "Pam," she whispered.

Rina pressed her hand. "Her funeral is later today."

"I'll find who did this," Yoshi promised. His hand patted her back in an awkward gesture.

Their reassurances felt like platitudes. "I'm going to sleep now," Lani said. Maybe when she woke up, she'd be able to see the blue sky.

two

Ben Mahoney stood at the busiest intersection in Kona. The light went from yellow to red, and the sound of traffic changed. He glanced down at Fisher, the two-year-old golden retriever at his side. The dog glanced up as if to ask if he was going to give the command.

A smile lifted Ben's mouth. "Forward," he said. Ben kept a tight grip on the leather harness and started to step out.

Fisher stepped in front of him and pressed against his legs, preventing him from walking into traffic. "Good boy," Ben said. He'd never seen a dog as quick to learn as Fisher. Intelligent disobedience was often tough to teach. He rubbed the dog's ears and waited for the light. When it was safe to cross, he gave the command again, and they hurried across the street.

The sun beat down from a cloudless sky, and steam rose off the pavement as the dampness of the night's rain evaporated. Ben saw Fisher look longingly at a mud puddle, but at least the dog didn't jump into it. That's what Fisher usually did if he didn't have the halter on.

A rainbow shave ice would hit the spot about now. Ben stopped outside the Scandinavian Shave Ice shop on Ali'i Drive. Most establishments allowed service dogs, and Fisher wore his working-dog vest with the patches that announced his occupation.

A figure hurried toward him. "I thought I recognized that ugly mug," Yoshi Tagama called.

Ben turned to see Yoshi jogging through the slow traffic. Yoshi had been his partner when Ben was still on the force. They used to get together for coffee, but as they each went on with life, the meetings became fewer. When had he seen Yoshi last? Six months ago at least.

Yoshi's dark eyes looked somber. He took off his cap and swiped his black hair into place. "I was going to come see you. You saved me the trip. I need your help."

"My help? I'm off the force, Yoshi. Don't go trying to drag me back."

"You're still the best."

"Flattery won't get you anywhere. What's up?"

"My cousin needs protection. Someone shot her a couple of days ago and left her blind, at least for now. But whoever shot her killed another woman. I doubt he'll want to leave a witness. There's no man in the house, just my aunt, my cousin, and my aunt's friend. They're clear out in the middle of nowhere. My aunt owns the Kona Kai Coffee Company."

"Which cousin?" Ben asked. Yoshi had three.

"Leilani."

Ben started shaking his head. The woman was a barracuda. "Look, I know she's your cousin, but she had her hooks in my brother once. And he's married, I might add. Then she moved on to Tyrone. Find someone else."

Yoshi's lips pressed into a thin line. "She's been through a lot, but she's trying to get her life in order. She's changed, Ben. You'll see it when you meet her. And as much as she could use your help with learning to navigate blind, it also makes a perfect cover."

"Cover? Why can't you just tell her who I am?"

Yoshi was shaking his head while Ben asked the question. "She says she doesn't remember anything, but I think she's blocking it out, or else she just doesn't want to tell me. Maybe she's protecting someone that she thinks might be guilty. You could get a lot further than I would. She'll trust the blind trainer who comes in."

Ben had no use for the woman, but he was a sucker for someone facing blindness. "What's the doctor say about her eyes?"

"When the swelling in the brain goes down, he's hopeful her vision will come back. But that will just make whoever did this more desperate. When her sight returns, she'll be able to identify the killer."

"I don't want to have anything to do with her," Ben said.

Yoshi poked his finger into Ben's chest. "Everyone makes mistakes."

Ben's gut clenched. His own mistakes dogged him. He relived the worst one most nights in his nightmares. The slick road, the headlights looming out of the rainy night, the sound of the tires shrieking on wet pavement. If only he hadn't been fiddling with the radio. Stupid, stupid. Ben's inattention had cost his best friend his eyesight.

He stepped away from Yoshi's prodding finger. "She almost runied my brother's marriage."

"Your brother wasn't innocent either," Yoshi pointed out. "Lani is a Christian now. She's different. You'll see."

Ben doubted it. While he knew God could change anyone, some things were too innate to overcome easily. The Lani Tagama he'd met was only interested in a good time.

"She's going to need to learn how to deal with being blind," Yoshi said. "You're the best teacher out there. Take her a service dog and work with her. Get her to confide in you."

The deception of it deterred him. He shook his head. "Get someone else. There's a woman in Hilo who might help you."

"I need you, Ben."

"Sorry. There's a waiting list for service dogs. If her blindness is temporary, it's hardly worth the work of teaching her to work with one."

Yoshi's gaze went to Fisher. "What about him? You could finish training him with Lani."

"Give it up, Tagama. I'm not going to do it."

Yoshi's partner called from the police car. "Hey, we've got a 10–19, Tagama."

Yoshi muttered under his breath. "I need you, Ben. I'll call you later." He ran to the car.

"Great, just great," Ben muttered. His cell phone rang, and he dug it out. His brother's number flashed on the caller ID. "Hey, Ethan, what's up?"

"Ben, it's Natalie." His sister-in-law's low, slurred voice came over the line. "Can you come over? Ethan is passed out, and I can't get him up."

She sounded about ready to pass out herself. In the background he could hear Meg crying. The toddler would be two next month, and she'd seen way too much strife already. "I'll be right there," he said. He clicked off his phone, then he and Fisher jogged back to the Harley.

He got the dog in the sidecar and kick-started the engine. The big motorcycle roared to life, and he drove to his brother's house. Fisher wore a doggy smile. He loved riding in the sidecar. Ben wished he could drop the dog at home first, but he didn't dare delay that long. The sound of Meg's cries still rang in his ears. He accelerated around the final curve.

Ethan lived in a small hillside house above the road that led to Kealakekua Bay, though the ocean couldn't be seen from there. Ben parked and stepped out into calf-high grass. Though grass grew fast in the Hawaiian sun, it had to have been a month since Ethan had mown.

He approached the house. "Stay, Fisher." The dog lay down in the grass, and Ben stepped to the porch. Through the open screen door, he could hear Meg still crying.

After rapping on the door for several seconds without getting an answer, he opened it and stepped inside. "Nat? It's Ben." He went down the hall toward the little girl's wailing. "Meggie, it's okay." He found the toddler sobbing in her crib and lifted her out. Her soggy diaper made him grimace. Carrying her out from his chest a bit, he went down the hall to his brother's bedroom. He stepped into the room and found his sister-in-law curled in the corner, asleep on the floor. He saw no sign of his brother.

Meg continued to cry. Her diaper needed to be changed, and it would be up to him to do it. And had she even been fed yet? His watch read ten o'clock; she had to be hungry. He went back to her room and laid her on the changing table. Though he'd never done it, surely it couldn't be that hard. He found a disposable diaper and went to work. The stench of urine nearly made him gag, but it wasn't Meggie's fault.

"It's okay," he soothed.

"Toast," she said, her blue eyes huge with tears.

"We'll get some toast in just a minute, baby girl." He slid the clean diaper on, then realized he had the tabs on backward and the bulk of the diaper bunched in front. Sighing, he corrected his mistake.

He left her pajama top on and her legs bare. She needed a bath, but first she needed food. She stopped wailing as he carried her to the kitchen. Crusty Cheerios and dried milk covered her high chair and the floor around it. Dirty dishes overflowed the sink. His brother lay sprawled on the tile by the back door. Even from here, Ben could smell the liquor oozing from his pores.

Still carrying Meg, he prodded none too gently with his foot. "Wake up, Ethan." His brother groaned but didn't move. Ben went to the cupboard. Toast was out of the question, since the only bread he found had green mold on it, so he got down the cereal. He'd feed Meg, then worry about Ethan.

Meg began to smile when she saw the Cheerios. "Eat," she said, reaching toward the cereal.

How could his brother be such an idiot? Natalie too. They were neglecting Meg. No child should have to endure this kind of treatment. She opened her mouth for him to slip in the first mouthful and kept asking for more. Poor baby. He had to do something about this, but what? His glance went to his brother. While he loved Ethan, the guy was an adult and could make his own decisions. Meggie had no choice in the circumstances.

Ben didn't want Meg to see her father in his disgusting state, so he carried her into the living room and sat on the couch with her on his lap, where he continued to spoon cereal into her eager mouth. Glancing around the room, he saw burlap bags of coffee heaped in the corner. They were stamped with the imprint of the Kona Kai Coffee Company. What would Ethan and Natalie be doing with so much coffee?

The new big-screen TV caught Ben's attention. High definition. There were other new items in the room: the couch, an iPod on the coffee table, and a Sony laptop. Where had Ethan found the money for these things? He'd been without a job for four months, and Ben had been helping out.

Meg finished her cereal. "Down," she said, wiggling out of his lap.

He let her go play and went to look at the bags of coffee. Opening one, he dug his fingers into the dark beans and grimaced at the smell. He hated coffee. His fingers dug down farther, but there seemed to be nothing in the bag but coffee. Ben closed the bag and stood. Ethan was going to tell him what was going on if he had to beat it out of him.

The baby was crying. Lani struggled to get to the child, but the blackness pressed in on her. Her hands reached for the baby but found only empty air. She bolted upright, her breathing erratic. She was in the hospital bed, but the darkness seemed so alien, so threatening. Outside her door, she heard the noises of normal life: the rustle of people moving past her door, the muted sound of a TV in another room down the hall, the rattle of a cart being wheeled along the linoleum. She lay like an island—alone and isolated, as distant from everything around her as she felt from God. *Why, why?* She wanted to scream at God. If he were here in front of her, she might even beat on his chest. If God had a chest. The unfairness of it pummeled her.

Wasn't her life supposed to be better now that she was a Christian? She'd been trying so hard to leave her past behind, to be a different person. The success she'd had this year had been heady. How could God do this to her? It had to be a mistake.

Maybe he meant to test her faith, and her condition would be temporary.

But what if the blindness was permanent—a punishment for her sins? "No!" she said to the darkness. The covers wrapped her legs like a shroud, and she kicked them off and sat on the edge of the bed. Opening her eyes as wide as she could, she willed herself to see. She stood and shuffled forward, believing her vision would come back if she just had faith. Her bare feet whispered across the cold floor.

Bam! She racked her knee on the rolling stand beside the bed. It rattled away from her. She heard something fall, then a wave of icy water hit her feet. Completely disoriented, she stood with the wetness spreading under her soles and tried to figure out which way she needed to go to get back to the bed. "Please, God," she choked in a low voice.

Water and ice slicked the floor as she tried to inch backward. Then her leg touched the bed, and she fell into it with a sob of thankfulness. The blankets warmed her cold, wet feet, and she wrapped her arms around her pillow just to have something to hang on to. Faith was a wasted exercise.

"My head hurts." Ethan put his head in his hands, turning his face away from the steaming cup of coffee Ben placed in front of him on the coffee table.

"Good." Ben didn't care if his brother had a hangover the size of a humpback whale. Something had to be done to wake him up to what he was doing to his daughter. Ben had tried to rouse Natalie too, but she hadn't stirred even when he poured cold water on her head.

Meg climbed back into his lap, and he jiggled her on his knee. She put her thumb in her mouth and leaned back against him. The urine odor hung strong around her. A bath was next on the agenda.

Ethan darted a glance at him. "You're real sympathetic."

"Who took care of Meg while you were out last night?"

Ethan made an obvious effort to think. "A girl down the street."

"Did she stay all night?"

Ethan shook his head, then winced. "Just until we got home."

"At five."

"I don't know what time it was."

"You're turning out just like Mom." Ben's lip curled. "You have a daughter to care for. I want you to go into rehab."

"I'm not an alcoholic!" Ethan's bloodshot eyes narrowed.

"What else would you call it when alcohol is more important than taking care of your baby girl?"

"I take care of her."

"Ethan, I got here at ten. Meg hadn't been changed and her diaper literally dripped. She hadn't been fed and I could hear her screaming as soon as I came in the front door. She stood crying in her crib when I got to her room."

"She's Nat's responsibility in the mornings."

"She's your responsibility *all the time*! Be a man, for once in your life."

"Get off my back." Ethan grabbed his coffee, sloshing it on his vomit-speckled T-shirt as he gulped it down.

"If you don't agree to go for help, I'm going to take Meg." What he'd do with a toddler, Ben had no idea, but he couldn't leave the little girl in an unsafe environment.

"You can't do that."

"Watch me. You either pick up the phone and call for an appointment, or I'm packing her things and taking her with me. If I hadn't shown up when I did, she'd still be sobbing for food in her bed."

Ethan eyed him and evidently saw Ben's determination. "Fine, give me the number," he muttered. "But I'm not an alcoholic."

"I'm not the one you have to convince," Ben said, dialing the phone and handing it to him.

He listened while Ethan stumbled through a request for an appointment, then carried Meg to the bathroom. He ran some water in the tub, then bathed and dressed her in a stained shirt and jeans that seemed at least partially clean. Her drawers held no clean clothes that fit her, only baby things she had outgrown.

The kitchen clock chimed two when Natalie stumbled into the living room. After lecturing her too, he waited until they were both bathed and coherent. Sweeping his hand around the room, he fixed them with a stern stare. "Explain all this."

"All what?" Ethan's eyes shifted away.

"The new stuff. The bags of coffee."

"I got a job." Ethan thrust out his chin.

"Doing what?"

"Delivering coffee by boat to the other islands."

"And it pays enough to buy five thousand dollars' worth of new stuff?" Ben didn't bother trying to hide his skepticism.

"Yeah." Ethan gazed over Ben's shoulder and wouldn't look him in the eye.

Ben smelled a rat. "Uh-huh. And what's the coffee doing here? Shouldn't it be in a warehouse or something?"

"I wanted to look at it," Ethan muttered.

"Look at it?" Ben glanced at the sacks of coffee. "What's to look at?"

"Never mind. It's none of your business." Ethan folded his hands across his chest. Natalie hadn't uttered a word. Her fingers played with the fringe on her blouse, and she gazed out the window.

Ben wanted to dump out the coffee beans and see what he could find, but it might not tell him what he really needed to know. There was a better way. He rose. "I'll see you later." He kissed Meg good-bye and went outside. He called Fisher and loaded him in the sidecar. Before he started the bike, he dialed Yoshi's cell phone.

Yoshi answered on the first ring. "Tagama."

"It's me. I'll do it."

"Great! What changed your mind?"

"I've got a thesis to do. I can see how long it takes Lani to progress through the stages of grief."

"Man, that's cold, Mahoney."

Ben didn't care. He kept his voice hard. "She doesn't deserve much consideration. Where is this place?"

"Off Napoopoo Road on the way down to the bay." Yoshi gave him directions. "She gets out of the hospital in the morning. Thanks a lot, buddy."

Ben was in for it now. He'd find a way to get Ethan out of whatever mess he was in even if it meant dealing with a woman like Leilani Tagama.

three

*L*ani felt as if she'd been gone an eternity. She wished she could see the ripening coffee cherries on the trees. "The trees are almost ready to harvest. I need to get well so I can help." She tightened her grip on her aunt's arm and walked along the path to the house. Her eyes stung from the vog. The blackness disconcerted her as it pressed in without a glimmer of light. With every step, she felt the ground might fall away.

"It's going to be a great harvest," Rina said.

Lani loved coffee harvest. She never tired of seeing the huge red cherries decorating the lush greenery of the coffee trees like ornaments on a Christmas tree. She stumbled when her foot struck the step to the porch.

"Hang on a minute. Let me open the door."

When the reassuring touch of her aunt's arm disappeared, Lani felt adrift in a sea of midnight. She reached out for some kind of support but found only air. The screen door creaked, then the scent of patchouli from inside the house preceded Rina's touch on her arm.

"Josie will have some green tea brewing. It will purge your liver of all the drugs that got pumped into you in the hospital." Rina guided her into the house. "Careful. You don't want to wipe out on the tile floors."

The strains of "American Pie" blared from a CD player somewhere in the room. Lani reached out with her other senses. She heard the *click-click* of the fan overhead and the whisper of feet on the floor.

"Where's that girl?" Josie's boisterous voice echoed in the room. Her work-roughened hands grabbed Lani's arms, and the next minute she found herself enveloped in yards of cotton that smelled of coffee, yeast, and the outdoors. Josie must have on one of her voluminous muumuus.

Josie clicked her tongue. "My, my, it's a shame what happened to you, my sweet girl. But Josie will fix you up. First thing we have to do is flush your body of all the drugs they gave you. I've made up some special homeopathics that help reduce swelling. We'll get you seeing again."

Hope surged in Lani's heart. Josie had studied every remedy known to man. A chemist by trade, she left the lab for the herbal garden, and Lani had seen her concoctions work wonders. "Thanks, Josie." She pulled out of Josie's hug.

"Josie, give her a chance to catch her breath," Rina said. "She hasn't even been to her room yet."

Lani nodded. "I wouldn't mind a nap," she said.

"Right this way." Rina led her on down the hallway.

The air turned cooler away from the big windows that let in the sunshine. Lani took small steps on the tile floor. Reaching out with her right hand, her fingers trailed along the wall for security.

Rina stopped. "Here we are."

Lani heard the click of the latch, then the scent of clean linens mingled with coffee blossom rushed at her. Fatigue descended at the memory of her room. It looked out on the garden where Lani had planted a bed of orchids. Someday she would see them again. She had to.

Rina led her onto the thick carpet. Lani's knees bumped against the bed, and she practically fell onto the quilt. "Thanks for letting me come home, Aunt Rina." She heard her aunt clear her throat. "I'll try not to be a bother."

Rina patted her shoulder. "You're never a bother, Lani." She paused. "You look so much like your mother. It doesn't seem possible Adele isn't here too with that laugh of hers that could brighten even a funeral. I miss her so much."

Lani hadn't thought about how hard her mother's death must have been for her aunt. Every time Lani looked at Aunt Rina, she saw her mother. Even the timbre of her aunt's voice made her heart clench.

Her aunt patted her hand. "You get some rest, *keiki*. Dinner will be in about an hour. I'll call you when it's ready."

Lani heard her aunt plump up the pillows. She leaned back against the thick feather bedding with a sigh. Now that she was home, maybe it would work its special magic, and she'd wake up with her sight back.

With Fisher, his harness, his food, and his bowls in the sidecar, Ben drove down Highway 11 to Napoopoo Road. The vegetation changed and grew thicker, with small coffee groves dotting the hillsides. He found the turnoff for Kona Kai. The coffee plantation spread out in front of Ben as he paused the bike at the entrance. Coffee trees covered the Mauna Loa slope in neat rows. Red cherries practically smothered the leaves. The bright red next to the deep green leaves looked downright festive.

"Pretty," he told Fisher. The dog woofed. Ben accelerated and drove through the entrance flanked by brick pillars that supported a sign: KONA KAI COFFEE COMPANY.

Coffee trees intermingled with orchids. Banks of ginger softened a wooden office building, low and bulky. Wide windows held displays of packaged coffee and coffee-brewing equipment. "Stay," he told Fisher. The dog whined but didn't try to jump out of the sidecar. Ben strode to the building. The aroma of brewed coffee hung around the screen door in an almost visible cloud. He was going to wish for a nose plug while he was here.

The Asian woman behind the counter wore a flowing skirt in soft blue topped with a red sleeveless blouse. A beaded headband over her forehead continued around the back of her straight black hair, which hung to her waist. Ben first thought her to be in her thirties, but as he got closer, he noticed gray streaks in her hair and tiny lines at her eyes and around her mouth. She was probably close to fifty even if she wore clothes a girl would have worn to Woodstock.

Her mouth dropped open at the sight of him, and she stared as though one of the Night Marchers had walked through the door. She blinked and put her hand to her throat. "For a minute there . . ." She shook her head. "Sorry, let me start over. Good morning. How can I help you?"

"My name is Ben Mahoney. I'm looking for Lani Tagama."

She continued to watch him as though she thought he might grow two heads. "Why?"

"I think I might be able to help her. I raise guide dogs, and I've brought her one."

"Guide dogs?" The woman glanced out the window. Fisher still sat in the sidecar even though he could have jumped out. "We hope Lani's blindness is temporary."

"Even if it is, she needs to be able to deal with life right now." As protective as she appeared, she must be the aunt, Ben figured.

"How'd you find out about her problem?"

"Yoshi is a friend. He asked me to help."

The woman hesitated. "Right now all she wants to do is sleep. She hasn't come out of her room all day." She seemed to make up her mind, because she held out her hand. "I'm Rina Hashimura, Lani's aunt." She smiled. "But just be warned. She may not welcome the help. Come with me."

Ben followed her to the door, where she put a closed sign up in the window. He stopped at the bike. "Come on, boy." The dog jumped out and wagged his tail, then sniffed Rina's shoes.

She smiled and patted Fisher's head. "Nice dog. If you can't get through to Lani, the dog is irresistible."

Ben and Fisher followed her across a soft green grass lawn, then down a lane to a house set back in a grove of olive trees. A single-story plantation-style with a big porch, it looked like it had recently received a fresh coat of white paint.

"Nice place," Ben said.

"It's choice," Rina agreed. "I'll never sell it. The trees are six years old. Their first harvest was a year ago. Since then we've had two more, and they've been really good."

She opened the door, and Ben followed her into a spacious room tiled in a light brown color. The two sofas looked to be from the seventies with orange and green flowers. Kind of hideous, but he held his tongue. The room's furnishings didn't do the house justice. Incense sent a lazy curl of smoke from a holder by the window. Beads hung in a doorway to another room. He wouldn't have been surprised to hear folk music twanging. This lady was definitely still mired in the hippie era.

"Have a seat, and I'll get Lani," Rina said. She went down the hall.

"Sit," Ben told Fisher. The dog settled on his haunches, and Ben sat on the misshapen chair cushion. He glanced around the room. The coffee table held pictures of a hippie commune on the beach. The six people in the photo all looked to be in their twenties, and they wore headbands, garish clothing, and identical carefree smiles. He glanced at the women, but none was his mother. In the background a tree house loomed, a full-blown house in the treetops. He'd seen it before. In fact, he'd been born there.

Ben choked back a gasp when he saw the man in the middle of the group. The guy looked just like Ben himself. How could that be?

"That's Taylor Camp," Rina said, stepping back into the living room. "It was the best time of my life."

He decided not to tell her of his own experience. "I've heard of it. On Kaua'i's north shore, right?"

Rina nodded. "I lived there in the early seventies." She studied him, then glanced at the picture. She pressed her lips together.

He put the picture back on the table. From her fascinated expression, he knew his resemblance to the man in the picture had been the reason for her shocked expression when she first saw him. He decided to let her bring it up. "Do you still see any of your friends from that time?"

"Oh yes. Several of them work for me here on the farm. You'll meet them at dinner." Her gaze went to the picture. "The boy in the middle, Ash, drowned a couple of years before the camp closed." Her mouth drooped.

Before Ben could ask more questions, Fisher's ears perked, and he stood, his nose turned toward the hall. Ben glanced in the same direction. He could hear someone approaching.

"Here comes Lani now," Rina said.

Ben stood with his hands in his pockets. A young woman came into view with her hand on the wall. She looked like a younger version of Rina, though her hair barely touched her shoulders instead of hanging to her waist. Only about five foot two, she was perfectly formed, with chiseled cheekbones, full lips, and dark eyes. He'd forgotten she was so beautiful, but he knew too much about her to be attracted.

"My aunt said you wanted to see me."

Low and somewhat husky, her voice sounded like it might belong to a folk singer. Her feet were tiny, the nails tipped in a faint shell pink. She wore shorts and a tank top, but he thought she would have looked more at home in a kimono.

Ben cleared his throat. "I'm Ben Mahoney. I brought someone for you to meet." He grabbed Fisher's lead and stepped to where Lani stood with her hand still on the wall. When he reached her, he took the hand hanging at her side and guided it to the dog's head. "This is Fisher. He's going to help you get around."

Lani tried to pull her hand away, but Fisher thrust his nose into her palm, and she stopped. Her hand roved over the dog's ears, and Fisher stood still. He gave a happy whine deep in his throat, a sound Ben had never heard before.

"I'd say he likes you," Ben said.

"He seems like a nice dog," Lani said. "But why are you bringing him to me?"

"He's a guide dog."

Her face went white, and she pulled away. "I don't need a guide dog. My blindness is only temporary." Her voice held a trace of desperation.

"Even if it is, you need some help getting around while you heal. I'm going to show you how to navigate. There's no reason to stay stuck in your room."

"Are you some kind of shrink?" she asked. Her tone was as frosty as the top of Mauna Kea.

"Not exactly. I'm working on my master's in occupational therapy to train those who are visually impaired, and I train dogs."

"Are you blind too?" Lani's face began to lose its haunted loneliness.

"No, but my best friend is. I got interested in teaching the blind how to cope after he lost his sight." Guilt played a part in that decision, but Ben didn't know her well enough to tell her the full story.

Fisher nosed at her hand again, but she pulled away. "I don't need your *pity*," she spat. "This is only temporary."

"What could it hurt?" Rina put in. "It's better than sulking in your room."

"Sulking? I'm *blind*, Aunt Rina. I'm not going to put myself on display for people to stare at."

Still the spoiled princess he'd met before. Ben barely prevented his lip from curling. "Self-pity won't get you anywhere." She turned in his direction, and the pain and desperation in her sightless eyes nearly made him change his mind about her.

Then she stamped her foot as if she were Meg's age. "I won't be blind. I won't!" She turned and shuffled back down the hall.

Ben frowned. Strike one. But this wasn't over by a long shot.

"Master?" Simi said in a timid voice. The big man dug in the dirt near a tall tree. Orchids bloomed in a sea of color. Mr. Kato didn't look up, and Simi tried again. "Mr. Kato, in letter for Mother, I would like money." He held out the envelope with the letter he'd painstakingly written. The creased and dirty envelope held all his dreams and hopes for the future, and he desperately wanted to include some of his pay. He'd been here three months and hadn't seen a single coin yet.

The man straightened. "Kid, you've been a worthless worker so far. You haven't earned more than fifty cents."

While Simi wasn't sure how much fifty cents was in relation to the Tongan *pa'anga*, he didn't mistake the disdain in Master's voice. A *kiu* strutted past and almost seemed to stare at Simi with the same contempt. Stupid bird. "Please, Master, I come to help my parents. They think I keep wages for myself." He looked down at the rags he wore. He'd been promised new clothes, shoes, a nice place to live— all lies, he was quickly finding out.

"I'm tired of your mouth, boy. You'll get paid when I say you do." He smiled then and slung his arm around Simi's shoulders. "You're getting there, kid. I'll have you trained in another month or two, and you'll be raking in the dough. Why, I bet I could pay you five dollars a week then. Just keep your mouth shut and do what you're told. I'll send them some money to keep them quiet. And here, this is a carabiner. I'll show you how to go down a cliff with it. When you go back to Tonga, everyone will be jealous. It's a great tool."

Simi stared in fascination at the metal thing. He'd watched the big man climb the cliff behind the orchid farm and marveled. The metal felt cool in his hand. It wasn't money, but this was all he'd get for now. There was no one to take up for him. If he went to the law, he would be sent back to Tonga or maybe even jailed. He was stuck.

four

The scent of roasting coffee from the building in the clearing hung heavy in the breeze. Thresh stood in the shade of a monkeypod tree and stared into the face of the man the sharks had taken thirty years before. At least they'd taken the dead body. Seeing this man was like peering through a mirror into the past. He had to be related to Ash in some way. Maybe he was Ash, reincarnated.

Thresh approached him, trying to appear nonchalant yet interested. Up close, the guy was even more exactly like Ash.

"Ben Mahoney." The man stuck out his hand.

The eyes seemed to look right through Thresh. It was all Thresh could do to maintain a smile. "You look familiar to me somehow."

"A couple of people here seem to think I look like a guy named Ash," Ben said. "They say everyone has a twin somewhere."

Thresh studied Ben's face. Ash was in there, laughing and yukking it up at everyone's expense. He was one of the *Huaka'i Po* now—a death marcher. Thresh had seen him, gliding along with his feet above the ground, many nights as he walked these roads.

In the nineteenth century, the historian Lord Acton said great men were almost always bad men. It had become Thresh's motto. Greatness demanded thinking outside the box and being focused on one thing: success. Failure wasn't acceptable, especially with his goal so close in sight. Ash's reappearance couldn't be allowed to derail the plan. If Ash had to die again, Thresh thought the act might be even more enjoyable the second time around.

Roosters crowed outside the bedroom window. Lani's eyes flipped open, but darkness still shrouded her. Dumb birds. She sat up and swung her legs out of bed, then reached over and flipped on the light. No light lit the room. Warmth touched her foot, almost like sunlight. Then she remembered. She was blind. She sagged back and covered her face with her hands. The darkness had to lift soon. It had to. She couldn't bear it.

She stood and felt along the wall to the window. If only she could stare into the blue sky with the sun on her face. This blackness was more claustrophobic than the room. She might escape these four walls, but she couldn't swim out of the dark sea she moved through.

That man hadn't left yet. He still played outside with the dog. He'd been hanging around for two days. He came every morning at nine and left after dinner. It was about to drive her crazy. Even pressing her palms over her ears didn't block out his shout and the dog's happy yips.

She'd always wanted a dog. Her mother hated dogs, and her father disliked all animals. Annie had endured a constant battle with him over her pet mongoose, Wilson. Lani wondered if she would have to give the dog back when she got her sight back. Because, of course, she would regain her sight. If only Annie were here.

Lani turned at a tap on her door. "Come in." Moving slowly back across the carpet, she felt the mattress and sat on its edge. A rush of air told her the door had opened. "Who's there?"

"It's me." Her aunt's voice had a happy lilt. "You've got a visitor."

"I don't want to see anyone." The door latch clicked, and Lani heard the whisper of her aunt's feet.

"You about ready to stop feeling sorry for yourself?" Rina asked in a clipped voice.

"I'm just tired. I was shot, remember?"

Rina's light steps came closer, then her hand touched Lani's shoulder. "Where's the spunky niece I love? You can do this, Lani. You have the willpower and the ability. Your nose is sharp—it always has been. You're the only one in the place who can smell when the coffee is roasted just right. Your other senses will begin to compensate for the loss of your sight. You're going to be okay."

Lani scowled. "Easy for you to say. Just leave me alone."

The door opened, and Lani caught the tinkle of jewelry and the faint scent of sulfur. She turned. "Fawn?" With Annie gone, it could only be her sister's friend and fellow volcanologist.

"I came as soon as I heard." Fawn Trenton's footsteps moved across the floor, and she sat next to Lani and enveloped her in a hug. "I'm here to help you. I took some time off work."

Lani clung to Fawn. "How did you hear?" Her sister Annie's best friend, Fawn, was as close as a real sibling. Only having Annie here would be better. Fawn's hair, pulled back in its trademark braid, smelled faintly of rotten eggs, the hydrogen sulfide gases she'd been working in. She must have come straight from the volcanoes.

"I ran into Yoshi in Big Save."

"I'll leave you two to visit while I help Josie with dinner," Rina said. The door clicked behind her when she exited the room.

Fawn pulled away, but Lani kept hold of her hand. "Rina tried to get hold of Annie, but the volcano on Montserrat is erupting and the phone service is out," Lani said.

"I know. Yoshi told me."

"Sounds like he told you a lot."

"We—talked a bit." There was a smile in Fawn's voice.

"Oh? Did he ask you out?" Lani couldn't help the hope in her voice. She'd love to see Fawn in the family. For the past six months, she and Annie had kept throwing Fawn in Yoshi's path. For all the good it had done them.

"Well, we got a Frappuccino together. Does that count?" Amusement gave a lilt to Fawn's voice.

"Awesome! Sure it counts. My boneheaded cousin might be wising up."

"I've got a date with another volcanologist on Friday."

Lani clutched her hand. "I thought you were staying with me." Fawn's appearance had lifted the gloom around her, and she didn't want to let her go.

Fawn laughed. "I can cancel it. I didn't want to go anyway." She put her arm around Lani. "Now tell me what you're doing sulking in the bedroom. There's a positively yummy man with an equally scrumptious dog in the front yard."

Lani tipped her head. "Really? What's he look like?"

"About six-three. Built like a linebacker. Thick hair the color of chestnut. Lashes I'd kill for. Is that his Harley in the yard?"

"I don't know," Lani said. "I only know he's trying to push the dog on me. Have you ever seen him before? His voice seems a little familiar."

"Nope."

"You're sure?"

"Honey, I wouldn't forget a man who looks like him. Now get your slippers on. We're going out there." She stood.

"I don't want to. They'll all stare."

"Is that all? People stare at me all the time. I'm used to it. They think I dress weird, but I don't care. I'm going to be myself, and you should too."

Lani tightened her grip on Fawn's hand. "Wait. I need to talk to you." She pulled Fawn back down beside her. "I thought when I became a Christian, things would get easier. What's the use of trusting God if he's going to let me go through something like this? Is this punishment for my past?" Her hand settled on her midsection.

Fawn and Annie had brought Lani to Christ. Fawn might dress in flowing skirts and wear T-shirts that would keep most people awake, but she was the wisest person Lani knew. Next to Annie.

"Where did you get the impression life would ever be easy, Lani?" Fawn's palm came down on Lani's hand. "As long as we have life in our bodies, we'll have trouble in this world. And God doesn't remember your sins anymore. Or mine. This isn't punishment, Lani."

"It feels like he hates me." She brushed the moisture away from her cheeks. "I sound whiny, don't I? But I just don't get it, Fawn."

"I don't either, sweetie." Fawn's finger trailed along her cheek. "I can't explain why babies die or young people get cancer. But I *trust* God. He knows things we don't."

She knew Fawn spoke the truth, but it didn't make her feel any better. Lani sighed and felt around on the floor with her toes. "Do you see my slippers?"

"They're right here." Fawn slipped them onto her feet. "Those bright green Locals are hard to miss. Let's go."

Lani stood, put her hand on Fawn's arm, and stepped cautiously along the floor. She'd lost track of time. In the perpetual darkness, she had no sense of the passage of the hours, no sun to mark the day's movement. With her other hand on the wall, she navigated the hallway. The scent of patchouli incense grew stronger, so she knew they must be passing through the living room.

"Hang on," Fawn said.

The screen door screeched, and Lani felt the touch of a cool breeze on her face. A babble of voices came across the yard. Several male timbres came to her ears, and she recognized the voices of her aunt's friends and employees. They were supposed to be here for a luau tonight. Her mouth watered at the aroma of the kalua pig in the *imu.*

"There she is." Her aunt's voice held a touch of eager nervousness. The babble of voices died. "I'm glad you decided to join us."

Had they been talking about her? Lani held her chin up, but doing so made her feel more off balance, and she clutched Fawn's arm tightly. "The food smells good."

"Let me get you a plate," Rina said.

A cold nose pressed against her leg. Lani reached out and touched the dog's soft fur. The dog's presence seemed to leach out her tension. He felt like a safe harbor to her. She sank to her knees and put one arm around him. The dog whined and licked at her chin.

"What's his name again?" she asked.

"Fisher," a deep male voice answered.

Lani scratched the dog's ears. "Are you a fisherman, big guy?"

"He loves fish," Ben said. "He's been watching for you. I've never seen a dog fall so completely in love overnight."

Did he think he could get her to agree to his help by flattering her with a dog? She'd handled flattery since she was five, and he was an obvious amateur. "He's pretty special."

"Here we are," her aunt interrupted. "You sit down right over here, Lani, and eat it while it's hot."

Lani heard the rustle of a chair being moved close, then Fawn placed Lani's hand on the chair back. "Your seat is here," Fawn said.

The dependency Lani felt was like being two years old again. As the baby of the family, she'd fought hard for her independence, and it had vanished as if it never existed. Curling her fingers on the metal chair frame, she wanted to pick it up and toss it across the yard, then sit down and drum her heels on the grass.

The din of conversation ebbed. Lani's face flooded with heat. People would be staring to see if she could hit her mouth. She wasn't even sure she could. All she'd eaten so far were sandwiches, because she didn't want to try to find her mouth with a utensil.

She shoved the chair away. "I want to go back to my room."

"Oh no, you have to eat first," her aunt said. The scrape of the chair came again. "Here, sit. I've got your plate."

"I'm not being paraded like some kind of freak," Lani said past a throat almost too tight to speak. "I want to go to my room."

"Let me help you." Ben spoke softly into her ear. "Sit down a minute."

Before she realized it, she found herself sitting down with a heavy plate on her lap. "Imagine this is a clock." He twisted the plate in her hand. "There's kalua pork at twelve o'clock. Huli-huli chicken at two o'clock, mac salad at four o'clock, a poi roll at six, sweet potatoes at eight, and mango bread at ten."

Surprised by the understanding in his tone, Lani turned her face toward him. Why did his voice seem so familiar? She couldn't put her finger on it. Ben put the fork in her hand, and she moved it toward the warm plate on her knees. Pork at twelve o'clock. The fork in her hand met resistance, so she knew she'd found something. Lifting the loaded fork toward her face, she prayed she didn't stick it up her nose or something equally humiliating. The pork on the tip of the fork hit her lips, and she quickly opened her mouth and ladled it in. Success felt sweet. After living on sandwiches, the taste of the slow-cooked pork made her close her eyes and savor the flavor.

The hum of conversation picked up around her, and the tension in her shoulders eased. A bit of her independent spirit seemed to be resurrecting its head. She took another bite. What was this guy's story? "So how did you get interested in doing this?"

"Doing what?" His voice held a note of warning.

"Never mind." She didn't want to deal with any more controversy in her life than she had right now. "How long will it take to learn to work with Fisher?" At the mention of his name, the dog pressed his nose against her knee. She started to give him a piece of pork, but Ben put his hand on hers.

"Dogs can't digest pork. He'd love a piece of your chicken, though." He guided her hand around to two o'clock.

She picked up a small piece and tossed it toward Fisher. His jaws snapped, and she heard him licking his chops. "I have a lot to learn about dogs."

"I'll teach you."

"How long will it take?" She nibbled on a bit of chicken. The thought of having her independence back was exhilarating. When she'd demanded to be taken back to her room, the fact was, she couldn't have found it by herself, but maybe with a dog's help, it would be possible.

"Usually about a month, but I have a feeling it will only take a couple of weeks with the connection you and Fisher have."

"I thought there was a waiting list for service dogs. Why do I get one when my situation isn't permanent?"

"Fisher isn't fully trained. And neither am I. We can learn

together. And he'll be a loan. When your vision comes back, he can help someone else."

Her fingers trailed through Fisher's silky fur. The thought of growing fond of the dog only to give him up bothered her. And was Ben using her in some way? She didn't like the idea of being a guinea pig. "I'll have my sight back before a month is up."

"Maybe."

She didn't want to consider the possibility that her condition might last. If only she could catch some small glimmer of light and dark, just shadows. But nothing showed in her vision except this awful black hole that sucked her into oblivion; it was like floating in an empty universe.

Rina's hand touched Lani's shoulder. "Lani, everyone wants to say hello."

How do you greet someone without seeing them? Lani held her tongue and tipped her head up. "Aloha. Are you all here?"

"The gang's all here. Arlo Beckett, Harry Drayton, Jerry Kapuy."

A chorus of male voices sounded in her head. The different voices seemed impossible to filter, but she had to make an effort for her aunt's sake. "Arlo?"

A soft hand took hers. "Right here." His high voice sounded almost effeminate.

"And Harry's here." A hard hand with calluses replaced Arlo's soft one. Harry squeezed her fingers, then dropped her hand. "You look more like your aunt all the time. I like the new shorter hair-cut."

Another hand picked up hers, so large it enveloped her small palm. "It's Jerry, Lani." His deep voice held a rich timbre. The compassion in his voice was from his longtime medical background. He was a holistic doctor, though he and Josie often disagreed on things.

She could hear the pain behind his words too. He'd been dating Pam, and she'd expected an announcement any day.

"I'm blind, Jerry," she whispered.

"Your vision will come back." Jerry squeezed her fingers. "If you don't mind, I'd like to talk with the specialist in charge of your case. Maybe there's something I could do on this end to help. Something complementary might work." His voice held no pity, just a calm acceptance of how things would be.

"Oh thanks, Jerry! You're the best." She gave him her doctor's name. "I—I'm sorry about Pam."

He squeezed her hand again. "Me too. I don't know what I'm going to do with the ring I got her."

"Oh, Jerry." Her eyes burned, and she heard him swallow hard.

His voice sounded thick. "I'd better let you eat." He pulled his hand away.

Ben's voice came. "So how did you all meet up again? Rina said you lost touch until a year ago."

Arlo's voice answered. "I ran an ad in the *Honolulu Advertiser* looking for people who had lived at Taylor Camp in the early seventies."

Josie sniffed. "You just wanted to find Rina. She's too good for you."

"Now, Josie," Arlo said in his squeaky voice. "I could never aspire to win her hand. But a guy can't help dreaming."

Now that she thought of it, his voice reminded her of Gomer Pyle. She hadn't heard this story. They'd all been on the plantation by the time she arrived, and she'd just accepted them as her aunt's friends.

"Were you all in love with Aunt Rina?"

Josie didn't wait for an answer. "Rina has always been like orchids to bees."

"And all the Taylor Camp residents called you?" Lani asked Arlo.

"E-mailed me. And we set up to meet. Your aunt hadn't changed a bit. Still just as pretty as ever." The smile in Arlo's voice grew. "We all met here, and the years we'd been apart melted away."

"What about you, Jerry?" Lani thought his friendship with her aunt seemed more long-term.

"I never lost touch with Rina," he said. "We shared a lot of the same interests—pearls, holistic medicine, organic food. We've been friends a long time. Josie too, though she doesn't often admit she likes me." He laughed.

"Why did you ever leave the camp?"

"They burned it!" Josie exclaimed. "Kicked us all out and burned it to the ground. I watched my tree house go up in flames and cried."

Lani gasped. "But why?"

"It was a legal wrangle with the state. Howard Taylor bought the land to build a house. The state wouldn't let him because they wanted it for a park, but they expected him to pay the taxes. He let us live there, and when he finally turned it over to the state, we were settled pretty tight," Josie said. "They didn't get rid of us easily, but they finally wore us down and we moved out. They wasted no time in burning our homes." Her voice cracked.

"It was a long time ago," Jerry said, his deep voice gentle.

Lani put her attention back on her food as the others drifted away. Taylor Camp must have really bonded them for their friendship to have stood such a long test of time.

Bikes lined the lot of the Harley Davidson shop. Ben mentally ticked off the various bikes to see if Tyrone had sold any. One black Softail no longer sat by the fire hydrant. A red Fat Boy was missing too. His bike rumbled to a stop by the door, and he dismounted and went inside. Customers meandered through clothing displays. Several men stood talking to Tyrone Brown at the parts counter. Ben nodded to sales clerk Monica Warren, then made his way back to parts, where he waited until Tyrone finished with customers.

Tyrone turned sightless eyes toward him. "That you, Ben?"

"Yep." It never ceased to amaze him how accurately Tyrone could catalog footsteps and small sounds. "Looks like you're having a good week. I saw a couple of bikes missing."

"Not bad. I tried to call you this morning." Tyrone was about Ben's age. They'd grown up together, gone to police academy together, and been best friends for thirty years. Tyrone had never wanted to go into business with his dad, but he didn't have much choice after the accident. He took over the Harley dealership last year, and it had thrived.

"I'm going to be gone a couple of weeks."

"Oh?" Tyrone's dark face lit with interest.

"Yoshi needs me to guard his cousin."

Tyrone's face grew guarded. "Lani?"

"Yep." Ben tried to reconcile the defiant young woman who'd interfered in Ethan's marriage with the hurting, vulnerable one he'd been seeing all week. "What went down with you two? You dated her for a while. What happened?"

Tyrone's hand crept along the counter to a pen that he began to twirl through his fingers. "I don't want to talk about it. Why are you getting involved? It must've been some problem to get you to help *her*."

"Ethan is mixed up with something." Ben told his friend about finding the coffee bags and the expensive purchases in the house.

"So you agreed to go help so you can check it out."

"Yeah."

"Maybe she's involved. She was always up for an adventure. Smuggling might be right up her alley."

Ben decided not to remark on the bitter tone in Tyrone's voice. "I took Fisher out to help her. I'll look around while I teach her how to function, do a little work on the master's, and just try to stay out of her way." Ben studied his friend's face. Tyrone never seemed to blame Ben for the accident that had blinded him. The first few weeks he'd railed against his fate, then he'd accepted it with quiet resignation. Ranger at Tyrone's feet had been Ben's first experience with the amazing blessing a guide dog could be.

"Let me know how she gets along."

Ben studied his friend's pensive face. "You sound like you still care about her."

"It's hard to turn off feelings. What she did . . . Never mind."

"It might help to talk about it."

"Not now." Someone called to Tyrone from the back room. "I'd better go. Keep in touch."

Ben watched him walk away, his white cane gliding along the floor, and felt a pang of guilt. No—in spite of everything, Tyrone was a success story. Ben had to remember that.

five

*F*isher whined and put his wet nose against Lani's knee. He'd been with her two days, and she was already hooked on his presence. She tangled her fingers in his fur. "Having Fisher here has made a big difference," she told Fawn. "I don't feel so alone in the dark when he's here."

"He seems to love you too."

"Ben never said he was mine. I have to figure out a way to keep him even when my sight comes back."

"Can you do that?"

Lani's fingers tightened in the fur. "I have to. He's part of me now. Ben has to let him stay with me. I'll buy him." She couldn't lose the dog.

"What if Ben won't sell him?"

Lani didn't want to consider it. The cell phone clipped to her waistband vibrated. She found it and flipped it open. "This is Lani."

The home show director came over the line. Michelle Landers always sounded as though she couldn't catch her breath. "Lani, glad we caught you. We're going to need those initial drawings for the garden by the first of next month."

Lani's fingers tightened around the phone. "But that's only two weeks," she blurted.

"Is that a problem? I thought we discussed a fast turnaround on the design." Displeasure coated the director's words.

"We did. It's fine." Lani knew she should tell Michelle what had happened, but the words wouldn't come. "I'll be in touch." She flipped her phone closed. "I don't know what I'm going to do," she moaned.

"The garden design?" Fawn asked.

Lani nodded. "They need the designs in two weeks."

"You should have told them what happened and asked for more time."

"I don't want to lose this project."

"But how can you design anything when you can't see?"

"I don't know, but I'll think of something. Where's Aunt Rina?"

"In the coffee building. Changing the subject isn't going to make your problem go away."

"I know that! But I need to think." She had reams of designs. Maybe she could adapt one with Fawn's help.

The purr of a car engine came to Lani's ears, then the crunch of gravel under tires. "Who's here?"

"Some big guy in a black Cadillac."

"Willie Kanaho," Lani said. The car door slammed, and she heard Willie's customary whistle. "Hey, Willie."

"Where's your aunt?" he asked.

"I'm right here," her aunt called. It sounded like she was still a ways off, then the whiff of her perfume floated in the air. "What are you doing here, Willie?" She sounded breathless.

"I came to say I'm sorry," he said.

"A man apologizing?" Fawn whispered to Lani.

Lani hid her smile with her hand. "You want to sit down, Willie?"

"I can't stay," he said, but his tone invited them to convince him.

"I just made some coffee, if you'd like a cup," Rina said.

"Well, maybe just one." A lawn chair groaned under his weight.

Her aunt's light steps retreated to the house. Lani shifted in her chair. "Are your trees ready to harvest?"

"We start tomorrow," he said. "Yours are almost ready too. Do you need a hand?"

"I'm sure we can get it done," Lani said. The last thing her aunt would want was to owe Willie anything. She had to wonder why he'd come here. Did he think sucking up to Rina would get her to drop the injunction?

"Well, if you need anything, just ask."

She heard the sound of the door opening, then her aunt's voice called. "You take it black, don't you, Willie?"

"Yeah."

Lani smelled the aroma of coffee. "What a rich, floral nose. Is it the new full-city roast?"

"It is. You're good, Lani." Rina pressed a warm cup into Lani's hand. "See what you think. Here, Willie, you too. It's really choice."

Lani sniffed the aroma. Deep and rich, the bouquet made her mouth water. She tasted it. "Perfect. Are these the aged beans?"

"Yes."

"The aging really added to the depth. We have to continue to offer this."

"It's pretty good," Willie said. He slurped again. "You aged these beans, you say? How long?"

"About a year," Rina said.

"I'll have to try it with my beans."

The front door banged, and Josie's voice called. "Rina, you're sharing your secrets with the enemy." Her voice grew closer as she spoke. "You want some cream, Lani?"

"Please." Lani held out her cup and tried not to show her relief. Her aunt was too trusting. Willie would steal their secrets, especially if Rina's injunction made him mad enough. The liquid splashed into her cup.

Josie's heavy steps went across the lawn. "Here are your supplements, Rina. You forgot them this morning."

"You're trying to kill me. I know it," Rina said with a smile in her voice. "Just shoot me now and be done with it."

"Bam," Josie said. "Now quit whining and take your pills."

"Jerry doesn't want me mixing these supplements with the ones he's trying."

"I'll talk to him about it. These won't interfere with anything." Josie's voice was stubborn. "I know you better than he does."

"I know you do, Josie. Don't get steamed over nothing."

An uncomfortable silence followed, and Lani assumed her aunt was doing as she was told. Rina suffered from lupus, but under Jerry's care she'd been doing well, almost to Josie's chagrin. Josie had wanted to be the one to help her best friend.

Her aunt finally spoke again. "What do you want, Willie?"

Willie cleared his throat. "I'm not your enemy, Rina. Actually, I wondered if you might want to go to dinner with me on Friday."

Lani heard Rina inhale sharply. "I don't know, Willie. We'd better not fraternize until this whole mess is sorted out."

Josie snorted. "If you believe his sweet talk, you're a fool, Rina Hashimura."

"Hush, Josie," Rina admonished her friend in a low voice.

"I'd like to show you my trees," he said. Rina didn't answer right away. "What do you say?" he persisted. "Let's put it behind us. You know how I feel about you, Rina."

"I'll think about it." Rina rose and headed toward the house with Josie.

Willie sighed, and his heavy tread moved away. The car door slammed. Then the motor roared to life and the car pulled away.

Lani wished she could see her aunt's face. Rina cared about Willie, Lani would bet on it. The sound of rapid steps came, then the screen door banged on the house.

"Wow," Fawn said. "There's no telling about love. We get fixated on a person and never move on."

Fawn's pensive tone struck a chord with Lani. How many men had she hurt over the years with her carefree attitude? But no more. "Hey, could you help me with something?"

"Sure, what's up?"

"I have to ask Aunt Rina what to wear every day. Could you help me organize my clothes? I thought if tops and bottoms were hung or folded together, I could pull out an outfit and know it matches."

"Good idea. I didn't want to hurt your feelings, but those two prints you're wearing don't exactly make the best fashion statement."

"Aunt Rina is color blind." The corners of Lani's lips tipped up. She thought this might be the first time she'd smiled since the injury. She took off Fisher's harness. "Have fun for a while, boy." Moments later, water splashed over her legs. "Is he trying to get in his water bowl again?"

"His whole face is submerged." Fawn chuckled and touched Lani's hand. "Let's go see your closet. We can't have you looking like a street person. You've always had fabulous fashion sense. I wanted to be you for years."

"I'm no one to imitate," Lani said. "You know, something happened that really woke me up. At the time it seemed so humiliating, but I'm not sure I would have realized who I really was if it hadn't happened."

"What was it?"

"I'd been dating this guy. His name was Ethan, but I didn't even know his last name. I didn't ask." She chewed her lip and looked away. "I knew he was married, but I told myself his wife must be pretty pathetic or he wouldn't be looking around."

"I see," Fawn said.

Lani stole a glance at her friend. Fawn would hate her now. "He bought me nice things, took me to fancy restaurants, and most importantly, he reminded me of a young Harrison Ford, and I love Harrison. So I didn't care who I hurt." She whispered the last words.

"You don't have to talk about this if it's too painful," Fawn said.

Lani didn't hear condemnation in Fawn's voice. She shook her head. "No, it's good for me to remember what I was, and how much I don't want to be that person again. Anyway, I left work one day and this guy stops me. He says he's Ethan's brother and shoves a picture in my hand of a pretty young woman and a darling baby that looked about a year old. 'This is who you're hurting,' he said. The contempt in his eyes just made me shrivel. I realized how small I was." She shuddered at the memory.

Fawn touched her hand. "Even a surgeon's knife hurts, but it heals too. It's great that you woke up."

Lani nodded. "I've never told anyone, not even Annie. Do you think I'm scum?"

Fawn's fingers tightened on Lani's. "Of course not. I love you. We all make mistakes."

"Thanks for listening." Lani gave Fawn's hand a final squeeze. "Now let's get me fashionable again. I've changed, but not *that* much."

Just as Ben had anticipated, Fisher and Lani were a perfect team. Just a few days into training, and it seemed as if they were attuned to each other in some mystical way. Fisher barely left her side, even when

Ben removed the harness. Ben began to show Lani how to grip the leather harness, how to be sensitive to the way the dog would press against her leg, the commands Fisher expected.

They walked along the narrow road past masses of ginger and proteas toward the Hula Orchid Farm just up the lane. Lani had improved daily at keeping her balance and stepping forward confidently with the dog at her side. A chorus of chirping crickets serenaded their passage.

"You don't like me, do you?" she said.

"I don't know you," Ben said. He'd maintained his guard around Lani. While she didn't seem the good-time girl he'd met before, he figured her seeming innocence was the bait that women like her used to entice men. He refused to allow himself to fall prey.

"I know. But your voice is often clipped when we talk. Have I offended you?"

"Of course not, but I'm here to do a job. I doubt we'll ever see one another when your training is complete."

She nodded. "Whatever you say. I could use a friend, though." She lifted her face to the breeze. "Speaking of later, um, what about Fisher?"

"What about him?"

"I don't want to lose him. How much do you want for him?"

"He's not for sale. When you don't need him anymore, he'll go to someone who does."

Lani's chin jutted out. "I'm not giving him up. We belong together. You even said he was specially attuned to me."

Ben didn't have an answer. Fisher was special. Even the thought of letting the dog go to *anyone* bothered him.

When he didn't answer, Lani bit her lip and turned her face up. "What's the sunset like tonight?"

"All pink and gold with a few wispy clouds," he said. "Inhale. Go ahead, do it now." He waited until she took a deep breath. "What do you smell?"

A tiny frown crouched between her eyes as she concentrated. "Fresh greenery, dew, the ginger and orchids in the flower bed. Um, fresh dirt."

"And just smelling them brings back what they look like, doesn't it? The beauty is still there, waiting to be called up to memory."

"Is this called blind psychology?" She laughed, putting her hand to her mouth. Fisher gave his happy whine and nudged her knee.

He found himself smiling and quickly wished he hadn't. Her wiles wouldn't work on him. "I want you to reach out with your other senses and realize you haven't lost everything. Just your vision. You still have touch, smell, taste, hearing. They'll become more acute."

Her smile morphed to that familiar pout. "This isn't permanent."

He wanted to point out that it had been a week and a half since the accident, and she didn't have a glimmer of light and shadow, but he kept his mouth shut. He stared at her pensive face. Now might be a good time to probe. "How much coffee do you ship out?"

"About sixty thousand pounds a year."

"Wow. Do you hire people to transport it for you?"

She blinked and raised her perfectly shaped brows. "Just UPS." She smiled.

So Ethan had lied, just as Ben thought. "How many people do you employ?"

"About ten, including Rina's friends. Some of the others are part-time. They may have to hire someone to take my place. It depends on how long this . . . problem lasts."

She still skirted the possibility her condition might be permanent. Ben remembered that Tyrone had done the same. "Let's look at the orchids."

"I can't look at anything."

"Sure you can." He stopped at the first bed. "What do you know about orchids?"

"Gardening is my passion. I have a garden full of orchids outside my window." Her tone grew wistful. "I'd thought to be a garden designer someday."

"Give me your hand." She held out her hand, and he guided it to the nearest blossom. "See if you can identify this one."

Her small hand caressed the blossom, running down the petals to the stem and leaves and back again. The orchid had light purple flower clusters that looked almost like lilacs. She knelt and took a whiff of the fragrance. "I think it's a *Honohono superbum*. It only blooms once a year, but you can't miss that perfume." Her hand moved to the next flower, which resembled a pansy. The white-tipped blossoms held dewdrops. "It's a miltonia. A pansy orchid." Her face, lit with delight, turned up to him. "You're right, I can see them in my mind. I wish I had a picture for later, when I get my sight back."

"My cell phone has a camera. I'll take a picture for you." He whipped it out and snapped a couple of shots.

She worked her way through the bed of flowers. Then they turned and meandered up the hillside, through a pathless meadow. They were trespassing, but right now, he didn't care. What she learned on excursions like this would be worth a scolding from the owner. At the top of the hill, more flower beds spread out in front of them. Ben wished she could see them. Glorious colors with delicate blooms.

Lani knelt by the first bed, and her fingers danced across the blossoms again. She caught her breath.

"What is it?" he asked.

"What does this flower look like?" Her low voice sounded intense. She thrust her nose into the blossom.

"It's real pretty. The top leaf looks kind of like a shield. The center is pale green, and the edges are pink. What's wrong?" Something rustled behind them, and Ben turned but didn't see anything.

"Go now," a small voice said from behind the tree.

A small boy, probably around eight or ten, gestured to them. He looked Polynesian, and Ben struggled to place his accent. Tongan, maybe? "Aloha," he said.

"He come. You go." The little boy swept his bony arm. "Go fast."

When he came out from behind the trees a bit, Ben frowned. The boy had welts across his bare back. Had someone been beating him? The kid wore only loose shorts that he had to keep hitching up, and it looked like he and a washcloth didn't have so much as a nodding acquaintance.

"Hey, you there. You're trespassing," a man shouted at them from the top of the hill.

The boy's face paled, and he scrambled back to the safety of the foliage. "Run," he hissed. "Must run!"

Ben glanced toward the sound of the voice. He couldn't see the man yet, but he grasped Lani's hand. "We'd better get out of here."

"I want to see the orchid again." She tugged her arm out of his grasp. Kneeling, she ran her fingers over the delicate blossom once more.

"What are you doing? Get away from there," the man shouted.

The guy stood six-six or so and probably weighed three hundred pounds. He reminded Ben of a Sumo wrestler. Ben watched him approach, and even the dog seemed to sense his menace. Fisher planted his webbed paws in the grass and faced the man. A growl rumbled in his chest.

"Easy, boy," Ben said. "Come on, Lani, we need to get out of here. We're in the wrong."

She stood and put her hand on his arm. "Take a quick picture of the orchid with your cell phone."

"Why?" Ben glanced back up the hill. The guy was only about thirty feet away, approaching with balled fists and a thunderous scowl.

"Just do it. Quick."

Ben slipped his phone out and quickly snapped the photo, then grabbed Lani up in his arms and strode toward the road. Fisher bounded after them. Lani felt as light as a China doll against his chest. Her hair smelled of something exotic like sandalwood. She trembled a little.

"I wish I could see." Her slender arms clasped his neck.

They reached the road. Ben glanced back. The guy still chugged toward them as though he had every intention of taking away the cell phone. "I'm going to have to put you down," he told Lani. He set her on the road. "Take Fisher and head back to your aunt's."

"Where are you going?"

"Don't argue. Just leave." He guided her hand to the harness. "Forward, Fisher." He watched her stumble after the dog. They'd walked this road plenty of times. She should be able to find her way back. He turned to face the big man, who had picked up speed and came rushing toward him.

The man held out a hand as big as a giant clamshell. "Hand it over," he demanded. "You got no right to be taking pictures of our flowers. They're proprietary."

"Look, I'm not giving you my cell phone. I'm sorry I trespassed. I don't want to fight you, but you're not taking my property."

The man lowered his head and bellowed as he charged Ben. Ben sidestepped and grabbed the man's elbow as he passed, flipping him to the ground. His eyes and mouth opened, but nothing but a grunt came from his lips. He rolled to his stomach and sprang to his feet, a graceful act for a big guy. He came at Ben with his fists up and jabbed a meaty paw toward Ben's face.

Ben danced back, ducking the blows as they came. If one connected with his face, he was in trouble. He wished he had a Taser like he used to carry when he worked the streets on the police force. Then the man switched tactics and charged Ben. His massive arms circled Ben's waist, and the two men went tumbling into the ditch beside the road. Bits of lava gravel dug into Ben's arms and back as he tried to loosen the man's grip. He managed to get his knee up and dig into the guy's stomach. He got one arm loose. There was a pincher move he'd learned in karate training. He positioned his fingers on the man's shoulder by his neck and squeezed.

The guy's face jammed so close to Ben's, he could smell his breath, reeking of garlic. Ben applied pressure to the nerve, and the man's face went slack. His eyes rolled back in his head, and he sagged onto Ben. His bulk just about pressed the air from Ben's lungs. Ben struggled to throw him off and finally managed to wiggle out from under him. When he'd staggered to his feet, he stumbled onto the road and headed back to Rina's. The guy would recover in a few minutes, and Ben didn't want to be anywhere close.

Was it possible? With her fingers tight around the dog's harness, Lani stumbled into something on the road, probably a rock, and nearly fell. Fisher shoved against her, and she regained her balance. She leaned against his soft fur and caught her breath. Maybe her mind was playing tricks on her. When she'd touched the petals, the vision of the rare orchid had flashed through her memory. And that fragrance! She couldn't be wrong. She'd seen the rare orchid in Thailand at an orchid show last year. She'd never forget its beauty.

Without Ben along, her confidence eroded. She stumbled along the pebbled lane. The crickets were louder now. Lani had never before noticed how there were different notes in the chirps, almost like an orchestra. The lightest sounds, bare whispers she'd never heard, brought vivid pictures—dark leaves rustling in the breeze, the flutter of birds' wings, the faint splash of fish in the pond that ran beside the road.

She heard a conversation and moved toward the sound. Fisher led her in the direction of Fawn's voice. Her steps quickened when she heard a man's voice too. "Yoshi, is that you?"

"Aloha, *kaina*. I thought I'd drop in and see how you were doing." Yoshi kissed her cheek.

She tugged on his arm. "Quick, you need to go check on the trainer. Some guy chased us." She pointed behind her, hoping her gestures pointed in the right direction.

"Ben's in trouble?" Yoshi's voice sharpened. "Where?"

"By the orchid farm." He didn't answer her, and Lani heard someone running away. She turned her face toward where she'd last heard Fawn's voice. "Did he go?"

"He's running down the road," Fawn said.

"How did he know Ben's name? Did you tell him?"

"No," Fawn said in a dreamy voice.

"You sound funny. Kind of breathless. Is everything okay?"

"Everything is perfect." Fawn's voice held a smile. "Yoshi invited me to dinner."

In spite of her anxiety for Ben, Lani began to smile. "It's about time he saw the light. When?"

"Tonight. I can't believe it."

"You sound like you're about to cry." Lani groped for Fawn's arm, found it, then squeezed her hand.

"Silly, isn't it? I wish Annie were here."

"Still no word from her? Do you think she's okay?" Lani just wanted to hear her sister's voice. Annie always knew what to do about everything.

"Yes, she's fine, according to the consulate. No one has been injured or killed. When the communication systems are back up, they'll get in touch with her. In the meantime, I'm sure she's in her element."

"She'll be obsessed. Poor Mano." Lani began to smile.

"He's probably right there with her."

Lani tipped her head to the side and listened. "Are the men coming back?"

Fawn didn't answer for a moment. "Sounds like it. Yeah, it is. I can see them now. Ben looks like he's been in a tussle. His shirt is torn, and his face is bloody. It's scratched or something."

As the men approached, Lani could hear them talking.

"You look like you've been wrestling with a bear," Yoshi said.

"I feel like it."

She planted her feet and turned to face the men. Yoshi had better answer her questions.

"I found him. He's fine. Just a dawdler," Yoshi said in a cheerful voice.

"I'm not stupid, just blind," Lani said. "What happened? I know we were trespassing, but the guy sure overreacted."

"He wanted my cell phone," Ben said.

"Why?" Yoshi asked.

"I took some pictures of his orchids."

"Are they proprietary or something?" Yoshi asked.

"It's not just that," Lani said slowly. "I think he's smuggling orchids."

"What?" Ben's voice was sharp.

"I'm sure that was an Asian slipper orchid. Fawn, you know a little about orchids. Look at the picture on Ben's camera." She heard the rustle as Ben got out his cell phone and opened it.

"Hang on, let me find it," he said. A few faint clicks sounded. "Here it is."

"It's kind of fuzzy," Fawn said. "But it does look like some kind of slipper orchid."

"It is," Lani said. "I'm sure of it."

"It's illegal to import and sell them," Fawn said.

"That's what I'm saying. The guy must be smuggling orchids. Just one Asian slipper orchid is worth thousands. Something shady is going on down the road, and I have to wonder if it's connected to Pam's murder. Two crimes virtually next door to each other? It can't be coincidental." She moved without thinking, bumped into a chair, took a step back, and stumbled over the dog. Caught in a vortex of gravity and awkwardness, she couldn't find anything to catch herself with. She went down on one knee. A strong hand caught her by the hand. Ben?

"You okay?" Ben's deep voice asked.

"Fine." She righted herself. "Or I would be if we could figure out what was going on."

six

Simi sat on the small cot in the basement and waited. Master had seen him. Simi cast a fearful glance toward the door. The man would hit him, but Simi could take it. He'd taken many bad things in the time he'd been here. Tonga seemed far away, a mere dream that he was having a hard time hanging on to. A tear slid down his cheek. If only he could go home. America was no land of gold, but a dark, fearful place.

Though Master said he would send money to Simi's family, Simi didn't trust him. Nothing else he'd promised Simi had happened. Simi hadn't seen the sea since he got here. There had been no day off, just pulling weeds and digging in the dirt.

The door flew open, and Simi cowered as Master burst into the room. The man's face was swollen. There was a cut on his lip. Simi whimpered as the big man came toward him.

"What did you say to them?" Master shouted.

The sound of his voice was so loud it made Simi's ears hurt. He held up his hands in front of his face. "Please, Master. I say nothing. Tell them to go away."

"You should have come to get me. They took a *picture*." Master paced around the room.

Simi didn't understand the word picture, but he'd seen the man pull out a hard thing and lean toward the flower. It must have been a bad thing, this picture. "Simi sorry," he said. More tears squeezed from his lids. His back still hadn't healed from the last time he'd angered Master.

"You're a poor worker, Simi. I think I should sell you to another master, let you see how hard it could be for you." Master took a step toward Simi.

Simi's chest hitched. He wanted to hide under the bed, but Master would just drag him out. The big man stood only two steps away when a voice called to him from the other room. He scowled and turned to charge back the way he'd come. "Come with me," Master snarled. He grabbed Simi by the forearm and dragged him toward the door.

The roar of his bike soothed Ben like a lullaby. Stress usually sent him to the road, where he prayed while he rolled along. He still felt unsettled as he kicked down his stand and dismounted in front of his brother's house.

It didn't seem possible to smuggle orchids in the coffee, but then, he didn't know much about orchids and how they could be transported. Maybe he could get something out of Ethan tonight.

Ethan answered the door at the first knock. "Hey, Ben. Do you know what time it is?"

Ben glanced at his watch, surprised to see that it read after eleven. "Sorry, I need to talk to you."

Ethan stepped out of the way. "Natalie is in bed. I heard your bike when I was getting a drink."

Ben sniffed as he followed his brother to the living room. He thought he smelled the yeasty odor of beer, but maybe he was too quick to jump to conclusions.

"What's this all about?" Ethan dropped into an armchair and crossed his bare legs. He wore only boxer shorts and a T-shirt. He didn't look like he'd shaved today.

"I want to know about the coffee."

Ethan sighed and ran his hand through his hair, causing his cowlick to stick up. "I told you I'm delivering coffee to the other islands."

"You're lying, Ethan. I asked at Kona Kai. They use only UPS."

Ethan dropped his legs to the floor and bolted upright. "You've gone too far this time, Ben! You're my brother, not my dad. I'm an adult. I can do what I want."

"Did you go to the counseling session?" Ben blurted.

His brother swore. "Would you get off my back? Yes, I went, and no, I haven't been drinking today. I heard you smelling me as we came down the hall."

Maybe Ben deserved that. "I only want what's best for you and your family."

"That's the kicker, isn't it? I have a family and you don't. You know what your problem is, Ben? You're so afraid of failing someone, you never try. At least I'm in the ball game. I'm swinging the bat for all I'm worth."

"You're swinging at a football when you should be taking aim at the baseball," Ben said dryly. "You're doing something illegal, Ethan. I can smell it. Tell me, what do you know about orchids?"

Ethan's laugh echoed with bitterness. "Orchids? We've moved from coffee to orchids?" He stood. "I think you're the one who's been drinking. Why don't you get some rest and come back when you're making more sense."

"What are you smuggling, Ethan? Orchid starts?" he guessed.

"I'm taking care of my family," Ethan said fiercely. "I'm not hurting anyone."

Ben realized this was the nearest thing to a confession that he was going to get. Ethan was up to his neck in something, but what? Ben sighed and slumped. "Can I peek in on Meg?"

Ethan's tight look eased. "I guess. But you've got to trust me a little, Ben. Everything is okay."

"I hope so, Ethan," he said. "I really hope so." He went down the hall and opened the door to Meg's room. He tiptoed to her crib. Her hair smelled fresh and clean when he bent over the rail to kiss her soft cheek. At least she'd been bathed. They must be trying to clean up their act a little. If only he could extricate his brother from whatever problem he faced.

"*Why wasn't someone* guarding the orchids?" Thresh glared at the big man, his bald head slick from a fresh shaving.

Kato spread his beefy hands. "The kid was supposed to be watching."

Thresh glanced at the boy, who cringed. "Did anyone kipe a flower?"

The boy's eyes clouded. "Kipe?"

"Steal. Are the orchids all there?"

Simi nodded vigorously. "No steal."

"Don't leave your post again, you understand?"

Though his blank eyes said he didn't, the boy nodded. "No leave." His dark eyes darted toward Kato.

Thresh glanced at the bruises on the kid's back. He should tell Kato to lay off, but handling the slave labor was the big man's worry.

It was up to him to bring in enough illegals for their purposes. The Tongans were the best. They were so desperate to send money to their families, they did whatever they were asked without complaint.

Thresh turned back to Kato. "Who trespassed?"

"Some guy. And a blind woman with her dog. I didn't get a close look at her."

Thresh studied the cuts on his face. "Looks like you got plenty close up with someone."

Kato flushed. "He caught me off guard. It won't happen again."

"What about the shipment?"

"Out the door already."

"Copacetic." Thresh didn't want to worry about business right now. Everything was under control, in spite of this little bump in the road.

Sitting in a lawn chair surrounded by the aroma of some Spam concoction Rina was making, Lani took comfort in Fisher's warm body leaning against her leg. "I hope Yoshi stops by to tell us he's gotten to the bottom of the orchid farm mystery," she told Fawn.

"I think he'll be by in a bit," Fawn said.

Lani's cell phone vibrated, and she answered it.

"Hi, Lani. It's Tyrone."

The deep voice made her fingers spasm around the phone. "Tyrone. What a—surprise." Her throat constricted. Why was he calling? She hadn't talked to him in two years.

"I've been thinking about you. How are you doing?"

"Okay. You?"

"Fine. The dealership is going good. I—I heard about what happened to you."

"Did you call to gloat?" The words sprang from her lips before she could call them back. "I didn't mean that. I was pretty nasty to you, Tyrone. I'm really sorry." Her eyes stung, and she blinked.

"I'm not gloating. I'm sorry about it. Blindness is no fun."

"I'm not permanently blind," she said. "This will pass when the swelling goes down."

"I held on to that hope for a while too."

She squeezed the phone so tightly her fingers hurt. "Look, why are you calling?"

"I'd like to take you to dinner. See if I can help you adjust."

"Why would you want to do that? I threw you over when you were blinded." *And worse.* She couldn't talk about that and prayed he wouldn't bring it up.

"I still care about you, Lani." His voice was husky. "Maybe there's still a chance for us."

She called to mind his image—tall, broad-shouldered, black hair and eyes, skin the color of a rich roast of coffee. A good man. She swallowed. "I don't know, Tyrone. There's a lot of water under the bridge."

"I've got a boat."

She laughed, an uneasy sound. She couldn't in good conscience blow him off. "Just dinner, okay? No promises."

"No promises. Tomorrow night?"

"Okay. Um, how do we do this? I can't drive, and neither can you."

"Ben will take us."

"You know Ben?"

"He drives a Harley, doesn't he? Of course I know him."

Great, just great. What had she gotten herself into? She closed the phone and clipped it back onto her waistband.

"What was that all about?" Fawn asked.

"It was an old boyfriend. I've got a date tomorrow." Lani searched for a change of topic. Fawn didn't know the whole story, and Lani wasn't about to go into it.

"Here comes Yoshi," Fawn said.

A chair scraped as someone settled into it. "Yoshi?" Lani asked.

"Yeah. How you doing?"

"Did you find out anything about the guy who attacked Ben?" she asked. Yoshi's heavy sigh came, and Lani wished she could see his expression. She could read him like the tide.

"The property is in a holding company. We're trying to find out the real owner. The housekeeper knows nothing, and we saw no one else around."

"Mind if I join you?" a voice interrupted.

"Hey, Arlo, pull up a chair," Yoshi said.

Metal screeched against concrete. "I'm bushed. We shipped out over two thousand pounds of coffee today. I'll be glad when you're back to work, Lani."

"So will I." He would be a good diversion, Lani decided. She didn't want to think about Tyrone's call. "I want to hear more about Taylor Camp. Did you love it as much as Aunt Rina?"

"I must have, since I was so set on getting us all together."

He had a way of speaking that made everything sound like a question. She hid her smile. "What was your favorite part?"

"We had a marvelous church," he said promptly. "The Church of the Brotherhood of the Paradise Children. No other church since then has rivaled it. Every idea about worship was welcome. We had Wiccans, Buddhists, Muslims, Christians, even atheists, all celebrating together."

"What about truth?" Ben asked.

When had he walked over? Lani turned in the direction of his voice. The way Fisher shifted should have told her he stood nearby.

"Truth is relative. We all knew there was something out there; it just had a different name to some of us. One of us would play the guitar, someone else pounded out the rhythm on the drums, someone played the sitar. My, my, it was quite delightful."

"Sounds like a broad path to destruction," Ben said.

"You don't believe in tolerance?" Arlo's voice went even higher.

"Not when it comes to truth. Everything needs to line up with Scripture."

"My, my." Arlo's seat rustled. When his voice came again, it was over Lani's head. "Well, I think I'll check on the food. Rina is making her famous macaroni salad."

A few moments later Yoshi chuckled. "Looks like you ran him off."

"I didn't mean to. I thought he might debate it with me," Ben said.

"I get the feeling he'd rather run than argue," Fawn said.

Lani hid a smile at the lilt in her friend's voice. She and Yoshi were supposed to go out to dinner in a few minutes, and Fawn's excitement could be felt even in Lani's black hole.

"Ready?" Yoshi asked.

The seat squeaked. "I'm ready," Fawn said.

Lani listened to them move away and thought about her own pending dinner date. How could she even talk to Tyrone? Especially with Ben along.

Jerry's voice interrupted her thoughts. "May I join you?"

"Sure, pull up a chair," Ben said.

The chair's springs protested, and Jerry spoke again. "I hear you had some excitement last night."

"Lani thinks some orchid smuggling is going on," Ben said. "Tell us about the orchid, Lani. What's a slipper orchid?"

Anything to get her mind off Tyrone. "The Asian ones are some of the rarest of the orchid genera. New ones are discovered in the wild sometimes, and there's a ban on exportation. Their habitat has to be preserved."

"I would think if they could be cultured, it would save them from extinction," Jerry said thoughtfully. "Though, of course, the natural ones are beautiful. Just like pearls."

She nodded. "It's a tricky issue to decide what's right. The orchids in the wild are beautiful and exotic—and worth thousands of dollars for one plant. But the fear is that they would cease to exist in the wild if they were allowed to be dug up for propagation."

"So people dig them up and sell them to private orchid collectors, is that it?" Ben asked.

"Yes. Sometimes."

"Fawn said it looked like an Asian slipper orchid," Ben said.

"But she's not an expert. I'd like to see it myself." The one she'd seen was the most exquisitely beautiful plant she'd ever personally encountered.

"Could we get someone in there to look at it?" Ben asked.

"Not without their permission. And I can't see that happening, can you?"

Ben's voice lowered. "You still think the smuggling might be related to the murder of the Aberstrom woman, Lani?"

"Maybe. It's just a gut feeling, though. I've tried to think, to remember something concrete, but there's nothing there."

Ben hesitated. "I thought . . . I don't know. I just thought maybe something would register—"

"Nothing registers. I don't remember anything." Why did everyone keep pressing her? The harder she tried to call up the events, the more they floated away.

"Do you really want to remember, Lani?" Jerry said gently.

"Of course I do! Do you think I want to forget what happened?"

"Sometimes it's easier to forget. Especially when we're trying to protect someone."

She leaned forward, furious, and felt Fisher's body tense. "I don't remember anything. I'm not trying to protect someone, either."

Jerry cleared his throat and gave an awkward laugh. "Hey, let's not fight." The chair groaned. "I'd better go see if your aunt needs me for anything." His steps crunched away.

Lani's cell phone vibrated again. Sighing, she answered it.

"Hey, girl. Where you been?"

"Hi, CeCe." She'd known CeCe would be calling anytime.

"Lani, how are you?"

"Well, I'm blind, you know."

"I heard. I'm so sorry."

"You never even called me, CeCe."

"I can't handle seeing you cry. But you're over all that, right? Now you can have some fun. I'll come pick you up for the party. Brad asked if you'd be there, and I told him you would."

Some friend. She was only concerned about her stupid party. Lani squeezed her eyes shut and ducked her head. "I don't think so, CeCe." Her fingers tightened on the phone. "I'm just not comfortable in that scene any more."

"Since you became a *Christian*? You're not dead just because you're going to church now." CeCe sounded disgusted.

Lani thought of CeCe's last party. What she could remember of it made her shudder. "Look, I have to go," she said. "I'm just not up for it."

"I'll call you in a couple of days. You'll be sorry if you miss this one."

Lani hung up. She should have told CeCe no in a firm tone. Knowing her own weaknesses, Lani knew she shouldn't be anywhere near that party. Would she always be chained to the old sins? She wanted the temptation to be gone.

"Everything okay?" Ben asked.

"Fine."

"Sorry if I upset you."

At least she could think about something other than her worthless life. She curled her fingers into her palms. "It's just that I really don't remember anything."

"I understand where you're coming from. We all want to protect the ones we love."

He didn't believe her either. She wished she could examine his expression. Was she imagining the pain she heard in his voice? "Have you ever failed protecting someone?" The silence went on so long she began to wonder if he would even answer.

"Yeah." He cleared his throat. "Who could we get to look at the orchid? Maybe we could sneak in after dark with a flashlight."

She knew her face had to reflect her disappointment. Even though she'd spilled her own story, he didn't seem inclined to confide in her. "The horticulture teacher at the University of Hawai'i could tell us. She's an avid orchid collector."

"Do you think she'd come?"

"For a chance to see an Asian slipper orchid? She'd be here tomorrow. But I can't ask her unless I'm fairly certain. We need a better picture to send her."

"I'll sneak back tonight and take one."

"You can't go alone." What was she saying? She'd be a burden, not a helper. He'd have to be worrying about a blind woman stumbling around behind him.

"Thanks, but I don't think that would be a good idea."

No surprise there—it didn't sound all that hot to her either. "My other senses are beginning to get more attuned. I'll be able to hear and sense things I don't see. So will Fisher." Why didn't she keep her mouth shut? Her tongue had a bitter taste. Danger in the dark was so much scarier.

"Thanks, but I'll handle it." His voice held a firm note of finality.

Stubborn guy. Relief tinged her disappointment.

Ben left Lani and wandered over to the coffee building. The stench of the coffee almost made him gag. Josie stood behind the counter making a drink for a couple goggling over the bags of roast coffee. Tourists, by the look of them. They wore matching aloha shirts, and the man had on tennis shoes with white socks that came to his calves. The woman had a sunburn that hurt Ben to look at.

Josie handed them their drinks, then rang up their purchases. Once they wandered back out into the sunshine, Ben moved closer to the counter. "Want a blended mocha or something?" Josie asked.

"About as quick as I'd want a shot of gasoline," Ben said. He grinned to take the sting out of his words.

"Philistine," she said, returning his smile. "We'll get you hooked yet."

"Don't count on it." He leaned on the counter. "How long have you worked here, Josie?"

"All five years Rina has been here." Her broad hands cleaned the counter with speedy efficiency.

"What'd you do before that?"

She tossed him a curious glance. "I was a chemist, then took some training in homeopathy." She smiled. "Some alternative-medicine people say coffee is evil, but I don't hold to that. It's full of antioxidants just like tea, especially when it's organic like ours. Here, I can enjoy working with something worthwhile. I was glad to leave the lab behind. Why do you ask?"

"I just wondered how easy it's been to build the business."

"It's always difficult at first, but our trees are bearing a huge crop this year. I hope to see us start to break even soon."

"This building looks new." Maybe money made from smuggling had paid for it.

"It is. We built it nine months ago and tore down the old barn we'd been using. Rina paid for it." She frowned. "Where are all these questions leading?"

"How well do you know the workers? The men from Taylor Camp and the others?"

She shrugged. "About as well as a boss ever knows the workers. Other than our friends. Rina and I both knew them in the old days. We lived together for five years, so we know them pretty well. It's hard to keep secrets when you've smoked weed together."

"People change," he said.

She sighed, an exasperated huff. "Are you accusing someone of something?"

"Could one of them have shot Pam Aberstrom?"

Her mouth dropped open. "Are you nuts?"

"Probably." He stood and wished he could level with Josie. Maybe she knew something about his brother's connection to the coffee farm. So far, everything seemed on the up and up.

"They're good men, and they care about Rina. Most of them, anyway."

"What about that Willie Kanaho?"

Josie gave an unladylike snort. She crossed her muscular arms over her chest. "He only cares about his bottom line. Rina doesn't see it, but he's not worth her little finger. She chooses men poorly."

"What do you mean?"

"Nothing." She scrubbed at a nonexistent spot on the counter. "Forget I said anything."

He wasn't going to get any more out of her. "Sorry to bother you," he said, heading for the door.

"No bother," she echoed as he strode away.

He stepped out into the sunshine just as his cell phone chirped. The caller ID showed Tyrone's number. "Hey, buddy, how's it going?"

"Pretty good. Just need a little help."

"You got it."

"I've got a date and I need wheels."

Ben grinned. "Who's the lucky woman?"

"Lani."

Ben couldn't believe what he was hearing. "She's already hurt you once, buddy. Wise up. Don't go looking for more."

"I'll be careful. But she's hurting now. And we have even more in common than we used to. Don't give me a hard time. Just help me out."

Ben's gaze darted back across the lawn to where Lani sat eating with the dog at her feet. He'd seen some signs that she wasn't as bad as he thought. She was intelligent, spunky, and she cared about her family. "Okay," he said finally. "What do I have to do?"

"Could you bring her to the shop tomorrow at six? We can walk next door to the restaurant, and you can pick her up in an hour and a half."

"I can do that." He hung up, unsettled for a reason he couldn't put his finger on.

seven

$\mathcal{B}$en wished a moon shone down tonight, but clouds obscured what light there might have been. He walked along the road that led to the Hula Orchid Farm with the wind at his back and Fisher trotting beside him. Lani insisted the dog go to warn him of anyone approaching.

A sound came from behind him, and he stopped and listened. Fisher glanced up as if to ask what was wrong. It must be just the wind. The night was still, with a gentle wind that misted his face with moisture. He turned up the lane and began to climb the hill. The wet grass soaked his feet, clad only in slippers.

He paused and looked around. "I think it was about here," he whispered to Fisher. He recognized the big banyan tree. He left the path and hurried through the wet grass. Banks of flowers lined the way. The orchids were hidden behind this rock wall, if he remembered correctly. Ah, there they were. He shone the flashlight on the flower bed, seeing only familiar orchids.

He searched for a full five minutes before he found the soft indentation in the ground where a plant had been removed. The only reason for them to move a plant was if Lani was right. They didn't want anyone to look at this orchid again.

Switching off his light, he headed in the direction of the buildings he'd seen in the daylight. Maybe the big guy had moved the orchid to a greenhouse. The quarter moon came out from behind the clouds and cast a meager beam on the ground. Not daring to turn on his flashlight, he picked his way up the hillside. When he reached the crest, he paused and peered through the darkness.

White orchid petals caught the gleam of moonlight. Kneeling, he touched the ground. The dirt felt fresh and moist under his fingertips. He dug out his cell phone and took a picture. The flash on the built-in camera illuminated the darkness. He glanced toward the house, a two-story that hulked at the top of the hill. A thin beam of light bounced along the ground toward him. Someone with a flashlight. He'd been found out.

Fisher growled, and Ben hushed him with a hand on the dog's head. The hillside sloped steeply down, and he almost lost his footing as he rushed toward the road. Glancing behind him, he saw the young boy who'd warned them when they first saw the orchid. He slowed his breakneck pace. The boy still hadn't seen him. Ben stopped and watched the kid wander toward him. He seemed to be on a routine examination of the perimeter.

When the flashlight beam touched Ben's boots, the kid looked up and saw Ben. His mouth dropped open, and he stopped. "You go!" He cast a fearful glance back toward the house.

"What's your name?" Ben stepped closer to the boy, who cringed back.

He gestured with the flashlight, and it wobbled over the hillside. "Go now. Hurry."

"Some guard you make," Ben said. He extended his hand. "I'm Ben."

The boy shook his head. "Away. You, away."

"You're turning into a broken record, kid. Look, I'm not going anywhere until you tell me your name and where you got those welts on your back." Though the dark hid the kid's bruises, Ben couldn't forget the livid marks. Someone had been beating him.

"Name is Simi," the boy said with another panicked glance behind him.

Ben stepped closer, and this time Simi held his ground. Ben touched his shoulder, and he winced. "Sorry. Why don't you come home with me and let me fix those bruises?" The first thing he'd do was call child protective services. The kid couldn't be older than ten.

"No, no." Simi tried to pull away, but Ben kept a tight hold on his arm. "Simi go now," the boy said. He jerked out of Ben's grip.

Ben grabbed at the boy but slipped on the wet grass, and Simi darted back up the hill before Ben could stop him. Lights blazed to life in the house. Time to boogie out.

Thresh stalked the windows of the dark house on Rina's property. Someone had been at the orchid farm again. They'd moved the most valuable plant, but these two meddlers needed to be stopped before they seriously derailed his plan. But how could he do it without having police swarming all over?

Lani was the more dangerous of the two. With her out of the way, dog boy would slink away with his tail tucked between his legs. That couldn't be allowed, of course. Thresh couldn't let Ash escape. He was in there with his mocking eyes.

Could she be goaded into helping with the cherry harvesting? She wouldn't be able to see to pick them, but she knew coffee cherries and could tell by touch which ones were ripe. There could be an accident when no one was around.

His thoughts roved to other ideas. Drowning, maybe? A picnic was planned for Saturday at Honaunau. If Lani got in the water, she would be a prime target. But would she go when she couldn't see anything? Doubtful. Still, the opportunity just might come up.

He peeked through the window at Lani. She was golden, just like Blossom when she was in her twenties. And maybe that was the real reason this killing would be so difficult. The room was closed in with darkness, not even a nightlight, but then, Lani wouldn't need it. Any day she could regain her memory. Any moment. She would remember it was his face she'd seen before the gunshot.

Through the open window, the dog's growl reverberated, then his nose touched the window screen. Thresh jumped back, and the dog began to bark. He turned and ran through the wet grass in bare feet. Nerve endings lit with adrenaline, Thresh felt twenty-five again. "Outta sight," he muttered.

Birds twittered from somewhere above her head, and late-afternoon shadows cooled Lani's arms. She stood with her hand on Ben's Harley.

"I'll put on the sidecar," Ben said.

Lani stroked the soft leather. "I've always loved to ride these. I'd rather sit behind you."

"Fisher will need the sidecar."

"Then I *need* to ride on the seat."

"If you like." His voice held a smile. "Let me load Fisher, then I'll get on and you can climb on behind me."

She listened to the rustle as he secured the dog. "You sure you don't mind doing this?"

"I don't mind." The leather seat creaked. "I'm on. Can you manage?"

"Let me try it." She ran her hand along the seat, then maneuvered close and swung her leg over. "I can't see where to put my feet."

"Let me help you." His warm fingers touched her ankles, then lifted her feet onto the footrests. "How's that?"

"Good." She settled into the wide, comfortable seat and leaned against the backrest. "I don't understand why you don't like me."

"Actually, I'm starting to think of you as a friend. You've got a lot of good qualities." He cleared his throat. "So are you and Tyrone an item?"

"This is just a friendly dinner. I have no plans for anything more with Tyrone."

He shifted. "Then why go?"

"Tyrone and I have some past issues we need to talk out."

"Don't hurt him. He's a good guy." The bike shook as he kick-started the engine.

His bossiness rankled Lani. "It's none of your business."

The bike took off with a jerk that made Lani grab Ben's waist to steady herself. The wind lifted the hair from the back of her neck. The bike rolled faster and faster, around the curves and into the straightaways. Exhilaration shot through Lani in a tidal burst. She leaned forward and clasped Ben tighter, laying her head against his broad back.

The muscles in his back and waist flexed, and she could smell his cologne. Her senses warned her off, and she leaned back again, but the road was too rough to ride without hanging on, especially with the disorientation she felt from not being able to see where she was going. Her pulse beat fast, but she ignored it. It was the excitement of the ride, that was all.

The bike slowed, and Lani heard other traffic. They must be in town. She smelled the exhaust and felt the pipes' heat against her legs. Other vehicles rumbled by, and she heard the bells chime on the town clock.

"We're here," Ben said. The engine died, and the bike tilted to the side. "Do you need help getting off?"

"Yeah, I think so." Her body still vibrated from the bike ride, and she wasn't sure how to get off.

"Sit still."

The seat under her moved as his bulk lifted from the bike. His fingers touched her ankle and guided it to the pavement. Holding on to his hand, she wiggled off the bike and stood. "Where are we?"

"At the Harley dealership. I can see Tyrone in the window."

Lani's resolve melted. She wasn't ready for this. Confession was good for the soul, but she didn't know if she could go through with it. Curling her fingers into her palms, she willed her breathing to stay even.

Ben pressed Fisher's harness handle into her hand. "Ready?"

"Sure," she said. Her lips felt wooden and stiff. "Forward," she ordered the dog. Fisher led her up the walk toward the building. The breeze blew the scent of the sea to her nose. Her stomach did a lazy rollover, and she swallowed.

"Let me get the door." Ben's arm brushed hers as he stepped past.

She heard the door open, and a whoosh of cool air hit her face. Keeping her head up, she navigated the steps into the building, smelling the scent of rubber and new clothes.

"There you are." Tyrone's fingers touched her elbow. "Our reservation is in fifteen minutes. It's just next door. We can get there from here, Ben. Pick Lani up in an hour and a half."

"Yes, boss," Ben said in a mocking voice.

"Idiot." Tyrone laughed, and Ben's chuckle joined in.

"Don't keep her out too late," Ben said.

"An hour and a half."

"I got it, I got it."

A dog nudged her left knee. Fisher was on her right. "Who's this?" She reached for the dog's soft fur.

"This is Ranger. He and Fisher are old friends. They'll enjoy their time together tonight too," Ben said.

"Shall we go?"

"Sure."

Lani mumbled a thank you to Ben before Tyrone stepped out and she followed with Fisher. The dogs seemed to know where they were going. They walked across the parking lot. Was it her imagination that the hum of conversation quieted when they entered the restaurant? After the host led them to a table, she felt along the chair back, then sat.

"I'm glad you could make it," Tyrone said. "To tell you the truth, I wasn't sure you'd show."

"I said I would." Her face burned when he didn't answer her. They both knew her word hadn't always been something to count on in the past.

The waitress brought water with ice tinkling in the glasses. She took their order and left them alone. Lani reached along the table, found her water glass, and took a small sip. The cold wetness gave her courage. She could do this.

"You smell good, Lani." Tyrone's voice was soft.

"Thanks." Lani put down her glass.

"So, um, do you have any idea who got our baby?"

Lani's heart rate accelerated. "You don't waste any time, do you?" Her hands shook, and she folded them together in her lap.

"Can you blame me? I've wondered all these months. Was it a boy or a girl?"

The wistfulness in his voice made tears well in her eyes. She wet her lips. "I don't know, Tyrone. I aborted it." Her right hand crept to her stomach, and she choked back the bile in her throat. She heard Tyrone inhale sharply. At least she didn't have to look at his face.

The words might as well have fallen into a void. The tinkle of tableware and the laughter and voices at other tables sounded distant as she waited for his response. If he called her every filthy name in the book, it would only be what she deserved.

"You killed our baby?" He didn't sound angry, not yet. His voice vibrated with disbelief. "All this time I imagined a little boy or girl growing up in some nice home."

"I couldn't go through with it, couldn't face the stares of my friends," she whispered. "But what I didn't know was how much I'd hate myself for doing it."

"It always comes back to you, doesn't it, Lani? All you care about is yourself." The anger was in his voice now, and the table vibrated as he slammed his hand down on it.

"You're right." Her words were barely audible. "You can't hate me any more than I hate myself. It was so wrong. I wake up in the night thinking I hear a baby crying." Hot tears rolled down her cheeks. "There's no way to take it back, to undo it."

"You're right." The chair screeched on the floor, then his voice spoke low as if to maintain some privacy. "I can't sit here and eat with the woman who killed my baby." His footsteps walked away.

Lani was sure everyone must be staring. She dabbed at her eyes with her napkin and took a deep breath. Tyrone's anger felt justified, a holy whip from God. It was a relief to have it out in the open. She'd told no one about the abortion except Annie. Her sister had cried, then tried to comfort her, but the comfort never took. Lani was still sullied with her deed.

Fisher whined and licked her foot. She reached down and rubbed his ears. "I'm okay," she whispered. But she wasn't. She would never be able to rub away the stain of her guilt.

Ben sat under a coconut palm by the water. The wind brought a salty spray to his lips as he listened to the sound of the surf. He'd dropped Lani off half an hour ago, so he still had an hour to kill.

His cell phone bleeped, and he answered it. "Ben here."

"Ben, it's Lani." Her voice was low and tearful. "Can you come get me?"

"Where are you?"

"At the restaurant."

"Where's Tyrone?"

"We—had an argument and he left." She took a ragged breath. "Can you come? I think people are staring."

"I'll be right there." He closed his phone and jogged to the bike. Tyrone wasn't the kind of guy to walk out on a woman. It must have been some argument. They sure didn't waste any time. He made it back to the Harley dealership in record time. Parking in the lot next to the restaurant, he saw Tyrone leaning against the twisting branch of a monkeypod tree. His shoulders slumped, and his head hung down. Ranger nosed at Tyrone's leg.

Ben walked over to join him. "What happened? Lani just called me to come get her."

"I don't want to talk about it." Tyrone lifted red-rimmed eyes toward Ben. "Just get her away from me." He grabbed Ranger's lead. "Forward," he snapped.

Ben watched him walk away then entered the restaurant. He found Lani still at the table with her food in front of her. Tyrone's plate was across the table from her. Neither had been touched.

He put his hand on her shoulder. "I'm here."

Her reddened eyes held a deep sadness. "Can we go now?" she whispered.

"Let me get a box for the food." He motioned to the waitress. She brought two boxes after a curious stare at Lani, then took the money he offered.

Lani and Fisher followed him out to the bike. Tyrone was nowhere in sight. He got Fisher and Lani installed. "Now what's this all about?" he demanded.

"I can't talk about it." She swiped the back of her hand across her eyes. "I just want to go home."

Ben sighed and kicked the engine to life with more force than necessary. One of them would tell him sooner or later.

eight

Pu'uhonua o Honaunau held a certain mystique Lani loved. The Place of Refuge had been a part of the islands since ancient times. If a commoner broke *kapu* and did something unpardonable, he could run here to make atonement. It had been a place of retreat and refuge for her, too, since she'd been a child. She would search the tidepools in hope of finding an oyster with the biggest pearl ever seen inside, but the most she ever discovered was a starfish or two.

She needed refuge after the encounter with Tyrone two days ago. Her spirit felt bruised and battered. The wind made a melody in the palms over her head, and the surf roared. Sand and grass softened the ground under her feet. She thought she saw a flash of light, but when darkness closed in tightly she decided it had been her imagination.

The picnic tables and barbecues were at the southern end of the state park past the tidepools. *Keikis* screamed with laughter in the shallow pools of water. She thought longingly of the great snorkeling just offshore, the brilliant blues, yellows, and reds of the fish. She could see the colors so clearly in her mind, and it seemed impossible that she might never see them with her eyes again, but she was beginning to wonder if she needed to face facts. The wind from the sea, clean and salty, brushed Lani's cheeks. The waves lapped with a gentle sound on the rocks. The sea must be mild today.

The wind carried Josie's voice to her. "The last one to hit the waves has to buy coffee!"

Lani heard Ben chuckle. "What?"

"You should see them all running for the water. They're all carrying surfboards. Even your aunt. Oh wow, Arlo just caught a terrific wave. He's a pretty good surfer. Your aunt is right behind him. Oh no, she just wiped out. Arlo just flipped off on purpose—I think to check on Rina." He gasped. "They're okay. Rina just gave the thumbs-up."

"Good play-by-play," Lani said, smiling. The sun beat warm on her shoulders. For the first time since her encounter with Tyrone, she felt at peace. Ben and Fisher guided her over uneven ground until she bumped up to a picnic table.

"I brought snorkel gear," he told her. "Are you up for a swim?"

Lani couldn't imagine anything worse than to be floating in the water without any idea of where the shore lay. "I don't think so. It would feel like swimming in an abyss." She shuddered.

"You don't have to give up the things you love," he said. "Fisher loves to swim. And I'll be with you every minute."

Her breathing quickened, and she fingered her mother's necklace around her neck. "No thanks. You go ahead. But if you could guide me to the big rock that juts into the water, I can sit there and listen to the sea."

"It sounds like it's a favorite spot."

"I used to come out here a lot after my mom died. Sometimes I thought I could hear her voice in the waves." Heat settled in her cheeks. Her confession was too intimate to share with someone who was a virtual stranger, especially one who held her at a distance the way he did.

"There's something lulling about the sea."

His voice sounded wistful, as if he had sorrows too. Lani wished he'd share something about himself. "Do you have any siblings?" she asked.

"A brother." His voice changed, grew grim. "Ethan."

She tried not to flinch. Every time she heard that name, she thought of her embarrassment. "Is he married?"

"Yeah, he and his wife have a little girl who's almost two."

"Are there problems between the two of you? You sound almost mad."

"I love my brother, but he's not being the dad he should."

"That's too bad. I know what it's like to have a dad who keeps me at arm's length. His research always comes first."

"I'm sure he loves you."

"A diplomatic thing to say." She smiled. "He probably does, as much as he's able, anyway. Annie has been my salvation, especially after our mom died."

"Hey, girl, let's get in the water." Fawn's voice broke into her thoughts.

Lani shook her head. "No way. I'm not going swimming."

"Yes, you are." Fawn grabbed her hand and hauled her up. "I even brought your swimsuit. I'll be with you every minute."

The breeze picked up and brought a stronger scent of the sea to her nose. Maybe it wouldn't be quite as scary as she thought. "Five minutes," she said. "But you have to hang on to my hand the whole time."

"Done." Fawn led her to the bath building, where they both changed into their suits.

At the first touch of the warm waves on her toes, Lani stopped. "I can't do this, Fawn. I don't even know where the rocks are."

Ben's voice spoke in her ear. "Reach out with your other senses, Lani. Hear the waves splash against the rocks. Feel the currents and trace them back to where they detour around the stones."

Lani fought back her jangling nerves and tried to do what he said. She strained to listen to the waves. There, a little curl of wave hit a stone to her left. Another sounded like a deep bell as a larger wave struck it. She waded in a bit farther, feeling along the bottom with her feet. The sand gave way to rock, and she stumbled and fell face-first into the water.

The ocean closed over her head, invading her nose, ears, and mouth with stinging salt water. Flailing, she struggled against the waves, not sure which way was up or down. Even with water clogging her ears, she heard a splash next to her, then something clamped onto her hair and an unseen force yanked in some direction. Her head broke the surface of the water, and her pinwheeling hands touched wet fur. Fisher had hauled her to the surface like a wet kitten. She coughed and gasped, sucking in a welcome mouthful of air. Her lungs and throat burned from the salt she'd inhaled.

A hand touched her arm. "Are you all right?" Ben asked.

Her eyes stung, and she tried to tell herself it was the salt. "I want to go back," she said. "You left me."

"I was right here. Fisher just got to you first. You were in no danger."

She bent over, coughing hard as the waves lapped at her knees. Didn't he realize she'd almost drowned? When she had her breath back, she stood and patted her leg. "Here, Fisher." She heard the splashing, then the dog pressed his wet nose against her leg, and she rubbed his head. Running her hands over him, she realized he barely had his head above water, but he still stayed close to her. "Good boy. You saved me."

He licked her hand, and she went to her knees in the water, letting him lick her cheek.

"I'm so sorry," Fawn said. "I tried to grab you as soon as you went down, but I stumbled too. Don't let this scare you, Lani. Five more feet and you'll be in water perfect for floating in the waves."

"I don't want to go in. Which way back?" She tried to sound rational and calm, but everything in her screamed for them to take her back.

"It's like getting back on a horse," Ben said. "If you don't go in now, you'll always be afraid to swim. Is that what you want?"

"I'm going to see again." If she could see him, she'd hit him.

"I hope so. But I don't want you crippled with fear, Lani. You have to conquer it."

She wasn't strong like Annie. But she heard the challenge in his voice. She wanted to be confident again, to laugh in the face of fear. "Five minutes," she said again. She held out her hand, and he took it.

"Hang on to me," he said.

Fawn moved to her other side. "Put your hand on my arm."

Lani grasped Fawn's forearm, and they began to wade through the waves. The ground sloped until she stood in water to her waist.

"I'm going to hold on to your hand. Lie on your back and float," Ben said.

Lani nodded. She took a breath for courage, then thrust herself back with her face up to the warming rays of the sun. The waves buoyed her, and she floated.

"I'm going to let go of your hand, but I'll be right here." Ben squeezed her fingers, then let go. "Now listen. You can hear the kids at the tidepools and the people at the picnic tables. Out in the water you can hear a boat engine."

He was right. Suspended in the waves, she knew the safety of the land lay to her right, and to her left stretched open water. She began to relax. The disorientation began to leave, and with it, her sense of terror. With some sense of her location, she floated on her back and let the waves lap over her. The sound of the surf soothed her.

"You okay?" Fawn asked.

"Yes, I'm not scared now."

"I forgot sunscreen, and I'm starting to burn. I'm going to go in a minute and put some on. I'll be right back. Ben is still here with you."

"That's fine," Lani said. Fawn sloshed off. Lani felt weightless in the water. She'd needed this time.

"Help! Help!" A faint scream came to her ears. She flailed in the water as she righted herself. "Did you hear that? Someone is in trouble."

Ben pressed her arm. "It's a kid. I have to help. You'll be okay, Lani. Stay right here. Keep the shore to your right."

The pressure of his hand vanished. "Don't leave me!" Lani grasped empty air and heard him splash off in the waves. Fisher nuzzled her hand.

His voice called from a distance. "No one else is close, Lani. I'm a strong swimmer. I'll be right back. Hold on to Fisher."

What could she say? Lani couldn't hold him back when someone needed saving. She stood with the waves hitting her in the chest. Shouts came from the shore as people realized someone was in trouble. Lani told herself she would be fine. Her feet were planted on the sand. Her hand gripped Fisher's collar. As long as she stood right here, the waves couldn't pull her out to sea.

She listened to the distant shouts from one direction and the sound of motorboats from the other. Ben would handle it. Her limbs were just beginning to warm after her initial terror when she felt a hard shove. Fisher barked. Her feet lost their purchase on the sand and slipped out from under her. Without thinking, she let go of the dog as if to prevent herself from falling. Waves closed over her head, and she inhaled a mouthful of water. Then hard hands pressed down on her shoulders, and her bottom touched the sand. And stayed there.

She tore at the hands on her shoulders, kicking out with her feet. The soles of her feet touched only water as her attacker stayed out of reach of her struggles. Her lungs burned with the need for oxygen. She had to breathe. Her hand brushed Fisher's fur. She reached out again and grabbed a handful of dog, but even with her fingers clenched in his fur, she couldn't get out from under the ruthless hands that pinned her to the seabed. A roaring filled her head.

She was going to drown. Fisher pulled away, and she felt abandoned. The pressure on her shoulders eased. The soles of her feet touched the sand, and she gave a great push up. Her head broke the water, and she began to gasp in huge lungfuls of air. Ben had been right. The first time she'd only choked down a bit of water. She had been in no real danger. This time she had come very close to drowning. Her lungs still felt on fire, and she felt weak.

She heard someone thrashing toward her in the waves. Was her attacker back? She listened for the sounds of children and moved with the waves toward the shore. Fisher barked and growled, and the sound of splashing moved away. Picking up her pace, she stumbled into shallow water. Then she reached the shore, where she collapsed onto the sand. Someone had just tried to kill her.

nine

Thresh stormed down the pier, still fuming about the failure. Ethan was waiting with his daughter, a cute little blond. If he thought her presence would keep him out of trouble, he was wrong. Thresh was in no mood for excuses.

Ethan's smile faded when he saw Thresh's face. "Everything okay?"

"Nothing I can't handle," Thresh snapped.

"I've been having some problems too," Ethan said. "My brother is close to finding out what I'm doing. You might have met him. He's helping the blind girl."

Thresh froze, blood pounding, feeling like a trapped bird. "Ben Mahoney is your brother? You don't look anything alike. You don't even have the same last name."

"We have different dads. Mom lived in a hippie commune on Kaua'i in the seventies, and she had Ben there."

Could it be? Peekaboo's last name had always been a mystery. "What about Ben's father?"

Ethan shrugged. "Someone Mom called Ash. He died. I guess she never knew for sure if he drowned or if sharks got him, but he went swimming once and never came back."

Thresh felt the blood drain from his face. So Ben was Ash's son, and Peekaboo was Ben's mother. What an unexpected surprise. Ben was the key to Peekaboo. No wonder the kid looked like Ash. Well, that settled it. Ethan would have to die. Thresh smiled at him, anger forgotten. Yes, Ethan would have to die for a greater cause, and the sacrifice would be a worthy one.

Maybe today hadn't been a total waste after all.

Ben eyed Lani where she sat on a blanket under the coconut palm. She still looked pale and kept coughing, even though she'd been out of the water over an hour. At first he'd wondered if she'd imagined the attack—until he saw the red blotches on her shoulders.

"Yoshi said he'd meet us at the station when you're ready," he told her. "He needs a statement."

"I can't tell him much. I didn't see who it was." Her tone tried for irony but settled for despair.

"I'm sorry," he said. "I promised you'd be okay."

"And I was." She lifted her head, her chin set with an "I am woman" resolve.

"Fisher has a bloody snout," Ben said. "I think he tangled with your attacker."

"Something drove him off."

He should have been there. She shouldn't have had to rely on the dog.

She tipped her head up. "Did you save the swimmer? I forgot to ask."

"It was just two boys clowning around. When I scolded them, they told me—" He stopped, suddenly understanding.

"They told you what?"

"That someone had paid them to pretend to be drowning," he said slowly.

Even more color leached from her face. "The killer planned this," she whispered.

"Looks like it." He turned and studied the crowd on the shore. Unaware of what Lani had been through, Rina and her former hippie friends were still out surfing. They'd been all over the water. Any of the other strangers here could also be the attacker.

A police car, lights flashing, came screaming up the lane. Ben turned and saw it skid to a stop.

Yoshi leaned over the seat and pushed open the passenger door. "Get in!"

Ben looked into the car. "What's wrong?"

"There's been a boating accident. It's your brother."

Ben felt his heart come to a stop before it began to pump blood through his veins again. "How bad?" Lani and Fisher came up behind him before Yoshi answered.

"I want to come too," Lani said. "I'm afraid." She clutched his hand. "Besides, you need someone with you."

Ben's hands began to shake. He realized he wanted her there, needed someone who cared. And she did seem to care. He opened the back door and helped her get in. He told Fawn to let Rina know where they went, then he hopped in the front seat. "Are they okay?"

"We don't know yet, Ben. There's been an explosion. I've got a Coast Guard boat waiting in Kealakekua Bay for us."

Don't panic. Ethan is probably fine. But his mouth went dry as he began to imagine the worst types of scenarios. He pushed away the ugly thoughts and prayed instead. God had this situation under control too.

The car drove down the winding shoreline to the bay. Kayaks

dotted the deep blue water. Yoshi killed the sirens and the lights and pulled the car to the road's shoulder. "I'll get Lani. You get on out there and see if they've found them," Yoshi said.

"Them?"

"A report said Natalie and Meg were aboard as well."

The baby. Ben vaulted from the car and ran to the water. A Coast Guard cutter was anchored offshore, and he waved to the boat. A launch separated from the cutter and zoomed toward shore. Two men manned the Zodiac. Ben kicked off his slippers and waded out to the craft. "I'm Ben Mahoney. Have you found my brother and his family? Driscoll, it's Ethan Driscoll."

"Not yet."

Ben turned to check on Yoshi's and Lani's whereabouts. They were nearly to the shore. He turned and slogged back through the water to the sand as they arrived. "No sign of them yet." At least their bodies hadn't been found. He could only hope that meant good news.

"Let me see what I can find out." Yoshi waded through the water to the boat.

Ben had Lani grab his arm, and he helped her to the boat. Once they were aboard, the boat banged against the waves as it zoomed back to the cutter. Yoshi stood talking to the petty officer, but Ben couldn't hear over the roar of the wind. He scanned the whitecaps but saw no sign of flotsam or debris. Yoshi hadn't said where the explosion took place.

They boarded, and the boat sped out to sea. Lani reached for his hand. He curled his fingers around her cold ones.

"I'm sorry," she said. "It's scary to think of such a little one being out here."

"She's not even two," he said. "Sweetest little thing with big blue eyes and blond curls." He wanted to tell her how close he'd come to taking her out of the home last week, but he couldn't face the guilt. If only he'd followed through. Ethan had eventually kept his appointment with the rehab center, but Ben had a sinking feeling that alcohol would be found to have played a role in today's accident. That particular monkey clung with tenacity to Ethan's back.

"They may have found everyone already," Lani said.

Fisher pressed his wet nose against Ben's bare calf. "I hope so," Ben said. He leaned forward. "I think I see some debris." He released Lani's hand and stood at the rail. Pieces of fiberglass boat began to appear in the choppy seas. Another Coast Guard cutter cruised the waters on the other side of the flotsam, and he could see several smaller boats as well.

Lani joined him at the rail. "I hear a chopper."

He hadn't noticed, but when she mentioned it, he heard the *whop-whop* of an approaching helicopter, and the rotors stirred the water. A petty officer handed him a set of binoculars, and he began to scan the waves. The choppy sea made it hard to search. Whitecaps rose and fell, and he had to try to see into the valleys of water.

Yoshi joined them on Ben's other side. "There are bags of coffee everywhere. The Coast Guard thinks Ethan was smuggling something. Drugs, maybe. You see any signs that he had more money than usual?"

Ben didn't want to squeal on his brother, but he couldn't lie. "Yeah," he said. "A few new things. I questioned him about it too. I saw bags of coffee in his house. He told me he had a job delivering coffee for Kona Kai."

"That's why you asked me about delivery," Lani said.

"I confronted him, but I couldn't get anything out of him."

"Why didn't you talk to me about it?" Yoshi demanded.

"I had no proof of anything." He sighed and rubbed his head. "Lame excuse, I know."

Yoshi looked back at the floating burlap bags. "If this coffee is from Aunt Rina's trees, I'll bet your shooting is connected to a smuggling operation, Lani."

Ben lowered the binoculars and looked at her. Was someone she loved involved too? Maybe she *was* trying to protect someone.

Lani's knuckles were white where she gripped the railing. "I know you think I'm hiding something, Yoshi," she said. "But I honestly don't remember anything."

Ben hadn't pressed her much on what she remembered, but he thought Yoshi had it wrong. If she remembered what happened that night, surely she'd say so.

"You're protecting someone, aren't you, Lani? Who is it?"

Her wide, unseeing eyes blinked in her cousin's direction. "I can't remember!"

"You can't or won't?" Yoshi pressed with relentless persistence. "Something is going on out there at the coffee farm, Lani. You and I both know it. Just tell me what you saw."

Lani pressed her fingers to her eyes. "Don't you think I've tried and tried to remember? If only I could identify the killer, I'd be out of danger. Someone tried to kill me today, Yoshi."

"We need to talk about that too." Yoshi glanced at Ben for confirmation, and Ben nodded.

"The accident is more important. I'm okay." She dropped her hand. "Let's worry about finding Ben's family right now. This can all wait."

Yoshi nodded and raised his binoculars to his eyes.

Ben blocked out everything and began to scan the water again.

This section of ocean held even more flotsam. He saw bits of cushion, something that looked like part of a cabinet, and the charred remains of a cooler floating in the whitecaps. Then he glimpsed a small face in a valley before another wave hid it from view.

"It's Meg!" He dropped the binoculars and dove into the water. Yoshi shouted something, but Ben ignored him. Kicking through the rough seas, Ben swam toward the debris. Meg had been just past the seat cushion. A wave tossed a piece of the boat's bow toward him, and he dove to avoid it. Salt stung his eyes as he surfaced and blinked the water away.

"Meg!" he shouted. "Meggie!" He heard an answering whimper. She was alive! He swam in the direction of the weak cry. Riding the crest of a wave, he slid down the blue-green wall into the dip. A bright orange flash caught his eye. A life jacket. He struck out toward it, then saw Meg's blond hair plastered to her head. His hand snagged the vest's tie, and he clutched it, dragging the little girl toward him.

Then he clasped her in his arms. She wound her small arms around his neck. "Mommy," she said, her face puckering.

He hugged her to his chest. "Hang on, Meggie. Let's get to the boat." She clung to him even tighter. He began to swim, the heavy seas breaking over his head with every fresh wave. He tried to signal the boat, but he wasn't sure if they could see him. At least her life jacket kept her head above water, though he had to have swallowed at least a gallon of seawater as he struggled to propel Meg and himself through the waves.

He thought he heard a motor, then saw the Zodiac cutting through the swells. With the seas heaving him up and down, he thought the men might have trouble finding them. He waited until the next wave lifted them to the crest, then shouted and waved. Yoshi sat in the small boat with the Coast Guard and acknowledged Ben's yell. Yoshi gestured to the pilot, and the Zodiac bounced over the waves toward them.

The boat reached Ben and Meg in a few seconds. Ben started to hand Meg up to Yoshi, but she shrieked and wrapped her arms and legs around him more tightly. "It's okay, Meg. I'm coming too." He finally succeeded in handing her up into the boat, but she continued to cry.

Exhaustion left him sinking in the waves without the strength to climb up himself. Two seamen grabbed him and helped him clamber into the boat, where he lay spent on the rubber deck. Yoshi put a squirming Meg down, and she flung herself onto his chest. "Mommy," she wailed.

Ben gathered her close and sat up and looked at Yoshi.

Yoshi looked away. "Nothing yet."

Ben's eyes burned, and he gulped. He sat with Meg in his arms. "Want some gum, Meg?" That usually distracted her.

Her tears stopped for a moment. "Gum?" She stuck her fingers in his mouth.

"In a minute," he mumbled past her salty, wrinkled fingers. The waves slammed into the rubber Zodiac, and it jolted over the tops of the whitecaps as it sped back to the Coast Guard cutter. A few minutes later they were all safely aboard. A smattering of rain began to fall, smacking into the water and onto the deck of the boat.

Ben's gaze found Lani by the railing. The wind whipped her hair around her head, tangling it around her throat like a noose. A shiver radiated along his spine at the image. The day's events included a murder attempt on her. Could someone have put a bomb on his brother's boat? The coffee implied some kind of connection. Or was he grasping at something that wasn't there? He didn't want to believe Ethan would put his family at risk by drinking on the boat, but maybe it was just that simple.

A seaman brought him a blanket, and he wrapped Meg in its warmth. Her lips were blue, and her eyelids fluttered, then closed. He settled onto the seat with her in his arms. He should put her down and let her sleep, but he didn't want to let her go.

Lani and Fisher moved to the seat beside him. "How is she?"

"Okay. Exhausted, of course."

"Poor baby." Lani groped toward him, found his arm, and followed it down to where Meg lay sleeping. She caressed the little girl's wet hair.

Yoshi joined them. "We fished some coffee bags from the water."

"And?" Ben asked. "Anything there?" Yoshi held out his hand palm up. Several pieces of deep blue coral lay in his palm. Ben picked up a piece. "It's beautiful."

"What is it?" Lani asked.

Ben took her hand and pressed a piece of coral into it. "It's dark blue coral."

She went still as she fingered it. A frown crouched between her eyes. "Something about this," she faltered.

"Sir." One of the seamen gestured toward Yoshi. Yoshi walked over to speak with him.

Ben touched Lani's arm. "Could you hold her a minute?"

"I'd love to." Lani held out her arms, and Ben deposited the toddler into them.

"Thanks." He kissed Meg's forehead, then joined Yoshi. "Is there news?"

"I'm afraid so, Ben." Yoshi put his hand on Ben's shoulder. "They've found Natalie's body."

Ben slumped against the railing. How did you comfort a two-year-old who wanted her mommy? "Ethan?" he whispered.

"Nothing yet." Yoshi's eyes were sympathetic.

"I'm not an idiot. I know the odds aren't good. It's a miracle Meg survived. They always made sure she wore a life jacket, but Ethan and Natalie hardly ever did." He realized he was speaking of them in the past tense and swallowed.

"Any ideas about the coral in the coffee?"

"There's a moratorium on selling blue coral. It's the richest color I've ever seen. Collectors will want it in the worst way," Ben said.

Yoshi nodded. "Orchid smuggling just down the road from the coffee farm, and now this. I feel certain Pam's murder is connected. I'm going to talk to Aunt Rina. Maybe she knows something. She won't like ratting out one of her friends."

Ben knew the interview wouldn't be pleasant for Yoshi. Rina was one of his only relatives. "When?"

"As soon as we get back."

Ben frowned and focused his attention on the sea. A fast-moving boat approached, slamming into the crests of the waves. It slowed as it reached the Coast Guard cutter. He could see something lying in the bottom. Natalie? But as the boat pulled up, Ben looked down into his brother's face. Ethan was quite dead.

Lani fingered the coral in her hand. The memory wouldn't come, but she knew she'd seen this coral somewhere. Her pulse fluttered whenever she tried to push past the darkness shrouding the recollection. Rolling the piece around in her fingers, she finally gave up. The harder she tried to remember, the more it eluded her.

"No!" A hoarse cry that sounded like Ben came over the roar of the wind and sea.

Lani tightened her grip on Meg and wished she understood the sudden hubbub. Had they found the rest of the family? She heard footsteps. "Who's there?" she asked.

"Seaman Lowell," a young male voice said.

"Can you tell me what's happening?" she asked.

"They're bringing aboard the little girl's daddy. He didn't make it."

Tears sprang to Lani's eyes. Other sounds came to her ears now—the harsh sounds of a man trying to choke back sobs. This had to hit Ben hard. The thought of losing her own brother or sister made her shudder. Ben was a good man, and a Christian. Why would God allow something like this to happen to him? Was her new faith a lie? She'd been trying hard to straighten out her life, and God had walloped her with blindness. And now he'd callously killed Ethan and Natalie and left Meg orphaned. What kind of God did something like that?

She knew she should pray for Ben, but the words died on her tongue. Why even pray or trust God when he brought this kind of trouble? Her life had been better before she became a Christian. She couldn't remember the last time she'd gone out with friends for a night of fun. Was this all her life was supposed to be about now—church, futile prayers, and misery? If only Annie were here to talk to. Lani felt lost and alone. She understood so little of this new life.

She heard feet shuffling on the deck, then a hand touched her shoulder. "Who's there?" she asked.

"It's me." Ben's gruff voice choked out the words. He sat beside her on the bench. "He's dead, Lani."

"I know. I'm so sorry, Ben." She felt for his hand and found it. His fingers clung to hers, and she felt him shudder.

"Can I have Meg back?" he whispered.

She held the little girl out to him, and he slipped Meg out of Lani's arms. The shoulder that touched hers shuddered again, and he began to rock back and forth a little. Lani wished she knew some comforting words, but found nothing worth saying. Maybe God could comfort him, but she couldn't.

ten

*T*hresh stood under the monkeypod tree wearing a smile of satisfaction. The death of her son should bring Peekaboo running. After all these years, she would finally pay for her sins.

Kato walked to the tree. "Why'd you sink the boat?"

"I can't stand whining. You are not to question my actions. Just follow orders."

The big man looked down. "You might let me in on it. Our most important shipment was on that boat. And the mother is missing. I think Ethan took it."

Cold rage gathered in Thresh's belly. "What? What happened?" If the greatest of all treasures was at the bottom of the sea, someone would have to answer for it.

"I don't think it was aboard the boat," Kato said quickly.

The churning in his stomach began to settle. "Find it. Search his house—tear it apart if you have to. But find it."

Ben clutched Meg to his chest. She was all the family he had now. He couldn't believe, couldn't grasp the fact that he would never see his brother again, never hear his laughter. The shudders that wracked his body had finally stopped, but he felt cold, so cold.

He sat in the backseat of Yoshi's squad car. Meg should have been in a car seat, but Ben did the best he could and strapped her into the seat belt between him and Lani. Rina had promised to run by his brother's house and pick up Meg's car seat along with some other things for the toddler. Ben wanted to do everything right, to fill in as best he could for his orphaned niece.

Lani ran her fingers over Meg's curls, dry now but still flattened against her head. "At least she's sleeping."

He nodded and pushed back his grief. If he didn't dwell on it, maybe the pain would begin to ease. His gaze lifted to her face. "How are you feeling?"

"A little sore." She removed her hand from Meg's head, and her fingers touched a mark on her upper arm.

"I'm sorry I wasn't there for you. Or for her." He hadn't been there for much of anyone lately. He'd failed his partner, failed his brother, and now failed to protect Lani when he'd promised he would.

"It's not your fault."

He swallowed and looked down at Meg. "Tell that to Meg when she grows up without parents."

"You're blaming yourself for this? There's nothing you could have done."

"I could have turned him in to Yoshi. At least he'd still be alive."

"It's no good to play Monday-morning quarterback. You could have locked him in his house too, but what good would that have done? When someone wants to do something, no amount of inter-ference from family will stop them."

"You sound like you know that firsthand." He stared at her and noticed the sad droop of her lips.

"Oh, I do. I've always liked doing whatever I wanted. No matter how much it hurt someone else." She turned her head. "No one ever talked me out of pleasing myself."

He wasn't sure what to say without revealing that he knew her better than it appeared. "You listen to your aunt, to Fawn, to Yoshi. And to me. I like the way we can talk." The fact of it surprised him. He couldn't remember ever talking so openly with any other woman.

"I've been trying to change, but after today, I'm wondering if it's worth it."

"What do you mean?" He adjusted his arm as Meg shifted in her sleep.

"You're a Christian," she stated.

"Yeah."

"If God loves us, why did your brother die?"

He flinched, feeling like the blow had come out of nowhere. "You're asking the same question Job asked. Why do bad things happen to good people? I wish I knew the answer. All I know is that I deserve God's judgment, not his mercy. Anything good I get in this life is just gravy. If it wasn't for his grace, I don't know how I'd get through this right now." His voice thickened, and he cleared his throat.

"But he could have stopped it from happening."

"We all have free will, Lani. God doesn't *make* us do anything. He wants us to love and obey because we want to, not because we have no choice."

She absorbed his words in silence. "What about my blindness? He could choose to make the swelling go down."

"He still might. Look inside yourself and see what he wants you to learn through this. Maybe it's to trust him in the hard times." He knew he should do the same in his own trial. He shared her questions and knew only that there were no easy answers.

Lani removed Meg's wet clothes and dropped them on the floor. The little girl smelled of sea and wind mingled with the freshness of the clean blanket wrapped around her. Meg murmured but didn't awaken. Lani slipped pajamas on the toddler—Aunt Rina had fetched some things—then pulled the covers up over Meg.

Lani connected with Meg at a deep level, understanding how it felt to be motherless like Meg. Her own child would have been only a year or so younger. She touched Meg's soft cheek, then folded her hands in her lap as she sat on the edge of the bed. Through the open window, the wind blew the scent of roasting coffee into the bedroom.

Lani tried to think, to analyze all that had happened today. Someone wanted her dead. Ethan was smuggling some oddly familiar coral in Aunt Rina's coffee bags. There had to be some way she could remember what happened before she fell and hit her head. The only possible reason for someone to make an attempt on her life was that she could identify the shooter. But even if she remembered, she was blind and unable to identify the killer. Unless it was someone she knew. She gulped.

Fisher's cold, wet nose probed her leg, and she rubbed his ears. "I'm okay, boy." But her agitation hummed along her nerves. She felt trapped in this darkness, unable to help herself. The murderer could be sitting across the table from her at dinner tonight, and she wouldn't know it. And behind one smiling face lurked the heart of a murderer.

A tap came at the door. "Come in," she said, careful to speak in a soft voice. She didn't want to awaken Meg.

"It's me." Ben came in. "How is she?"

"She didn't stir, not even when I changed her clothes. Have you found out anything more?"

"Yeah." The wicker chair across from the bed rustled as he sat. "I identified both bodies. They reeked of beer."

The pain in his voice made her want to touch him. She clenched her hands together in her lap. "I'm sorry."

The bedding beside her shifted. "Gum?" said a little voice.

Lani's heart melted at the plaintive voice. Her hand moved along the quilt until she touched the little girl. Meg kicked off the covers and crawled into Lani's lap. She didn't stay long but slid to the floor. Her feet pattered to her uncle.

"Gum?" she said again.

"Do you have any gum?" Ben asked Lani. "She's going to ask for it until she gets some."

"I think I have some in my purse." Lani stood and felt along the bed to a cedar chest at the foot. Her purse sat on top of it. She opened it and began to dig around inside. She inhaled the aromas of lipstick, money, the metal of keys, and leather. Her aunt was right— she *did* have a sensitive nose and always had. God hadn't left her without resources for this journey.

Taking another sniff, she caught a whiff of her aunt's coffee-blossom cologne, probably on the handkerchief she'd loaned her after her near drowning. A faint cinnamon scent told her the gum she sought was in the corner closest to her. She brought it out with a triumphant flourish. It felt good to know she was getting the hang of this.

"Gum!" Meg's feet pounded across the carpet, and she grabbed Lani's legs.

Lani scooped her up and handed her the gum. She heard the rattle of paper as the little girl unwrapped it.

"Say thank you, Meg," Ben said.

"Tank oo."

"You should see her. She has red juice running down her chin." Ben's voice was close.

"Mommy?" Meg said. "Daddy?"

Lani's fingers tightened around the little girl. If only she could fix it all.

"Are you hungry, Meg?"

"Eat," Meg agreed.

She lurched away, and Lani had a hard time holding on to her.

"I've got her," Ben said. The weight of her lifted.

"What's going to happen, Ben?"

"To Meg, you mean? I guess I'll take care of her. It's a cinch I can't let her go to my mother. Or to Nat's parents either. Her dad has been in and out of jail more times than I remember. But man, I have no idea what to do." He fell silent. "I love her, but I feel lost. What do I feed her? I know she likes mashed potatoes, but that's about it. And gum."

"Gum," Meg agreed.

Lani could hear her chomping away on the gum, and she couldn't help smiling. "I used to work in a day care. I like kids. I'll help you with her as long as you're here. Maybe by the time you leave, you'll be an old pro."

"I wouldn't count on it," he said in a gloomy voice.

A tap came on the door, then it opened. "Dinner's ready," Rina said. "Oh, the little girl is awake. Hello, precious. You want to eat?"

"Eat," Meg said. "Mommy?"

Lani winced. The requests for her parents were going to get more and more frequent. Her aunt took Meg and went down the hall with her and Ben. Lani listened to Ben talking to Meg and felt a stirring. Every other man she'd been with, she'd found physically attractive. This pull she felt toward Ben was based purely on another plane. His tenderness toward his niece made her feel like a toasted marshmallow inside.

Lani's cell phone vibrated, and she answered it.

"Hi, Lani, it's Michelle Landers. We're having a meeting next

Tuesday and wondered if you could bring some preliminary ideas to it? I know you've got another week before they have to be in, but we'd like to talk about some of our other ideas. Any chance you can come?"

"A—a friend was killed today, and I think the funeral will be Tuesday," Lani stammered.

"Oh, that's too bad. Well, I'll shoot you an e-mail about our new ideas, and maybe you can incorporate them into the design. We'll just take a peek at the scheduled meeting. Talk to you soon." Michelle hung up.

Lani flipped her phone closed. There had to be some way to pull this off. She hadn't even thought about the design. Getting to her feet, she shuffled to her closet, opened it, and found the shelving on the right side. Her sketchbook, notebook, and landscape plant books should be on the second shelf. She lifted them out and carried them back to the bed. Opening the top plant book, she ran her fingers over the glossy pages. If only she could see the plants!

Her doorknob rattled. "Hey, girl, are you okay?" Fawn asked.

"Oh, Fawn, I need some help."

Fawn's steps came closer. "What's wrong?"

"I just got another call from the home show director. I've got to figure this out, Fawn. I can see the design in my mind, but I don't know how to put it to paper."

"How can I help?"

"I don't know." Lani put her head in her hands. "Maybe if we work together, I could tell you what plant I had in mind and where to put it. There's a scaled drawing of the area on my computer."

"Let me take a look." Fawn moved from the bed, and the computer began to hum. The familiar Windows chimes sounded, then she began to tap on the keyboard. Lani told her the file name. "Here it is."

"There might be an e-mail from Michelle too."

Fawn continued to tap. "Yeah, it's here."

"See what suggestions she has."

"I'm reading it. Hmm, it sounds like she wants you to incorporate a rock waterfall somewhere in the design. And a gazebo."

"I can do that. Listen, I have an idea. Print out the layout and bring it to me."

"Okay." The printer began to whir.

Moments later, Fawn thrust a paper into Lani's hands. "Here you go. Now what?"

Lani traced the edges of the paper and visualized the layout. "Is this the front door?"

"You're amazing. It is!"

"And the walk here?" She stabbed a finger.

"Almost." Fawn guided her finger over a hairsbreadth.

"I think I can do this!" Lani's voice went up a notch. "I've been thinking about the design for weeks. All I have to do is get it down on paper with your help."

"I'm game."

For the first time in two weeks, Lani felt in control. Her future wasn't going to slip away. Not just yet.

Ben had as many blobs of food on him as Meg had down her front and in her hair. She had stuff in her ears, up her nose, and even on her feet. Were kids always this messy? He didn't remember Meg having stuff all over her when Natalie fed her. She shuddered at the sweet potatoes he spooned into her mouth and spat them back at him. She picked up the green beans with her fingers. The poi she wouldn't even try.

"She's been raised on hamburgers and French fries," Ben said.

Josie put her hands on her hips. "The poor child needs to learn what real food is. You'll stay here with her until she settles down some. She needs some women around. She'll be missing her mama."

"At least she's healthy," Jerry said. "Not a scratch on her."

"Thanks for taking a look at her," Ben said. "I don't know how long she was in the water." He stood. "I'd better give her a bath," he said.

"I'll do it." Lani rose and laid down her napkin.

Ben liked to encourage independence, but this one thing might not be possible for her to do. How could she see if Meg was clean? "I'd better figure it out," he said. "But you can help." He carried Meg to the hall bathroom. Lani followed with Fisher.

Warm terra-cotta covered the bathroom floor. A dolphin border ran around the ceiling and caught Meg's gaze. "Fish," she said, pointing.

"Dolphin," Ben said.

"Fish," Meg insisted.

He grinned and turned on the tap. Meg wiggled to be put down. She sat on the floor and pulled her bottoms off over her small slippers, then began to try to tug her pajama top off.

"Off," she said.

He removed her pajamas, and she bent over the side of the tub in her diaper. "In," she insisted.

"Just a minute." He checked the water. He liked water scalding hot, but what temperature would be best for a child? "Is this okay?" he asked Lani.

She swished her wrist in it. "It's just fine." She touched Meg, traced down her tummy to the diaper. With two tugs on the tabs, she had the diaper off, then lifted Meg into the tub. Even blind she seemed to know the procedure.

A bark came from behind him, and he turned to see Fisher running for the tub. "Look out!" he said. Fisher zipped between his legs, and Ben tried to grab him, but the dog moved too fast. Fisher bounded to the rim of the tub and jumped into the water with Meg. She shrieked and tried to scoot away.

"What's happening?" Lani asked.

"Fisher decided to take a bath too." Ben watched Fisher duck his head into the water and come up flinging water droplets. He looked ecstatic. Meg quit screaming and began to smile as she watched the dog. Fisher made a happy whine deep in his throat.

"He makes that sound when he's excited," Lani said.

Ben grabbed the dripping dog and lifted him from the tub. Fisher's wet fur soaked through his shirt. "Hand me a towel, will you?"

Lani turned and reached for the shelves that held the towels. She found one and handed it to him. He toweled off the dog and set him down. "Stay," he said with a stern edge to his voice. Fisher gave him an aggrieved look.

Ben turned back to the tub to hide his grin. "She's got stuff in her hair," he said. "I'd better wash it. Can I use my shampoo?"

"I'll use mine." She ran her hand along the back of the tub. "You'd better do it, though. I don't want to get soap in her eyes."

"What do I do?" He stared at Meg, who lay on her stomach in the shallow water, splashing madly.

"Get a cup to rinse her hair with. She's probably got her hair wet already."

"Uh, yeah. She's soaked." He grabbed the drinking glass from the sink. "Flop over on your back, Meg. Let's wash your hair." Meg rolled over, and he lathered her hair.

"Rinse it with the water in the tub for now, but when she's ready to get out, you can turn the tap back on and get some clean water for a final rinse."

It took some doing, but Ben eventually managed to get the shampoo in and out of Meg's hair. "I guess it's clean."

"I'll finish up." Lani pressed past him and felt along the tub for the washcloth. "We'll get some baby wash tomorrow."

Ben had never felt so out of his element. The task of raising Meg seemed overwhelming.

"Could you get some clean pajamas from my room?"

"Sure." He exited the bathroom and drew in a breath. It was a sad day when a man got so scared of a little thing like a bath. What happened when Meg had a dirty diaper? No way could he see himself changing something like that. Maybe he could get Lani to potty train her.

He found the small bag of her things and fished out a pair of pajamas and a clean diaper. His hand connected with something unfamiliar in the bottom of the bag. What on earth? Pulling it out, he saw a doll. Only as big as his hand, it wore a white dress with a weighted hem and had an innocent smile. It almost looked like Meg. *This should comfort her tonight.*

Carrying the doll, he went back to the bathroom. "See what I found, Meg?" He held up the doll.

"Dolly," Meg said, reaching for the doll.

"Let's get dressed first." Lani lifted her onto the towel in her lap.

"Dolly," Meg said again. The little girl began to wail for the doll. Kicking and screaming, she tried to escape Lani's grasp, but Lani held her firmly and didn't seem at all rattled by the commotion. Ben wanted to hightail it out of there.

Lani slipped to her knees and finished drying off Meg. "Give me the diaper."

Ben slid it into her outstretched hand. She felt for the tabs, then quickly dressed the squirming child. As soon as she tugged Meg's top over the girl's head, Ben slid the doll into Meg's arms.

She grabbed it, then flung it aside. "Mommy!" she wailed. She drummed her heels on the floor. The shrieking cut through Ben like sharp coral. He knelt and picked her up. "It's okay, Meggie," he soothed. But it wasn't. And Meg knew it too.

"Let me rock her," Lani said. She held on to the wall and made her way back to the bedroom.

Ben followed with the sobbing child. "The rocker is to your left," he told Lani.

She nodded and maneuvered to sit in the rocker, then held out her hands. "I'll take her."

He deposited Meg into her arms. She crooned to the toddler and began to rock. Meg's sobs eased. "Maybe she'd like her blankie." He dug through her things and pulled out the tattered pink satin blanket and nestled it around Meg. She grabbed a corner of it, popped her thumb in her mouth, and closed her eyes.

"I'll be outside," he whispered. Lani nodded, and he eased out of the room. He could hear Yoshi's voice. Watching Meg had reminded Ben of another child he needed to do something about. He followed the voices until he found Yoshi talking with Fawn in the living room.

"Sounds like she's settling down," Fawn said. She sat beside Yoshi on the sofa, and he clasped her hand.

Ben nodded. "Once she had her blanket, it was all over." He settled into an armchair. "Hey, Yoshi, I need to report some child abuse."

Yoshi raised his brows. "Who?"

"There's a kid at the orchid farm. An immigrant named Simi. He looks like a Pacific islander, maybe Tongan. If I was guessing, I'd say he's illegal. I saw bruises on him, and he seemed scared to death."

Yoshi frowned. "I'll turn it in to child protective services."

"Do it right away. The kid looks really mistreated. I should have remembered to tell you sooner." There seemed to be no end to his failures.

Yoshi made the call, and Ben went to the kitchen and grabbed a bag of chips. His stomach felt hollow. Back in the living room, he began to munch. Fisher sat back on his haunches at Ben's feet. "You little beggar," Ben said. He tossed a chip to the dog, who practically inhaled it.

Yoshi dropped his cell phone back into his pocket. "They're sending someone out."

"Thanks."

The front door opened, and Rina stepped inside. She stopped when she saw them. "You startled me." Her mouth turned up in a smile, and her color rose.

"I waited around to talk to you," Yoshi said.

"Oh?" She went to the chair by Ben and sank into it. "Has something else happened?"

"Something is going on here, Aunt Rina. Burlap bags of Kona Kai coffee were found around Ethan's boat. He claimed to be delivering coffee for you."

She shook her head. "We don't hire delivery people like that."

Ben examined her expression and thought she looked sincerely puzzled. "How do you explain the bags of coffee on the boat?"

She spread her hands. "I can't explain it." Someone tapped on the door, and she got up to answer it.

Ben heard a deep voice, then Willie stepped into the entry. Rina invited him inside.

Willie stopped at the front door. "I didn't mean to intrude."

"Come on in," Yoshi said. "Maybe you can shed some light on this."

Willie went to a chair, and Rina followed him. "On what?" he asked.

"It appears my brother may have been smuggling protected coral in bags of coffee," Ben said.

Rina gasped. "Smuggling coral!"

Yoshi sent Ben a warning look and took over the questioning. "Have you noticed any missing coffee from your farm?"

Willie shook his head. "I run a pretty tight ship. No one comes into or out of my shop unless I know about it."

"The bags are marked Kona Kai," Yoshi said, shooting an intense glance toward Rina.

"Are you accusing Rina of being involved in smuggling?" Willie's voice rose. "I've never heard anything so stupid in my life." He balled his fists. "Your own aunt?"

"No," Yoshi sounded weary. "I don't think for a minute that Aunt Rina is involved. But someone connected with the farm is. I've questioned all the employees. Nothing has shown up yet, but I'm convinced the answer is here. I'm just trying to get to the bottom of it."

"The bottom of what?" Josie stepped out of the hallway. A bright red cotton robe clad her stolid figure.

"Someone is using Kona Kai coffee to smuggle coral," Rina said in a shaky voice.

"That's nonsense," Josie said. "Now all of you get out of here. We need to get to bed." She shook her finger at Yoshi. "You, of all people, shouldn't be tiring your cousin or your aunt. We have a big day Monday."

Ben had forgotten about the coffee harvest starting in the morning, not that it would affect him. He had funeral arrangements to make. And he needed to locate his mother.

eleven

$\mathcal{E}$arly Monday morning Lani rode in the truck with her aunt toward the coffee orchard. The air still smelled of dew. Workers of every nationality crammed the bed of the truck behind the back window. Her aunt's friends were coming in another vehicle.

"I hope I can tell the ripe cherries from the green," Lani told her aunt. She slung her arm around Fisher's neck, damp from his morning splash in the water bowl. She'd never seen a dog who loved water so much.

"I'll help you get started. You've picked coffee cherries enough to recognize the feel," her aunt said. "I really need every hand this week. I thought I'd be able to get more workers, but Willie snatched them all."

"You think he did it on purpose? Surely he didn't need that many workers. His farm is half the size of this one."

"I'm trying not to wig out about it. I'll get my cherries harvested if I have to do it all myself."

"Are you sure you're up to the day? You sound tired." Lani knew the lupus often sapped her aunt's energy.

"I'm not tired, not really. Not since Jerry started me on his newest supplement a few weeks ago." Her aunt's light laugh came.

"Josie hates them, but they work. It hardly feels like I have lupus anymore."

Lani wet her lips. Maybe Rina would tell her more than she'd been willing to share with Yoshi last night. "I know you told Yoshi you didn't know anything about Ethan's coffee, but there might be some clue you've missed. Anyone lurking around the packing room? Any break-ins?"

"No. I can't imagine how someone got our burlap bags, either. Do you think the attacks on you and Pam are related to the smuggling?"

"I don't know. But with three people dead, it's not out of the question. And we think the orchid farm down the road is smuggling Asian slipper orchids."

"But we know less about that than anything. Are there other orchids of that type that aren't forbidden to be sold?"

"I'm sure it's an Asian," Lani said. "But the coffee, Aunt Rina. I touched some of the beans that were recovered from the boating accident. They were large like ours. Ours are the biggest ones in the area, thanks to Sonic Bloom. I think those bags were filled with our coffee."

Her aunt didn't answer for several long moments. "They didn't come from my trees," she said finally.

"Could Willie be involved in something more than engineered plants?"

"I don't believe it," Rina said.

It took Lani an extra second to decide to go out on a limb. "I wonder if he's trying to implicate you, get you out of his way."

"You sound hesitant," her aunt said. "We've always liked Willie, at least until he started this engineered-plant business. We've been friends a lot of years. Do you really think he could be involved in something so underhanded?"

Lani tucked her head down. "I don't know, but you have to admit it's a possibility."

Her aunt didn't answer, and the truck slowed. "Looks like the other group is here." The truck stopped.

Lani heard the murmur of voices. "Is it light yet?" she asked.

"No, it's still pitch dark, but I can see a glow in the east," her aunt said. The truck door slammed shut. "You know, Lani, it's been a gas watching you blossom and regain your confidence. You're an inspiration."

Her—an inspiration? "I still want to see again," Lani said.

"Of course you do. But at least you know you can cope if your sight doesn't come back." Lani heard Rina move off to speak to other workers.

Could she endure life in this black sea? Maybe. Lani opened her door and felt for the ground with her foot. "Come on, Fisher," she said. Holding open the door, she waited until the dog pressed against her leg, then grabbed the harness. She faced the direction of the babble of voices. "Forward," she said with confidence.

Fisher didn't move. "Come on, boy." She shook the harness. "Forward." He still didn't move, so she started to take a step herself. Fisher planted himself in front of her and began to bark. "What's wrong with you?"

"He's protecting you." Fawn's voice spoke to her left. "There is a deep ravine right there. If you take a step, you'll fall. Don't move."

Her initial confidence burst. So much for independence.

Fawn touched Lani's hand. "This way."

Lani put her hand on the back of her friend's elbow and followed. The voices grew louder. "Who's got Meg?" she asked the group. The toddler was already out of her crib when Lani got dressed. Ben was making funeral arrangements, and Rina had told him to leave Meg at the farm.

Josie answered, "She's with me. She was none too happy about being awakened so early, but I gave her some gum and she was good to go."

Lani reached out for the little girl. "Hey, Meg," she said.

"She's not saying much yet," Josie said. She took Lani's hand and guided it to Meg's shoulder. "Say good morning, Meg."

The sound of chomping gum made Lani smile. "It's amazing the way she doesn't swallow it. Most kids her age would. Are you going to help us pick coffee cherries, Meg?" she asked.

"Doggie," Meg said clearly.

She bumped into Lani's legs in her eagerness to get to Fisher. The sound of licking made Lani smile as much as the toddler's giggling. "You must have needed a bath, Meg."

"Bath?" Meg said.

"If you'll all gather around, I'll explain the process," Rina called.

Lani moved toward her aunt's voice. Josie's and Meg's feet crunched through the gravel beside her.

"I'm ready to go back to bed," a man's voice murmured in her ear.

She recognized Harry Drayton's voice. "I don't think you're scared of some hard work," she said, thinking of the hard calluses on his hands.

"Is that a challenge?" His voice sounded cheery and alert.

"I imagine you'll pick three times what I can."

"Quiet down," her aunt called. "Here's the skinny on our job today. Some of you have harvested before, but for the newbies here, I'll go over it again. These trees produce premium arabica beans. We want only ripe coffee cherries. Green cherries will make the coffee bitter. We don't want them overripe either. If they're dark, almost black, they're too far gone. The cherries will grow in clusters, so you can grab several at a time. Put them in the burlap sacks I'll be passing out. We have to get the bulk of them picked before they get too ripe. Any questions?"

"What about the cherries at the tops of the trees?" a voice called.

"Most of the trees are trimmed to six feet. You should be able to reach them all since they don't grow at the very top. Thank you all for coming. Now let's get picking!"

The crowd moved as one. Lani found herself with a burlap sack in her hands. She waited until her aunt finished answering questions. "Where do you want me?" It had been useless to come out here. Maybe she should go home with Meg.

"Come with me." Rina waited until Lani rested her fingers on the back of her elbow, then walked forward.

Lani gripped Fisher's harness with her other hand and stumbled a little on the uneven ground. The reality of her situation was beginning to get to her. When would her sight come back? She watched every moment for some glimmer of light.

"Here we are." Her aunt took Lani's hand and guided it to the coffee tree. "Touch the cherries, Lani. See if you can tell which ones are ripe. I'll tell you if you're right."

Lani stroked her fingertips over the coffee cherries. She pictured them in her mind. Plump and red, shiny skin glistening with dew. The two seeds in the middle would make sweet, delicious Kona coffee, the best in the world. The taste made it worth every effort.

Gently squeezing several cherries, she fingered one. "I think this is ripe. This next one is too, just not quite as ripe but good enough."

"You're right! There's a blackened one here too. See if you can find it."

Lani ran her fingers over the clustered cherries. "This one?" she asked.

"I knew you would be able to do it. Don't worry about speed.

Do what you can." Her aunt patted her hand. "I'd better get busy on my tree. These are easy trees since I've pruned them. The cherries cluster in clumps that aren't too high. Just be careful. There's a ravine about ten feet away. Stay close to the trees."

Lani heard her aunt walk off through the grass. She began to pluck the cherries and drop them into her bag. Having to examine each cherry by touch took longer, but at least she felt useful. Every tree she managed to harvest would be one less her aunt had to do.

Ben started his Harley, then he and the bike roared away from Aloha Mortuary. That was the hardest thing he'd ever done in his life. His hands were still shaking. Even the wind in his face didn't lift his depression. The thought of his brother in the casket he'd picked out made him want to throw up.

He drove to the attorney's office. This would be nearly as uncomfortable as making funeral arrangements. The receptionist took his name, and Cliff Grayson waved him back to the office a few moments later.

Cliff shook his hand and pointed to a leather chair. "Hey, Ben, so sorry to hear about your brother."

News traveled fast. "Thanks." He sat in the chair and leaned forward. "I need to find my mother. The funeral should be tomorrow, but I've pushed it back to Thursday."

"You don't know where she is?"

Ben shook his head. "The last I heard she was in Michigan, but that was a year ago. I tried the last number I had, but it's been disconnected." Having to talk about the depth of his family's dysfunction hurt.

"I'll see what I can do. What's her name?"

"Nancy Anderson. Or at least I assume it's still Anderson. She might have ditched the current husband and found another. There's no telling."

Cliff nodded but didn't comment. "I'll call you when I find her. Do you want to tell her the news yourself?"

"No, you can do it." It was the coward's way out, but right now, Ben couldn't bear the thought of hearing her voice. He rose and shook Cliff's hand. "Thanks. You've got my cell number. Oh, and check on getting me custody of Meg."

He escaped into the fresh air, but he couldn't escape the memories so easily: The afternoons when he would come home from school to find his mother passed out on the couch—or worse, in bed with some stranger. The days when the refrigerator held nothing but moldy leftovers. She never hit him, but her words could cut deeper than any knife.

Ethan had always been her favorite, though even he didn't enjoy much favor. Ben held on to a thin hope that she had changed in the five years since he'd seen her last. While it wasn't likely, it was possible. God was in the business of changing people.

He drove his bike to the police station and went inside. Several officers stopped to talk and express their condolences, so a few minutes passed before he managed to get down the hall to Yoshi's office. His friend sat with the phone pressed to his ear, and Ben dropped into the chair opposite the desk. Yoshi held up a finger to indicate he'd only be a minute.

When he hung up, he leaned back in his chair. "How're you doing?" His brown eyes were warm.

Ben cleared his throat, then swallowed. "Okay. I just made . . . funeral arrangements."

"I'm so sorry, buddy."

"Me too." Ben looked down at his hands, then back up. "I wondered what you found out about Simi and who owns the orchid farm."

Yoshi bent over his stacks of papers. "Child protective services couldn't find anyone around other than a housekeeper, who insisted there was no child in the house. The worker called a police officer, who searched the house but found nothing. We still can't figure out who's behind the holding company. We're trying to get to the bottom of it and not having much luck yet."

"There has to be a connection, Yoshi. And someone tried to drown Lani at Honaunau. Have you checked out Pam's background?"

Yoshi kept his head down and riffled through more pages. "She doesn't seem to have had any enemies, and her record is spotless. One employee—Joey Babao—has a track record. Just petty stuff." He squinted at the paper. "Reckless driving, a count of shoplifting, and a stolen car when he was sixteen. We're checking him out a little deeper. You ever see Ethan with him?"

Ben shook his head and stood. "Keep me posted. I need to get back to the coffee farm. They started harvest this morning, and your aunt has Meg."

"How's she doing?"

"About as well as you'd expect for a baby who cries for her mommy." Ben rubbed his burning eyes. "Thanks, Yoshi." He walked out the door and down the hill to his bike. Maybe he could outride the pain in his heart.

The fragrant breeze caressed Lani's face and cooled the damp sheen on her skin. She could tell when the sun came up and the orchard began to warm with its rays.

Fawn had been working at a nearby tree, but she'd left a few minutes ago to run to the bathroom. The other pickers were on the opposite side of the orchard. Maybe Rina had started them there so it wouldn't seem as though everyone were rushing Lani. She enjoyed the time of harvest. The slight popping sound the cherries made as they came loose from the tree mingled with the hum of insects. She heard the roar of Ben's Harley. He'd be a good worker once Rina showed him what to do.

A cry came from behind her. It sounded like a child. "Meg?" The sob came again. Lani turned and called again. "Meggie, you okay?" A whimper came back on the wind. "Fisher, here." She patted her leg, and the dog came at once. She grabbed the harness. "Forward." Moving slowly, she shuffled through the grass. "Meg, where are you?"

The sound had come from this way, she thought. "Meg?" She heard the whimper again. Fisher suddenly stopped in front of her. "What is it, boy?" He barked, a frenzied sound. The cry came again, and Lani pushed past the dog. "Come on, Fisher." The dog tried to pull back on the harness, so she dropped it. She had to get to Meg with or without the dog. He shoved her back, but he was at an angle, and it made her stumble in the direction she'd been walking.

Her foot came down but touched nothing. She flung out her arms and tried to grab something, anything, but found only air. Then she was falling into space. She screamed, her hands reaching out for something to grasp. She hit the ground hard, and the air flew from her lungs as her body collided with the rocks. Rolling over and over, she tumbled in the darkness. Stones cut her face, but the pain didn't penetrate her panic.

Branches lashed her face. She clutched at hard objects she couldn't identify as she hurtled down the slope. The idea of falling had always terrified her, but the reality paired with the disorientation of being blind was even worse. A flash of light came along with the blurred impression of something passing by her face. Then her head banged a rock, and as a reflex, she grabbed at it. Her body came to a jarring halt with her arms wrapped around the rock. Her head ached, and the vague images were gone.

She had no idea where she was. Her body throbbed in a hundred places. Lying on the ground, she didn't know if she dared move. If only she could see! She strained to see past the black blanket that covered her vision. Debris rattled past her cheek, then the dog whined by her head and licked her arm.

"Fisher," she said. "Get Ben. Go find Ben." The dog barked, then stones rattled with his passage back up the slope. Did Fisher know what to do? She could only hope and pray he did.

The rough lava rock cut into her cheek as she clung there. She didn't have any sense of being up or down or sideways. Her head swam with the disorientation. *Send Ben, Lord.* Her arms were getting tired, and she didn't know how much longer she could hang on. Maybe she lay at the bottom of the ravine, or maybe she hadn't rolled all the way down. Her shoulders ached with the strain.

A few minutes later she heard Ben call her name from above. "Lani, where are you?"

She raised her head and shouted. "Here, I'm here!"

Debris began to roll toward her, and she heard him scrambling down the slope. Then his hand touched her shoulder. "I'm here, but don't let go. You're on a ledge, and a sharp drop-off is below you."

She heard more movement, and tiny pebbles rained on her cheeks. "I've got to get a rope. Hold on."

She wanted to cry out for him not to leave her, but she clamped her teeth against the plea and tightened her grip on the rock. The blackness around her seemed even darker. She heard something rustling through the underbrush, then Fisher's wet nose touched her cheek. He whined and licked her face.

"Good boy," she said. The touch of something else alive gave her courage.

"I'm here, Lani," Ben called from above her head.

She heard him moving down the slope again. Moments later his hands touched her arm.

"I'm tying the rope around your waist." His swift, sure fingers slid the rope under her and tightened it. "I'm going to help you climb up while people topside pull, okay?"

She nodded, unable to speak past the rock in her throat. Every nerve tingled and throbbed. She heard the loose pebbles skidding away and knew she could go with them at any moment.

"Okay," he shouted. "Pull now, but take it slow."

"We're here, Lani," Fawn called down. "You're going to be okay."

"Let go of the rock now and take my hand." Ben's warm fingers closed around hers. "I'm going to be above you lifting you up. Push with your feet."

She did as he instructed. The strength of his hand reassured her, and they began to move inch by inch back up the ravine. Every muscle groaned as she followed his lead.

"We're almost there," he panted.

Pebbles rained on her again as he grunted. Then both of his hands came under her arms and lifted her to her feet.

"You're safe now," he whispered.

He didn't release her right away, and she clung to his bulk and listened to his heart thud under her ear where it pressed against his chest.

He pulled away and cupped her face in his palms. "Are you okay?"

"I think so. I hit my head." She reached up and rubbed it.

"Thank God, you're okay," Fawn said in a choked voice.

Lani barely felt her friend's touch on her arm. Everything hurt too much. She heard the rest of the group exclaim over her—her aunt, Jerry, Arlo, and Harry.

When the bedlam died down, she pulled away from Ben and tipped her face up. "Ben, I saw just a little before I hit my head. It wasn't much, just light and shadow and the impression of movement as I fell."

"That's great! Maybe it's starting to come back. Let me see the bump." His fingers lifted her hair, and the breeze cooled the back of her neck. He probed the tender spot on the back of her head. "It's bleeding. You whacked it good. That might be why your vision went back out. It's pretty swollen." He dropped her hair back onto her shoulders.

She realized her face was still tilted up to his. If only she could see his expression. His voice sounded almost tender, but maybe it was her imagination. She wished she dared lean into his embrace again. In the old days she would have done just that, but she had to be on her guard not to fall into the same bad behavior. She felt safe with Ben. She'd been used to sudden wild infatuations, but her relationship with Ben felt more real—like their friendship could last forever.

"What happened?" he asked. "Fisher should have kept you from the edge."

"He tried, but he pushed in the wrong place on my leg, and I reeled forward."

Ben's fingers tightened on her arms. "His mistake could have cost you your life."

"He tried," she insisted.

"Why did you go to the ravine anyway?"

"I thought I heard Meg crying in this direction. She kept whimpering."

"How weird," her aunt said. "Meg played at my feet the whole time. Are you sure it was her? Maybe you heard a cat or something."

"It sure sounded like Meg's voice," Lani said.

"I'm going to have a look," Ben said.

She heard him move away. "Fisher," she called. The dog pressed against her leg, and she patted him. At least he was safe too. "Where's Meg now?"

"Napping under my coffee tree on a blanket. Joey is watching her," her aunt said.

"I found it!" Ben's voice called. A few moments later, the grass rustled. "Was this what you heard?"

She heard a click, then a child's cry sounded. "That's it!"

"It's a recording of Meg crying." He sounded distant, preoccupied. "It was no accident. Someone tried to lure you to the ravine."

Not an accident. Lani wrapped her arms around herself. Someone seemed quite determined to shut her up. It was almost laughable since she couldn't remember anything and was blind even if she did. "He has nothing to fear from me. Why can't he just leave me alone?"

twelve

hresh looked carefully over the scene. So close. If only Lani hadn't landed on that ledge, all his worries would have been over. The plan had seemed so brilliant. Lani was a sucker for the little girl—no way could she ignore the crying.

This was turning into a comedy of errors. Kato was no help either. All Thresh heard from him were excuses. Did any of the Taylor Camp crew know about Blossom's stint in federal prison? Would they all care for her if they knew? Maybe he should make sure that little detail came to light. If she had no one else, she would turn to him for sure.

Thomas Carlyle, another brilliant historian, said that a man without a goal is like a ship without a rudder. The goal was finally within reach. It had to be karma. That was the only explanation for how all the pieces were here now. They could be moved around like chess pieces. Peekaboo would pay too, now that she'd been flushed from her hidey-hole.

Ben paced the waiting room while the doctor checked out Lani. Stopping to flip through a magazine, he tossed it back to the table and circled the room again. Fisher walked with him, looking up occasionally as if to ask if everything was all right.

"You're making me nervous," Rina said. "Sit down."

Fawn sat on a leather love seat with her legs curled under her. "Annie finally called. She's going to try to get a flight home tomorrow."

"Lani will be upset she's messed up Annie's research trip," Ben said.

Yoshi gave him an appraising look. "You seem to know my cousin well."

"Well enough."

"Has she told you what she remembers of the shooting?"

"She doesn't remember anything. I think it's time you started listening to her, Yoshi."

"She hasn't always been truthful in the past."

"Maybe she's changed." He wasn't sure he believed Lani had changed until he heard Yoshi questioning it. Lani wasn't the same young woman who had flirted with his brother. He almost wished she were. It would be easier to resist her. His change from wariness to care had been imperceptible.

"She has changed." Fawn swung her legs to the floor. "Lighten up, Yoshi."

Yoshi colored. "I can't protect her if I don't know what's going on." He stood up and cracked his knuckles. His uneasy gaze rested on his aunt. "Would you mind answering some more questions, Aunt Rina?"

She leaned back against the leather sofa. "What now, Yoshi? Haven't we been through enough today?"

"Do you want me to just stand by and let someone kill Lani?"

"Of course not! What do you want to know?"

"Where were you all the years we didn't see you?"

She blinked and looked away. "Here and there."

"But where? I asked my parents, and they were both evasive. You disappeared from the family for years—just dropped out completely."

"It's a private matter, Yoshi. I don't stick my nose into your business, and I'll thank you to give me the same courtesy."

Yoshi looked down and muttered something under his breath. He began to pace the room and almost collided with the doctor as he stepped into the waiting room. "How's Lani?" he asked.

"She's going to be fine. She's suffered another slight concussion, which isn't good, but I think she'll recover."

"What about her sight? She said she had some slight vision change," Ben said.

"What?" Yoshi moved to Ben's side. "No one told me that."

"I forgot until just now." Ben told him about her impression of movement and the flashes of light.

The doctor didn't smile. "That's very encouraging, but I'm afraid the new blow to her head has delayed her progress. It may be several more weeks before we can tell if the damage is permanent or not."

Ben winced. Lani had been so hopeful. He turned to Yoshi. "I forgot to ask. Did you find the boys who were paid to pretend to be drowning? This is the third attempt on Lani's life."

"I tried. No luck yet. You didn't get their names, and no one knows who was out there that day." He turned to the doctor. "When can we take her home?"

"I'd like to keep her here overnight. You can take her home tomorrow."

"What about her dog?" Ben asked. The two would be miserable apart.

"Sorry, we can't allow him to stay. The nurses will care for her. You can bring him with you when you come to get her in the morning."

Ben nodded. "I'd better go get Meg." He and Yoshi looked at each other, and Ben saw the same fear in Yoshi's eyes. The little girl might be with whoever murdered her parents. It was someone at the coffee farm.

Lani listened to the machines beep in the room. The night sounds of the hospital closed around her. She ached for her dog. If she had Fisher by her side, she wouldn't feel so alone. It wasn't fair that he was banned. The nurse came and went, her rubber-soled shoes squeaking on the tile floor. A baby cried in the room down the hall. Low voices passed her door.

She flopped onto her back from her side. The sheets were scratchy and smelled like bleach. A whisper of sound caught her attention. A soft *whump* muted the noise in the hall. The nurse must have shut the door to try to let Lani get some sleep. She still felt wide awake.

Footsteps approached. "You okay?" Ben's voice came at the foot of her bed.

"Ben!" She couldn't help the glad ring in her voice.

His steps came closer, and he took her hand. "I had to run home a minute and get Meg."

"Where is she?"

"Asleep right here in my arms. Lay back, and I'll put her in bed with you."

Lani settled on her side, and Ben lay the small, warm body next to her. She inhaled the little girl scent and snuggled Meg close. The toddler murmured but didn't awaken. With her chin on Meg's soft curls, Lani felt the tension drain out of herself. The peaceful in and out of Meg's breathing lulled her. "Maybe I'll be able to sleep now." Was it her imagination, or did Ben press his lips to her hand?

Ben's words whispered close to her ear. "I'm glad we're friends now."

She blinked and opened her eyes. "Me too. I'm not sure when it happened."

"I think it was the night you saw Tyrone. I saw you'd changed even if he didn't realize it."

"Did you ever talk to him?"

"No. If it's something I should know, you'll tell me."

"Have you ever done something so bad you wonder if God can ever forgive you?" she whispered.

"Yeah. But you know, there's nothing he won't forgive. The hard part is forgiving ourselves."

"Did you ever manage it?"

There was a long pause before Ben spoke. "Sometimes I think I have. It's in the night when I struggle the most. But I know deep down that God is my daddy. He's always happy to have me climb on his knee and say I'm sorry."

A smile tipped her lips. "Were you close to your own dad?" She heard Ben inhale sharply.

"I never knew him. My mom is a free spirit, antiestablishment all the way, baby."

"I used to think I wanted no restrictions on my freedom, no responsibility. But I hurt a lot of people when I was like that."

"My mom still does. When I joined the police force, she called me every rotten name in the book. Told me she'd never speak to me again. Come to think of it, I don't think we've been in contact since then."

"Oh, Ben, I'm so sorry." She stretched out her hand, and he took it. "I suppose the right course is somewhere in the middle. It usually is."

"'And everyone who competes for the prize is temperate in all things.' First Corinthians 9:25." He squeezed her fingers. "You should get some rest."

Lani snuggled her chin into Meg's hair. She could get used to a friend like Ben.

Looking at Meg curled up in Lani's arms, something Ben didn't recognize stirred inside him. He wanted to kiss the curve of Lani's cheek, run his hand over the black curtain of hair that draped the pillow. The friendship he felt seemed to be changing once again. Did he want it to? Watching her breath stir Meg's hair, he realized this was the kind of love that could last a lifetime. The steady kind that you could build a world on.

Ben sat in the darkened room and watched the peaceful faces of Lani and Meg. Lani had shown a lot of spunk, even faced with the loss of her vision. Until she remembered the day of the shooting, she was going to be in danger. The attacks on her were intensifying. This latest one right at the coffee farm came close to killing her. Who would keep guard over her? While he had Meg, it was hard to be there with Lani every minute.

Maybe he should step back and let someone else take over. Fawn, maybe, or Yoshi. But the thought of leaving her at a murderer's mercy didn't go down well. He realized he wanted to be her hero, to rescue her. He bit back a chuckle. This wasn't a movie where he was going to ride in and save the day. It would take all of them to uncover the murderer.

The long hours passed, and Ben prayed for them all. Dawn's light began to slant through the blinds. He stood and stretched. Nearly seven. The doctor would release her, and they could all get out of here. His cell phone chimed, and he stepped into the hall to answer it. Leaning against the wall by the door, he flipped it open. "Ben here."

"Sorry to bother you so early." His attorney's deep voice sounded gravelly, as though he hadn't had his coffee yet.

"I wasn't sleeping. What's up?" Maybe Cliff had found his mother.

"We have a problem. Natalie's parents are seeking custody."

"What?" Ben's loud voice caused a nurse walking the hall to frown and put her fingers to her lips. He lowered his voice. "They don't have a leg to stand on, do they?"

"Well, you're a bachelor. Taking custody of a little girl might be questionable in the minds of some judges. They might think she'll need a woman."

"She needs me. Besides, Natalie's parents are not—suitable."

"Any proof of that?"

"Look up the grandfather's record. He's got a rap sheet as long as my arm."

"That should help." Cliff's voice was tempered and rational. "But if he can prove he's been above reproach, he might still have a shot."

Ben began to pace the hospital hallway. "But that's ridiculous. I love Meg. She knows me. Her grandparents live on the mainland, and they haven't seen her since she was six months old. She wouldn't know them. It would be too traumatic for her."

"They're flying here for the funeral. It's the day after tomorrow, right?"

"Yeah."

"Be prepared for a battle."

He would not give her up. "What can I do to make sure I keep Meg?"

"Pray," Cliff advised.

"I will." Ben turned toward Lani's door. "What else?"

"Find her a good child counselor who will know how to help

her. That will look impressive. It might not hurt to move into Ethan's house for stability."

Ben nodded. "What about my mother?"

"I found her. She took the news well."

"Of course she did." Ben's lip curled. "Is she coming to the funeral?"

"She didn't make any promises." Cliff went silent a moment. "I'm sorry. I know that's not the answer you wanted to hear. I told her I'd call her tomorrow and see if she needed anything."

"I'll pay for her flight," Ben said.

"I thought you might." Cliff cleared his throat. "I'll keep you posted."

Ben closed his phone and slipped it back into his pocket. Looking at his situation realistically, he knew it didn't look good. An ex-cop who got his partner blinded, an unmarried male who drove a Harley and trained dogs. On the surface he wouldn't award a kid to someone like him either, but he loved Meg. She belonged with him. Besides, he'd caught Ethan in some shady dealings with his father-in-law in the past. Ben paused before reentering Lani's hospital room. What if Natalie's dad was involved in the smuggling?

thirteen

*B*en brought Lani home from the hospital and got her settled in the recliner by the window. He went to get Meg cleaned up and dressed for the day. Restlessness had taken hold of Lani and wouldn't let go. The birds sang in the trees outside the window, but she barely noticed. Her cell phone lay in her lap, and she toyed with it. The temptation to call CeCe plagued her. What would it hurt to talk to her friend?

So far all she'd done was answer the phone, so it would take some doing to dial out. She turned over the phone and carefully figured out the number pad, then dialed the familiar digits. Her heart beat fast, and something inside told her she shouldn't be doing this.

CeCe answered right away. "Lani? Tell me you've changed your mind and are coming to the party."

Lani pushed away the guilt. She was entitled to have some fun after the nightmare she'd been living lately. "Can you pick me up?"

"Sure! I'm so glad you saw the light."

Back out now! Lani ignored the internal voice. "See you Saturday!" She hung up and told herself it would be fine.

She heard Yoshi's voice at the door, then the screen opened and slammed shut again.

"Where's Aunt Rina?"

"Getting ready to pick cherries. Why?"

"I need to talk to her."

"Your tone of voice says it's serious." Lani rose. "I think I'll go to my room."

"I want you here, Lani. Someone is trying to kill you. You know Aunt Rina better than me, and you can tell if she's lying."

Lani sighed and settled back on the couch. "Okay." Fisher's fur pressed against Lani's left foot. The warmth comforted her. She strained to see but could make out nothing past the dark veil. That flash of light had been like a glimpse of paradise.

Her aunt's voice spoke from behind her. "Yoshi, I didn't hear you come in. Have you come to help me today?"

Yoshi cleared his throat. "Have a seat, Aunt Rina."

"What's this all about?" her aunt asked. "I've got cherry picking to do. And the cherries we picked yesterday need to be processed."

"This won't take long. We'll help you when we're done." Yoshi's voice sounded grim.

The front door opened, and Josie's voice floated inside. "Rina, are you coming?" Her slippers slapped the tile. "What's going on here?"

"We just have some questions. Rina will be right out," Yoshi said.

"I'll wait right here too," Josie said. The springs on the rocker screeched, then the rhythmic rocking started.

"I'll be fine, Josie," Rina said. The rocking didn't stop, and she sighed. "Let's get this over with. You're keeping me from my work."

Lani wanted to slip her hand over and squeeze her aunt's fingers, but she kept her hands in her lap. Something was going on here she didn't understand.

"I talked to my parents again last night," Yoshi said.

"I love you, Yoshi, but if you're going to start grilling me again, you can just leave. I told you all I chose to the other night."

Lani heard her cousin inhale sharply. Chewing on her lip, she waited for Yoshi to explode, but he simply cleared his throat.

"Just tell me straight up," he said. "I ran a check on you, but I'd rather hear it from you."

Josie's rocking stopped. "She was innocent!" Josie said. "She took the rap, but she didn't do it."

"Josie," Rina's voice held a command. "I'll handle this."

"You want to give me your side of it?" Yoshi asked.

The sofa springs rustled. Lani wished she could see Rina's face. She curled her fingers into her palms and prayed for her aunt to have a good answer. Could it be true? Lani gave a gentle shake of her head. There was no way—she wouldn't believe it.

"I don't have to answer this," Rina said.

"Either here or at the station." Yoshi's voice had gone from warm to steely.

"You wouldn't arrest me!"

"I don't want to, but it's your call."

"I'll tell you," Josie said.

"Josie, let me take care of this." Rina's voice had gone from confident to weary. "I wasn't guilty. I suppose you hear that all the time, though."

"What happened?" Yoshi asked. "My parents said they weren't surprised there was smuggling going on out here."

"I knew nothing about any smuggling ring. Not now and not at Taylor Camp. The six of us were living at the camp in the best tree house on the beach. Life was good." The words began to pour from Rina in a tide of confession. "I saw a flashlight one night on the beach, over by the church. I couldn't sleep, so I decided to commiserate with whomever it was."

"Had you seen any evidence of drugs?" Yoshi asked.

Rina laughed, a wry sound. "I was a hippie and lived among hippies. We had weed, LSD, you name it."

Yoshi shuffled on his chair. "Any dealing?"

"Sure. That's how some of the members lived." She cleared her throat and went on. "I heard a sound, like a car backfiring. When we got to the church, I saw Mary lying in the sand, covered in blood. A gun lay on top of her. I picked it up to move it out of the way so I could try to stop the bleeding."

"I thought none of you went by your real names," Lani said. "Who was Mary?"

"Mary wasn't her real name. We called her Madonna Mary, but most of us just shortened it to Mary."

"Why didn't you call for an ambulance?" Yoshi asked.

Rina sighed. "I just wanted to help her. She opened her eyes once, then closed them and died right in my arms." She drew in a deep breath. "I was stupid and tried to cover it up. I washed off the blood and wiped the gun before I called the fuzz in. They found traces of blood on my hands, and my fingerprints on her belt. And in the bag beside her, the police found marijuana and heroin. When they got a search warrant, they found more. It looked bad. But I knew nothing about it. You have to believe me." Her voice broke.

"You said 'we,'" Lani said. "Were you with someone?"

"Yes, another girl."

"It was all *her* fault," Josie said. "That girl was always trouble."

"Who all were there at the camp?" Yoshi asked.

"The same ones who backed me in the coffee business. Arlo, Harry, Jerry, Josie. Oh, and Willie Kanaho. But he's not involved in the coffee farm. At the time there were about sixty residents at the camp."

"The guy you filed an injunction against," Yoshi said with a sharp note to his voice.

"Yes."

"What happened that you were on the outs for a while?"

Rina sighed. "He asked me to marry him, and I refused. He took it hard."

"Why did you turn him down? Did you suspect him?"

"No, of course not. He is . . . rather overpowering. I've fought all my life to be my own person, to chart my own course. I cared about him, but I knew if I married him, he'd soon have me jumping to his every command. And there was my lupus."

"But you're dating him again," Lani put in. "Have you decided you were wrong to turn him down?"

"No." Rina cleared her throat. "Actually, he asked me again the other night. Then he asked me to drop the injunction, and I figured out the real reason he was hanging around." She sniffled.

The rocking stopped again. "What?" Josie whispered. "You want to marry that dude?"

"I was going to tell you about it, Josie, but I haven't had the time. But it's clear he just wants me to drop the injunction."

"Rina, Rina." Josie's voice was soft. "You have the worst judgment about men." She sighed. "You never seem to learn. At least you found out this time before it was too late."

"I think I'd better have a talk with him," Yoshi said. "So you went to prison for murder?"

"Yes."

"Is there anything else you can tell me?"

"Nothing. Now please, I need to get to work, or I'm going to lose this crop. Come on, Josie." The rocker stopped, and slippers slapped against the tile as they left the room. The door banged.

"I believe her," Lani said. She tried to sense Yoshi's mood.

"Strangely enough, so do I," Yoshi said. "One of her friends isn't a friend at all."

Lani shuddered. Not only did the people who seemed so friendly to her hide secrets, but she couldn't even gauge expressions. How was she supposed to figure out who was a friend and who was a foe? The blackness around her was a heavy blanket of menace.

She heard the patter of small feet, then a warm little body climbed into her lap. "Hey, Meg," she said.

"Eat," Meg said.

"She always wants to eat," Ben said, his heavy tread moving across the tile floor. "I just fed her an hour ago."

"I wouldn't say no to a peanut-butter sandwich myself."

"Sanich," Meg agreed. She slid from Lani's lap, and her steps moved in the direction of the kitchen.

Lani rose from the sofa and grabbed Fisher's harness. "Forward," she said. She could picture the room in her mind, the layout of the furniture, the location of the door openings. For an instant, it was as though she could actually see those things. Living in her memories would surely grow easier with time.

"You seem confident with him now." Ben's footsteps followed her.

"I trust Fisher," she told him. She reached the kitchen door. If she remembered right, there was a slight step up from an uneven floor. Navigating carefully, she stepped into the room. The kitchen table and chairs should be to her right.

"You want a drink, Fisher?" She dropped his harness, and a few moments later she heard him slurping. Then water sloshed and several drops hit her feet.

"Fisher, you're making a mess," Ben said.

"I think you knew him before you named him," Lani said, smiling.

"He's soaked, and the bowl is empty now." Ben's voice held resignation. "I'll fix a snack."

"I'll do it. I'm figuring out how to take care of myself." She felt for the edge of the counter, then followed the line of it to the end cabinet. She opened the overhead cupboard and touched the inside of the door. A rack on the door should hold the peanut butter. Her hand touched a large jar with a plastic lid. "Is this it?"

"You tell me."

She smiled and unscrewed the lid. The rich aroma of Jif filled her nose. She set it on the counter and trailed her fingers to the bread drawer. She could feel Ben's gaze on her. "Quit staring," she said.

"You're so beautiful."

He cleared his throat, and she realized he hadn't meant to say that much. Her cheeks warmed. "I haven't even been able to put on makeup." She pushed her hair out of her face. Even caring for her hair was a study in illusion. She had to guess what it looked like from the feel of it.

She held a sandwich down at her side. "Here you go, Meg." The sandwich was snatched from her hand.

"Tank oo," Meg said. A thump came from the floor.

Meg must have sat down. Lani carefully maneuvered around her toward where Ben's voice had come from. "What do you look like, Ben? I don't even know how old you are."

"I'm thirty-five." He took her hand and guided it to his face. "I'm nothing to write home about, but you can take a look."

Her fingers pulsed with sensation as she trailed their tips along a strong jawline, across firm lips and chin. His nose had a slight bump on it. Her fingers continued to explore the planes of his face. She dropped her hand. "What color is your hair?"

"It's red, kind of chestnut. Brown eyes." His voice sounded distant.

"I like your face," she said.

"I like yours too."

The warmth in his voice brought heat to her cheeks. She was flirting with him and enjoying it way too much. "Why aren't you married?"

"I watched my mother jump in and out of relationships like a flea hopping from dog to dog. It pretty much put me off marriage."

"You sound a little jaded."

"You might say that. Last count she'd been married six times."

"I heard you say you spent your early years at Taylor Camp. What do you remember about it?"

"I was four when we left, so I just have bits and pieces of memory. Like running around in swim trunks day and night. I remember the tree house. It had windows and a door just like a real house. Rugs, furnishings, a roof. I've got a couple of pictures from that time with me and Nancy at the dinner table. I swam a lot, dug for clams, picked up seashells."

"Nancy?"

"My mother. She never liked us to call her Mom. She thought it made her sound too old."

Lani tried to keep sympathy out of her voice. "Were you there when the woman died that Rina supposedly shot?"

"What woman?"

"Oh, you weren't in the room. My aunt was in prison. For murder. She was accused of killing a woman she called Madonna Mary."

He gave a low whistle. "Wow. I'm sure I was there. I remember a day when the beach was crawling with cops. That was probably it."

"Your mother has to know the rest of them. Is she coming for the funeral?" She wanted to meet the woman.

"I don't know. She hadn't decided, according to my lawyer."

"You haven't talked to her?" Lani disliked his mother more and more with every new revelation about her.

"No, and I'm not eager to see her. You still don't get what kind of mother she was, Lani. She's a drunkard who never cared if I had enough food to eat."

She heard his feet shuffle, and she realized the subject made him uncomfortable. Still, it often helped to talk about something. "I'm sorry. Another instance of what we talked about the other day. God let you grow up in a house like that, and I don't understand why."

"It made me stronger," he said.

"But why? Why would God let innocent children go through things like that? Why doesn't he intervene?"

"I don't know, but I trust him to work it all out for my good."

"That's easy to say, but harder to do," she pointed out. "With your history, I'm surprised you have that much trust."

"If I didn't, I couldn't handle my life."

Why did he find it so easy to trust, while she, who had lived with a loving mother, found it so difficult? She laced her fingers together to keep herself from touching his face again. "You're a good man, Ben Mahoney."

"If you're done eating that sandwich, we'll go help with the harvest."

She hadn't taken a bite yet, but suddenly she wasn't hungry. She heard a tap. "What's that?"

"Someone's at the kitchen door."

His steps moved across the tile, then the door squeaked open.

"Hi, Willie. If you're looking for Rina, she's out picking cherries. We're about to head out there ourselves."

"Come on in, Willie," Lani called.

"You okay, Lani?" Willie asked. "Rina told me about your accident." The scent of the outdoors wafted in with him.

His voice grim, Ben answered for her. "It wasn't an accident. Someone tried to kill her."

"You'd better stay close to her then," Willie said. "She's important to Rina. To all of us," he added.

"I hear you popped the question," Lani said. She forced her lips into a smile.

"Yep." He shuffled his feet. "I've loved her since we lived together at Taylor Camp. Now she's turned me down again."

Everything seemed to funnel back to Taylor Camp. "Were you there when the police arrested Aunt Rina for murder?" Lani asked.

"Yeah." The laughter faded from Willie's voice. "I tried to tell the cops she didn't do it, but they seemed sure they had their perp."

"Do you know what really happened?" Ben asked.

"I got my suspicions. I told the cops to talk to Peekaboo, but she talked her way out of it."

"Peekaboo?" Ben's voice sounded strained.

"I don't know her real name. She and Rina found the body together, but then Peekaboo refused to tell the cops she was there. I personally think she had someone kill Mary for her."

"Why would she kill the girl?" Ben asked. His voice sounded upset, and Lani wondered why it seemed to matter to him.

"Peekaboo didn't like her. Said she gave her the creeps. Mary quoted the Bible constantly."

Lani raised her brows. "Yet she lived at a commune. That seems like strange behavior for a Christian."

"Mary was different," Willie agreed. "She camped on the beach in a tent that blew down in the summer and got flooded out in the winter storms. She carried her rosary everywhere. She didn't drink or do drugs. No sleeping around. I think she saw herself as a missionary among heathens. And I guess we were pretty heathenish. I was pretty bummed someone killed her."

"So was Taylor Camp a drug-smuggling operation?" Lani asked.

He laughed. "Oh, there were drug sales around, but I don't know that I'd call it smuggling. Smuggling implies something going on in secret, and this was right out in the open."

"How did they convict Rina?" Ben asked.

"Paranoia ruled the climate in those days. Woodstock had hit the news, and the Manson family had killed Sharon Tate and the others. The country was in a frenzy about the dangers of people like us. The cops were all too ready to believe anything."

"You're a staunch defender of my aunt," Lani said. Willie had a pretty level head. This was the first time she'd had a conversation with him. She was beginning to wonder if she'd been wrong about him.

"I'd better go defend her from the coffee cherries," he said. Moments later the door banged.

"Uh-oh," Meg said.

"That doesn't sound good," Lani said. She slid her hand down the front of the cabinet and knelt on the floor, then trailed her hand out to find the toddler. "What'd you do, Meg?"

"Ucky," Meg said.

"You're yucky all right," Ben said. "She's got peanut butter smeared in her hair and all over her clothes."

"There's no time to bathe her. We need to get out to the coffee trees. Just get a washcloth and we'll clean her up. She'll just get dirty outside anyway."

"You don't realize how bad it is. Her hair is—matted with it." His steps retreated.

Lani touched the little girl's hair. "Daddy?" Meg said. "Mommy?"

"You want to go play with Fisher?" Lani asked, hoping to distract her.

Meg pulled away. "Mommy," she demanded. "Daddy."

Lani pulled her onto her lap, but the little girl pulled away and began to wail. "Mommy," she sobbed.

Fisher's nails clicked on the tile, then he whined, pressing his nose between Lani and Meg. Lani could feel his agitation. "It's okay," she said, rocking Meg back and forth.

Ben's footsteps came hurrying back. "What's wrong?"

"She wants her parents."

"Here, let me have her."

But Meg went from squirming to get away from Lani to clinging to her neck and screaming all the louder. "Mommy! Mommy!"

"You're making it worse," Lani said. "Quit pulling at her."

"Meggie, let's go play ball," he said in a coaxing voice.

But nothing distracted her, and she continued to sob for her parents. Lani finally succeeded in handing her over to Ben, then got to her feet. "Let's take her outside."

She called the dog, and he came at once, the metal tags at his neck jingling. They followed Ben as he carried the wailing child out the door.

"Maybe she'll fall asleep as we walk toward the orchard. I've still got the washcloth. I'll try to clean her up," Ben said. Meg's wails intensified along with huffs of frustration from Ben. "Well, she's not spotless, but she looks better."

"Let me have her a minute," Lani said, stopping and holding out her arms.

"Lani," Meg sobbed.

Lani felt her lunge into her arms, then Meg's small hands clutched her neck. "Mommy," she whispered in Lani's ear.

"I know, sweetheart, I know." Lani rocked her back and forth in her arms and wept with her.

fourteen

Meg had finally fallen asleep, and Ben laid her down on a blanket under a tree before going to work on picking coffee cherries. Ben fingered his chin and glanced at Lani as she worked steadily at the tree next to him. The touch of her fingers on his face had been as light as fireflies yet had carried an impact that still shook him. Tearing his gaze away, he focused on his work. The plump cherries dropped into his hand and then into the bucket.

He'd told her he'd keep her in sight. In the meantime, he could check out some of the other Taylor Camp residents. He edged around the tree until he positioned himself next to Jerry. With a trunk nearly as big as the tree, Jerry scooped up coffee cherries in his big hands with calm efficiency. He didn't look like a doctor today.

"Hot day," Ben said. He paused and wiped his brow.

"Yeah." Jerry's thick black hair fell over his forehead in a shaggy style the ladies probably found attractive. About fifty-five, he had a muscular build that showed he worked out.

"You all seem to have known one another a long time," Ben said. "I lived at Taylor Camp when I was a kid."

"No kidding?" Jerry's hands paused, then he began to grab handfuls of coffee cherries again. "When?"

"Early seventies until they burned it. I was born there."

"I had to have known your mom. What was her name?"

"Nancy Anderson. Peekaboo." He was still rocked by the way Willie seemed to think his mother had something to do with the old murder.

Jerry appraised Ben. "You don't look like her."

"My mother said I looked like my dad." Loser that he was. Every time he looked in the mirror, Ben thought of his dad and vowed never to be like him.

Jerry gave him a long, slow look. "You look like Ash."

"So I've been told. I think he might have been my dad."

"Where's your mom now?"

"Last I heard she was in Michigan. I haven't seen her in five years."

"Hard feelings," Jerry observed.

"You might say that." Ben saw no reason to reveal that his mother had been distant at best and neglectful at worst. She'd never even sent a birthday or Christmas card over the years. "There's so much water under the bridge I'd need a life jacket to survive."

"When she comes back for your brother's funeral, maybe you'll be able to patch things up." Jerry's glance held sympathy.

"I'm not holding my breath. She hasn't decided if she's even coming, and the funeral is tomorrow." Ben really didn't want to talk about his mother. His chest felt hollow whenever he thought about her. He watched Jerry move off to empty his bucket into the burlap sack. His practiced bedside manner had Ben talking more than he liked.

He glanced toward Meg and saw she was stirring. She sat up and rubbed her eyes. At least she wasn't crying. "Hey, baby girl," he said in a soft voice. Her sweet smile broke his heart. He would do all he could to protect her from further harm. She held up her arms, and he scooped her up.

Meg patted Ben's hair, then laid her cheek against his neck. He caught a whiff of something. A dirty diaper. Holding her at arm's length, he wrinkled his nose. "You couldn't have eaten that," he told her.

She giggled. "Eat."

Her diaper bag sat on the blanket. He laid her down, then retrieved a diaper and wipes and began the process. The odor nearly made him gag. He wasn't sure why. He'd trained puppies and cleaned up after them plenty of times. Meg smiled up at him in such a trusting manner that he felt like a heel at his reaction. He took a deep breath. Mistake. The unpleasant aroma filled his nose with a distinctive stench he didn't know if he'd ever get out of his lungs.

He heard something behind him and turned to see Lani approaching with Fisher. "Where you headed?" he asked.

"I need some water. The cooler's around here somewhere, isn't it?"

"Sure. I'll get you a bottle." He reached into the cooler beside the blanket and pulled out a cold, wet bottle of Hawaiian Springs. "Here you go."

"Thanks." She uncapped the bottle and took a swig.

Ben chuckled. "You should see the look on Fisher's face. I think he wants to play in your bottle."

Lani smiled. She tipped the bottle up and let some dribble out. "Did I hit him?"

"Yep, he's smiling." Ben glanced back at her. His gaze caught on the smooth, firm line of her neck. "Um, I'm changing Meg."

"Oh, that's the smell."

"Yep." He eyed her. She wasn't rushing to offer help. "I think I need some guidance here."

A slow smile lifted her lips. "You haven't changed a dirty diaper yet. I've noticed how you've managed to get out of it every time. You need to learn."

His gorge rose as the stench intensified. Stuff oozed from the side of the diaper too. She would laugh as he made a fool of himself. "I can hardly wait." He didn't bother to hide the sarcasm in his voice.

"It's easy. Got some wipes?"

"Yeah." He glared at the wipes. They looked pretty flimsy, not really big enough to protect his hands much.

"Just clean her up good and put a clean diaper on. Hold your breath through the worst part," Lani advised. She moved closer, then stepped back. "Whew, that's a bad one."

"You're telling me," he muttered. He turned his head into the wind, filled his lungs, then plunged into the task. When he had to take another breath, the dirty diaper was rolled up and lying on the blanket, but the odor still hung in the air. He tugged on the diaper tape and managed to get it snug enough not to fall off, then pulled up Meg's jeans. Smiling, he lifted her in his arms like a trophy. It felt good even if Lani couldn't see his victorious gesture.

"You did it." Lani's proud smile came quickly.

Ben dragged in more fresh air. "It isn't something I'm eager to repeat. Could you potty train her?"

"She's too young. You shouldn't start until they're two or so. Whenever she starts telling you she has to go or starts bringing you a diaper to change her, then you'll know she's ready."

"She'll be two in a few days," he protested. "My mom always said my brother was trained when he was eighteen months."

"That's very rare for a boy," Lani said.

"How do you know all this stuff?"

Her smile broadened. "Remember, I worked in a day care for a while."

Maybe women just knew this stuff naturally. It was all gibberish to Ben. He popped Meg back into her carrier and shrugged his arms into it. Walking back up the hill to the coffee grove, he matched his steps to Lani's measured pace.

"I heard you talking to Jerry. What do you think of him?" she asked.

"Seems like a nice guy. They all do. None of them seems likely to be a murderer. Or a smuggler. Harry doesn't drive a flashy car. He dresses like Jimmy Buffet and seems pretty easygoing. It's hard to imagine him aiming a gun at someone. And Arlo loves everyone."

She twisted her hands together, and her mouth turned down. She began to run. The dog loped along to keep up. He kept glancing up at Lani as if to ask her what was wrong. Ben jogged along after her, waiting until she tripped. He caught her as she stumbled.

She buried her face in his chest. "I feel so helpless. I need to see so I can figure out who's doing this. This is punishment. God hates me."

He gave her a gentle shake. "You know that's not true."

"It is true," she wept. "You don't know what I did. I killed a baby. My own baby. I let a doctor sweep it away like it was so much trash." She buried her face in his shirt, and sobs wracked her.

He went still, his hand running over her sleek black hair. An abortion. Sorrow sifted through him, but who was he to judge her? He'd killed his friend's sight. His fingers stilled. No wonder Tyrone had been upset. "God still loves you, Lani. He isn't punishing you."

"I deserve punishment," she whispered.

"Sometimes I think we'd feel better if we took what we deserved. But that's not the way it works, and it leaves us in debt to Jesus."

She raised her head. "I want the pain to go away."

"It may never go away. When we sorrow for our sin, we know

we really belong to God." He smoothed her hair. The fragrance of pikake blew away the diaper smell that still clung to his nostrils. Her tears soaked his shirt. She felt warm and pliable in his arms. He stared down into her face, his gaze lingering on her lips. Bending his neck, he leaned down to kiss her.

Her fragrant breath mingled with his, and he brushed her lips with his. Just a tiny kiss, but it was enough to send adrenaline shooting through him. He lifted his head. "We'd better get to work," he whispered.

"I know." She opened her eyes. "Thanks, Ben. I guess I just have to live with it."

"We all do." Something wet dribbled in his hair. He jerked. "What?" He twisted around to look at Meg. "You drooling in my hair?"

The toddler giggled.

Lani did too. She pulled back, and the moment ebbed away.

Ben dropped his hands. "Ick."

"Get used to it. It's just the beginning of your education." She laughed and widened the distance between them.

Ben wanted to pull her back against his chest, but he dropped his hands. "So what about the other Taylor Camp people? What do you know about them?"

"Arlo Beckett is my favorite. I think he has the hots for Aunt Rina. He's always watched her a lot. Does he still?" she asked.

"Yeah, now that you mention it. He's a goner over her."

Lani smiled. "She's well preserved for her age. What do you think about Harry Drayton?"

"He's an okay guy. Hard worker."

"He told me once he never married because he couldn't find anyone like Aunt Rina. I think they're all smitten by her. Jerry worries about her all the time and is always trying new medicines on her. But it seems no one wants to move in on Willie."

"Willie is the one I don't know much about. You know him well, don't you?" He found he loved watching her, the way she moved, the tilt of her smile, the length of her lashes.

Lani shook her head. "I've known him for about a year now, but he never said more than two words to me before today. I don't like the way he orders Aunt Rina around. And she lets him usually. Until this whole genetically altered coffee thing came up."

"How does she feel about Willie?"

"Well, she was almost ready to marry him. But I don't know. In case you haven't noticed, she's pretty closemouthed. If not for this injunction thing, I think she might say yes."

He nodded. "Did finding out she'd been in prison change your mind about her innocence in all this?"

"No," she said, jutting her chin up.

She was a loyal little thing. He smiled at her even though he knew she couldn't see. His gaze lingered on her lips.

Meg tugged on his hair. "Gum," she said.

"I've got some in my backpack." Lani felt around for it then pulled it out of the contents. "Here you go," she said, holding out a piece.

Meg took it and giggled. Ben set her down beside Lani. Fisher sniffed her neck, then licked her. Her peals of laughter made Ben smile more. His cell phone rang, and he looked at the display. A hard knot formed in his stomach. He didn't recognize the number, but it was a stateside area code.

He clicked on the phone. "Ben Mahoney," he said.

His mother's voice came over the line. "Ben, I just heard about Ethan. The least you could have done is call me yourself."

"Hello, Nancy," he said. "You don't keep me posted with your phone numbers, so I had to have my attorney track you down."

"I need you to get me a ticket," she said. "I don't have the money."

She never had the money. "I'll take care of it," he said. "Which airport do you want to fly out of?"

"Chicago O'Hare. I need to leave today to get there in time."

"Did you just now decide to come?" He knew it was a mistake to question her, but the words slipped out.

"I had things to arrange. Call me back when you have the ticket." She clicked off without saying good-bye.

Ben flipped his phone closed and stuck it in his pocket. After all this time of dealing with his mother, he'd have thought his hands wouldn't shake anymore. He put them in his pockets.

"A problem?" Lani asked.

"My mom is coming to the funeral." Was his voice shaking?

"I think it's a good thing. You need someone from your family."

"It's going to be hard enough to hold it together without her there. She didn't sound too broken up about it, but I bet she wails like a professional mourner at the service."

"You didn't even know where she was?"

Ben shook his head, then realized she couldn't see it. "No."

"I'm sorry." She sounded as though she was, too.

"The last time I heard from her, she was getting married again and wanted money for a dress. I didn't get a wedding invitation either, even though I sent her the money." Aware his voice sounded bitter, he cleared his throat. "Not that I wanted to go. I'd already been to four or so. I lost count."

She touched his hand. "Were she and Ethan close?"

"I don't know that anyone has ever really reached her heart. I used to wonder what made her so hard and self-centered, but then I got to where it didn't matter anymore." If anyone touched her heart, it wouldn't be him.

"I don't think I believe that," she said softly. "It sounds like you're just trying to convince yourself so it doesn't hurt."

"I've got my own life, and she's got hers. That's just the way it is."

"You'd better make her reservation if she's going to get here in time for the funeral."

"I'll have my lawyer do it." He pulled out his cell phone and dialed Cliff. The receptionist put him right through.

"Ben, I just picked up the phone to call you," Cliff said when he came on the line.

"Did my mother call you too? She needs a ticket leaving yet today."

"I'll take care of it, but that's not why I'm calling. I found out more about the Waldens' suit. They're claiming you're a dangerous driver and would endanger Meg's safety."

"What?" Meg puckered when Ben shouted, and he put his hand on her head and patted her curls. "It was an accident."

"But someone was blinded, and you were ticketed for negligence. We know it's not fair, but it might sway a judge."

He began to pace across the grass. "What can I do?"

"There's nothing we can do. It's a matter of public record. We'll go before the judge and present our case and hope he listens. Would Tyrone testify on your behalf?"

"I'm sure he would."

"That would help, but even then, it will depend on what the judge thinks is best for Meg."

"I want what's best for her too," he protested. "But being hauled off by strangers would crush her." *And me.* "And what about the rap sheet on Natalie's father?"

"I've got that, but he's been a model citizen for five years. I'll keep you posted," Cliff promised. "Let me get your mother's ticket. Do you want to pick her up at the airport?"

"No, she won't ride on my bike. It would mess up her hair."

"I'll take care of it, then."

"Trouble?" Lani asked when Ben hung up. She sat down with Fisher's head on her lap. The dog had a blissful expression on his face as her fingers ran along his ears.

Ben envied the dog. "Yeah. Natalie's parents are claiming I'm unfit to have custody of Meg."

"How can they say that?" Her voice rose, and she pushed the dog off her lap and stood. Fisher gave her a look of outrage.

"It's not too hard when it's my fault a man is blind," he blurted out. He waited to see her recoil.

She was extending her hand to him but dropped it at his words. "How?" she whispered.

"An auto accident," he said in a hard voice. "I was driving, fiddling with the radio and not paying attention. I missed a curve and rolled the truck. It was my fault Tyrone was blinded." He wanted to see her turn away in horror. Maybe that would kill the budding infatuation he felt.

She reached out for him. He made no move to take her hand, but instead stepped around her and scooped up Meg. "I'm going to get back to work." He strode away without looking back.

fifteen

With clenched fists, Kato stomped into the room where Thresh sat going over books. He looked up. "Did you find it?"

Kato shook his bald head. "I searched the Driscoll house again. It's not there. I'd say it's at the bottom of the ocean somewhere."

His euphoria vanished. "Have you sent down divers?"

"It's blue hole there. The bottom is too deep."

Thresh swept everything to the floor with one hand. "You have to find it! Do you have any idea what that's worth? Could he have given it to his brother? Did you search there?"

"Yeah. I came up empty."

"Ethan has to have it at the house. We'll look again, and this time, I'll go with you."

Silence enveloped the car as they drove to the Driscoll house. Thresh fumed with the need to find the treasure. It was for Blossom when all this was over. Streetlamps illuminated the dark night. The clock on the dash read twelve fifteen. He pointed out a parking spot down the street. They got out of the car and sneaked along the quiet streets to the back.

"Break the lock," he snapped. Kato nodded and threw his shoulder against the door. The jamb splintered and the door flew open.

They stepped inside, and he wrinkled his nose at the stench. "It smells like they haven't taken out the trash in weeks."

Kato's flashlight swept the room. "Turn on the lights. I doubt anyone will notice," he said.

He was right for once. Thresh flipped on the light, and they began to tear the house apart. But two hours later the treasure was still missing.

"What about the kid?" he asked. "Maybe he hid it with her stuff. How did he know it was in the bags of coffee anyway?"

"He started to take the bags we were using for camouflage. I think he got suspicious when I stopped him from taking them."

"I don't care who gets hurt at this point. I'm not about to give up my treasure. Find it!"

When Ben didn't find Tyrone at the shop, he walked along Ali'i Drive. Traffic rumbled by, and he could hear the sound of the surf on the other side of the road. His pace quickened when he saw the Mokuaikaua Church ahead. He turned in and passed under the lava-stone arch into the grounds. This first church built on Hawaiian soil held a mystique for Tyrone, and often he could be found here with his rosary beads.

Ben stepped inside and gazed around the interior, paneled with koa wood. Tyrone sat in the front pew. He lifted his head at the slap of Ben's slippers on the wood floor.

"I figured I'd find you here." Ben slid into the pew beside him. Ranger nosed at his foot, then lay down on the floor. "Lani told me what she did. She's torn up about it, Tyrone." What was he doing— trying to get the two of them back together?

"Maybe she is." Tyrone slumped against the pew back. "I'd like to blame her for all of it, but I can't. It was just as much my fault. I turned my back on everything I knew was right, just for a pretty face. Now I have blood on my hands."

Ben put his hand on Tyrone's arm. "Guess we're all in the same boat, buddy. We're always going to fail at something we think we should have done better. Even Paul did. I've been thinking a lot about this lately. God doesn't want us to be bound up by guilt. Jesus died so we would be free from that."

Tyrone rubbed his forehead. "I guess you're right, but man, it's low to feel so weak and ashamed."

A familiar emotion to Ben as well. But he was beginning to understand his own failings. "Let's go get a shave ice."

"I'm game." Tyrone stood and grabbed Ranger's lead. "What are you doing taking Lani's case? I thought you couldn't stand her."

"We've become friends."

"Friends, huh? Maybe more than that?"

Ben put his hands in his pockets. "Would it bother you?"

"Dude, you kidding? Of course it would bother me. I still care about her, chump that I am. But don't let that stand in your way. She and I have too much past to get over. I'd like to see you happy." Tyrone leaned forward and slapped Ben on the back. "I'll dance at your wedding, even if I cry in my beer a little."

Ben chuckled. "I'm not thinking along those lines. We're just friends." He shook his head. Who was he trying to kid?

Lani sat on the shore beside Fawn at the Place of Refuge. She tossed the Frisbee. "Go get it, boy!" She had no idea where it went, but Fisher's paws kicked sand at her as he ran off. His happy bark floated back to her, then a loud splash came. "Uh-oh, I must have thrown it in the water."

"Yeah, the wind caught it."

Shadows cooled her arms, and she knew the sun must be going down. Lani traced her fingers over the sketch pad in her lap. "Do you think it looks okay? I usually have colored-pencil sketches of the different colors in my design. This black-and-white won't be very impressive."

"Then what I bought should be just the ticket." Fawn placed a book in her hands.

"What is this?" Lani ran her hand over the slick cover.

"It's orchid stickers. Punch-out ones of different colors and varieties. It might not have all the ones you planned, but it should have most. You chose standard Hawaiian varieties of plants. I ordered it last week when we got started on this."

"Fawn, you are a genius!" Lani hugged the book to her chest. "You'll have to help me."

"I can do that." Fawn took the book and riffled through the pages. "Here are the phalaenopsis orchids. Let's do those first."

The women set to work sticking clumps of orchids onto the design sheet. The sound of the surf lulled Lani. Life wasn't so bad. She had good friends, her family. And Ben. That was a new thought. She lingered on it a moment. Their friendship might lead to more, but she didn't want to count on it. Still, the possibilities made her heart thump like the surf hitting the rocks.

Flash. Lani winced and blinked her eyes. The bright flash of yellow came again. She inhaled sharply.

"What is it?" Fawn asked.

"I don't know," Lani said slowly. "I saw a flash of light, like golden sunshine."

"Your vision?"

"Maybe."

Fisher's paws pattered on the ground, and droplets of water hit her legs. Her dog. What would happen if she got her sight back? She couldn't give him up.

She heard the roar of a Harley. "Is that Ben?" she asked Fawn.

"Yep. Hey, Ben!" Fawn's voice moved away. The bike's motor changed from a roar to a growl, then died.

Footsteps crunched in the sand. "Fawn said you saw light?" Ben asked.

Lani nodded. "Just a flash. It's gone now."

"You'd probably better go see the doctor," Fawn said, her voice worried.

"It's after hours. I'll call Jerry when we get home."

"You don't sound very happy about it," Ben said.

"I'm trying not to get my hopes up. Maybe it's something normal for blind people. Has Tyrone ever mentioned it?"

"No."

Lani touched Fisher's head. "What if I get my sight back? I can't give Fisher up, Ben. You can't expect me to do that."

"Look, we've discussed this before. Fisher is still in training. He could give someone else the freedom you have with him."

Lani knelt and put her arms around Fisher's wet neck. He licked her cheek. "He's mine, and I'm not going to give him back. Never ever." Maybe it was selfish, but Fisher was part of her now.

Later, when Jerry couldn't see any improvement with her vision, she didn't know whether to laugh or cry.

It was too lovely a day to bury Ethan and Natalie. Thursday morning Ben sat in the third pew close to the open window, next to Tyrone. The breeze held the scent of ginger and plumeria that blended with the oppressive fragrance of roses from the flowers covering the caskets. He kept glancing back at the door and realized he wanted Lani with him.

The door opened, and she came in with Yoshi on one side and Rina on the other. Her hand pressed against Yoshi's elbow; she hadn't brought Fisher with her. Lani walked with a tentative stride. The place was unfamiliar, and Ben watched her take small steps.

"Here," he said in a hushed voice. He stepped out of the pew and let them step past him. He settled beside Lani, and she reached out her hand for his. He didn't need words from her—the comforting press of her fingers was enough.

His mother hadn't made it. Maybe she'd run into an attractive man at the airport and decided she had better things to do. She normally ran from anything that resembled responsibility. Loneliness left him isolated in spite of Lani's touch. Ethan had been his only sibling, and while Ben didn't approve of the choices he'd made in his life, the void he left loomed huge in Ben's life.

The caskets stood open, and he'd walked to them when he first came in to say good-bye. If only he could have done something, helped Ethan to get out of the mess.

Natalie's parents were in the aisle across from him, but they hadn't so much as glanced toward him. He'd met them at Ethan and Natalie's wedding, so he doubted they'd have trouble remembering him. They would likely demand to see Meg as soon as the service concluded. The Driscolls' next-door neighbor had a little girl Meg liked to play with, and the mother had offered to keep Meg during the funeral.

The preacher stepped to the podium and looked out over the crowd. "You've all come today to pay your respects to Ethan and Natalie Driscoll."

The back door of the church banged open, and a wail escalated into a keening shriek. Ben turned and saw his mother stagger up the aisle. She wore a black suit and heels. Mascara ran down her face with the tears that flowed from her eyes. She lurched toward the coffins, her cries growing louder. "My boy, my boy."

Ben rose and tried to intercept her, but she darted to the casket and threw herself on top of Ethan's body. The casket shuddered, and so did Ben, envisioning the collapse of the stand. But it held. He moved quickly down the aisle to grab his mother. "Come sit with me," he said softly.

She tried to shake off his hands. "My baby boy. How will I survive this?"

He hung on to her hand and pulled her insistently back to the pew. Everyone stared as they made their way down the aisle, which was what she wanted. In spite of her great show of grief, anyone who knew her well realized the only thing she loved was Jim Beam.

Ben settled her into the pew. All through the service, she kept her gloved hands folded in her lap and her gaze straight ahead. He tried to do the same, but the minister's words went over his head. He had hoped to draw comfort from the service, but his mother's appearance left his thoughts churning.

As soon as the service ended, his mother rose from the pew. "I want to say good-bye to my son," she announced in a loud voice. "I'm sure *some* of you will understand." She tossed a pointed glance toward Ben.

He choked back his response and followed her to the caskets again. She wasn't going to make a spectacle of the funeral if he could help it. To his surprise, she merely touched Ethan's forehead, then turned and walked toward the back of the church with her head held high.

Ben stared into his brother's face one last time. His throat felt thick, and he couldn't have spoken if his life depended on it. *Good-bye, Ethan.* His eyes burned as he turned to follow his mother out of the church. He nodded to Natalie's parents, but they didn't respond. Would his mother's behavior be used against him in the custody suit? He exited the church, blinking when he stepped into the bright sunshine. Tyrone was getting into a car with some employees from the Harley shop.

His mother met him on the front steps. "Ben, where is my granddaughter?"

"With a friend."

"She should have been here."

"I decided she was too young."

"You decided. I should have been consulted."

"Well, that decision fell to me." He refrained from pointing out that she had no right to make any decisions about a grandchild she'd never seen.

"Don't curl your lip at me," she snapped. "Show me some respect. I'm still your mother."

If she only knew how hard he was trying to be respectful. The Bible's mandate on respect demanded it, but it was a struggle when she'd done nothing to deserve it. "I'll go get her after the interment."

"You'll go get her now. I want to see if she looks like me." She fluffed her black hair.

It was darker than he remembered and had not even a strand of gray. The wings of white at her temples had changed to fully black. And he'd never seen her in a suit. She appeared imminently respectable. What had happened?

He offered her his arm. "Meg looks like Natalie, not you."

"And you sound pleased about that," she said, her eyes tearing. "I'm not the ogre you like to think, Ben. I did the best I could."

He merely nodded. "I'll pick her up on the way to the meal at the church. I'm not going to miss the interment."

She pressed her lips together but didn't argue. He smelled whiskey on her breath when she took his arm. That hadn't changed. Lani, Yoshi, and Rina came up behind them, and he stopped to introduce them.

"Blossom!" his mother said. "Oh my, I can't believe it."

Nancy made a move to hug Rina, but Rina stepped away. "I never expected to see you again, Peekaboo."

Lani's eyes widened, and he knew she was remembering the things she'd heard about Peekaboo. He should have admitted she was his mother long ago.

Nancy pouted. "Are you still carrying a grudge, Blossom?"

"What do you expect?" Rina backed away.

"It's been over thirty years. I'd expect you to get over it."

"Your lies put me in prison those thirty years, Nancy. That's pretty heavy."

Nancy shrugged. She turned to Lani with a smile and held out her hand. "I'm Nancy Mahoney. And you are?"

"Leilani Tagama." Lani held out her hand.

"But everyone calls you Lani, of course." His mother took Lani's hand.

"Your son has been a big help to me. He brought me Fisher."

"Fisher?"

"A Seeing Eye dog," Ben put in. He winced at the way his mother turned to stare at Lani once she knew the younger woman couldn't see her.

His mother turned from her perusal of Lani and appraised him with a curious glance before turning back to the others. "Oh, Ben is a wonderful son. So helpful."

Ben raised his brows. He'd heard many descriptions from his mother about him. Helpful and wonderful had never been in the mix. "We'd better get going," he said, noticing the hearse idling.

The day grew longer by the minute. He ran down the window and let the wind blow in his face. Ethan had loved the wind. He said it blew away the pain, but it didn't seem to work for Ben. His mother chattered away, but her words were like gnats buzzing around his ears. They turned into the cemetery. A police car parked in front of the hearse, and Yoshi got out and waved to him. Ben walked over to meet him.

"I know this isn't the best place for this, Ben, but you said you wanted to be kept up on the investigation," Yoshi said.

Ben nodded. "What is it?" Ben's stomach soured at the look on Yoshi's face. Ben didn't know if he wanted to hear this.

"The boat was rigged with explosives. It was no accident."

Someone had murdered his family. Ben balled his hands into fists. "Who?"

"No idea." Yoshi squeezed Ben's shoulder. "I'm sorry, buddy. I'll do my best to find out who did this."

Ben nodded, his throat thick. Murder was such an ugly word, and an even uglier deed. Someone had callously snuffed out two young lives. The killer hadn't even cared about the baby. Meg's survival had been a miracle.

Cars and trucks began to arrive for the interment. He nodded to Yoshi. "I'll talk to you later." Right now he had to focus on saying good-bye to his brother, then he'd make sure whoever had ripped his family from him paid for it.

Standing on the neighbor's sidewalk with Meg in her arms, Lani listened to Ben's mother chatter to him. He answered mostly in monosyllables, and though he said nothing disrespectful, his curt tone made it clear his mind was with his brother, not his mother.

So she was the infamous Peekaboo. Lani told herself it didn't matter that Ben had kept that news to himself. Maybe she would have too. It wasn't something he'd want the world to know.

Lani hugged Meg gently. The little one didn't realize they had buried her parents today. She still asked for them constantly. She'd been happily playing when they picked her up a few minutes ago, but she'd called for her mother the instant the door opened.

"Baby," Meg said, thrusting her doll into Lani's hands.

Lani took the doll and ran her fingers over it. "Pretty baby. Just like Meg. What's her name?"

"Baby," Meg said again.

Lani tried to give her back the doll, but Meg shoved it away. "No!" she proclaimed loudly. "Daddy. Mommy. Baby." Meg tugged at the doll. Lani relinquished it.

"That child will be a handful," Nancy said.

"I'll carry her inside," Ben said. "We'll get a few things and get out of here."

Ben lifted Meg from Lani's arms. Lani laid her fingers on the back of his elbow and followed him.

"The living room is this way," Ben said.

Lani wrinkled her nose. The house smelled stale and shut up with the unpleasant fumes of garbage left too long. Ben stopped, and Lani nearly bumped into him. The muscles in his arm grew rigid. "What's wrong?" she asked.

"Someone's been in here," Ben said in a tight, strained voice. "All the stuff from the end tables and drawers is on the floor. I want you both outside while I check it out." He led them back to the warmth of the sunshine. He handed Meg to Lani. "Hold her until I get back."

Lani cuddled the little girl and shuddered. The atmosphere nearly writhed with malice.

"Vandals," his mother said. "People have no respect anymore. Breaking into the house of the dead."

Lani didn't answer. She strained to hear sounds from inside the house. Ben shouldn't have gone in alone. What if the intruders were still there?

Ben's voice broke the silence. "This was more than vandals," he said. "They were looking for something. The TV is still here. Natalie's rings are on the table."

He led them inside. Lani wrinkled her nose at the smell. Under the odor of rotting garbage, she smelled stale perspiration.

"Mommy," Meg said. "Daddy?"

Lani's heart clenched at the hope in the small voice. "We should have sent her on with Rina and Yoshi," she said softly. "Want to see your toys?" she asked in a fake, cheerful voice.

"Mommy!" Meg called. "Down."

She squirmed so hard, Lani almost dropped her. She put Meg down. As soon as her small feet hit the floor, she ran through the house calling for her parents. Her cries echoed down the hall, and Lani's eyes filled with tears. "Come here, sweetheart."

Meg's sobs grew nearer. "Mommy," she sobbed.

"Mommy's not here, Meggie." Lani knelt by the sobbing child and tried to gather her in her arms.

Meg pulled away. "No," she sobbed. "Mommy."

"I have gum, Meg," Lani said with a trace of desperation. She wanted to fix it, to heal her pain, but there wasn't much she could do.

The sobbing tapered off. "Gum?" Meg asked.

"Right here in my purse. Come here, sweetheart." She sat on the floor and pulled the little girl onto her lap, then found some gum.

"Bribing a child," Nancy said. "She's going to have to know her parents are dead. You should tell her, Ben."

"She's too young to understand the concept of death, Mother," Ben said.

"I know that," Nancy said, her voice indignant. "But you can tell her they went away and they're not coming back."

"That's just cruel," Lani burst out. "We told her they went away for a long trip. She can't even understand that much."

"It's cruel to let her go looking for them," Nancy said.

"She's too young to understand," Ben repeated.

Lani tipped her head to the side. "I think someone is at the door."

"Probably Natalie's parents."

The pounding at the door matched the throbbing in Ben's head. The day could hardly get worse, but he had a feeling something worse hovered on the fringes of it. Sure enough, the Waldens stood on the porch looking smug.

"We've come for our granddaughter," Jessica said.

Ben backed away from the door. "Come in." He led the way back to the living room. "Mother, you remember Natalie's parents." Meg ran to him, and he scooped her up.

"Hello." His mother shook Steve's and Jessica's hands.

"I want to hold Meg," Jessica said, holding out her arms.

Ben started to hand the child over, but Meg clung to him and started to whine.

"Don't you know your grandma?" Jessica coaxed. She began to tug on the little girl.

Meg wailed louder, and Ben moved out of reach. "She doesn't want to go. It's been a long day for her, and she's tired."

Jessica pressed her lips together. "Surely you see the impossibility of raising a little girl by yourself."

Ben shook his head. "No, I don't. I love Meg, and she loves me. We've been just fine."

"A little girl needs a woman's touch," Steve interrupted. "No judge will award you custody. You tool around on a Harley. That's not safe."

"I realize that," Ben said. "I'll buy a car. And you're hardly a model father. You've been in jail."

Steve stiffened. "That's in the past."

Jessica sniffed. "Meg needs a mother. Who will care for her during the day?"

"I will," Lani said.

Ben's head jerked to stare at her. They'd never talked about her watching Meg. A wave of emotion rose in him.

"I don't mean to be unkind, but you're blind. You won't be able to see to keep her out of danger. What if she gets into cleaning supplies under the sink? What if she falls and hurts herself?" Jessica asked, her voice firm.

"My vision is coming back," Lani said in a no-nonsense voice. "This is just temporary."

"Well, even so. Meg needs the stability of two parents. We'll do everything in our power to gain custody."

"Then get ready for a fight," Ben said. "I'll never give her up."

Steve looked around. "We'd be glad to help pack up the things."

"I can handle it," Ben said. Could they be looking for something here? Ethan had to be shipping the smuggled goods somewhere. Could Steve be involved? It would explain why he was so eager to get Meg when they'd made no effort in the past to get to know her. He didn't like the suspicion, but it wouldn't go away.

sixteen

The car stopped in Rina's drive, and Lani swung open the rear passenger-side door but stayed in her seat. "Meg's sleeping," she said. After the arguments at Meg's house, she'd been exhausted herself. Meg had refused to interact with her grandparents, and Ben hadn't forced her. Steve and Jessica would be hard to dissuade. The custody decision would probably have to be made by a judge.

"I'll try not to awaken her," Ben said. The front driver's-side door opened. He whistled, and an answering bark came.

A few moments later, Fisher pressed his wet nose against Lani's leg. She rubbed her fingers in his soft coat. "I missed you, boy."

"Hang on, let me get your harness," Ben said.

Lani heard Ben move off toward the house. His footsteps moved fast.

"How well do you know my son?" Nancy asked. "Years?"

"He's a good friend," Lani said. "He's helped me a lot since I lost my sight. It's only temporary," she added hastily.

"Did you know each other before you were blinded?"

"No." Where was this headed? Lani wasn't sure she wanted to know. "Ben's a good man," she said.

"Then you don't know him well. He's hotheaded and impetuous.

182

He'll never settle down with one woman, if that's what you have in mind. And he has no patience for illness. When I was sick in bed, he always wanted something. He's a rolling stone, just like his father."

The bitterness in the older woman's voice tipped Lani off that her words might not be the truth. She kept silent, because she didn't know how to reply.

"I don't want you to get your heart broken like I did. I saw the way you looked at him."

The woman was like Fisher with water: she just couldn't leave the subject alone. "What do you mean? He's just a friend," Lani protested. "Besides, I'm blind. I can't 'look' at him."

"Honey, I saw the way you turned your face toward him and your expression, so don't try to bandy words. I've been in love too many times to count. I know the look." Nancy laughed.

Lani prayed for Ben to get back. This conversation felt way too uncomfortable. "I'm not getting hurt," she said.

"Good, because it looks like you've been through enough. Ben's the type to love them and leave them. Men like him have never been good at sticking around."

"Ethan had been married five years," Lani pointed out, quoting what the minister said at the funeral.

"He was more like me," Nancy said. "Ben's like his dad, looks just like him and acts just like him. Being around him is like looking at his father."

"I think you haven't looked under the surface with your son. You're getting hung up on his appearance," Lani said. "I can't see the outward, but the inward is beautiful." Admitting her admiration to Nancy, Lani realized how much she was beginning to care about Ben. It hurt to hear his mother tear him down.

"Honey, don't tell me what he's like. I raised him."

"What happened to his dad?"

"Supposedly he drowned. Or the sharks got him."

Cigarette smoke wafted over Lani's face. "You doubt that?"

"He was a good swimmer, Olympic ability. I think he bugged out. Just that morning, I told him I was pregnant. It would have been just like him to run off. He didn't like being tied down."

"Maybe you took out your bitterness on Ben since he looked so much like his dad," Lani said. She probably shouldn't have said it, but no mother should talk about her son that way.

The car door slammed. "How dare you! You know nothing about me and my son."

Lani heard her tromp off toward the house without another word. Just as well. She'd been finding it hard to hold on to her temper.

The sound of another car motor growled beside her, and she lifted her head. A familiar voice called her name. Annie! She gasped and stood.

"Lani!" The muffled creak of the car door came, then Annie's arms encircled Lani, and they hugged fiercely.

All the sorrows and frustrations of the past weeks welled up in Lani's eyes. She folded herself into Annie's smaller frame and buried her face in her older sister's neck just like Meg had done with Lani earlier. Her eyes burned, and tears trickled from them. Everything would be all right now. Annie was here. She'd always taken care of things. She didn't want to cry, but she couldn't help herself.

Annie rocked her back and forth a little. "There, there, Lani, it's going to be okay. God's in control here. You know that."

Even though Lani acknowledged the truth of Annie's words, she rebelled at the thought. If God had things in control, why had he let this happen to her? Couldn't he see how much she was trying to change? The tears came harder and faster. Her muffled sobs intensified. "I want it to be the way it was a month ago," she whispered between hiccups. "I can't see, Annie. Did they tell you that? Nothing. It's all black." She strained to see through the darkness, to look at Annie's face.

"But you're still alive, Lani." Her sister pulled away and took her by the shoulders. "What would I do if I ever lost you? You're alive, and I thank God he spared you."

Lani's tears dried. She rubbed at her wet cheeks. "Is Mano here?"

"I'm right here," a deep voice said. "I wouldn't let my new baby sister go through this without me." Her brother-in-law's beefy arms enveloped her in a hug.

Lani clung to him. Mano always smelled like the sea, like a monk seal. Annie was fire to his water, but they made a perfect couple. She ached to see her sister, to look into Mano's warm dark eyes. Would she ever see them again? "Sorry for watering your shirt," she said when she finally pulled away.

"I had a spot on it anyway." His voice deepened with amusement. "Hey, who's the kid in the car?"

"Ben's niece. Her parents were killed." Lani told them the events that had been happening. "Ben should be back with my halter for Fisher any minute."

"Here he comes now," Annie said. "Fawn is with him."

A moment later, a wet nose touched Lani's leg while the two women greeted each other. "This is Fisher," she said when the excited talking had quieted a decibel. The dog barked, and Lani put her hand on his head. "Quiet, boy." He licked her hand.

"I've got your harness," Ben said.

The harness clanked, and he slipped the handle into her palm. "Thanks," she said. "I'd like you to meet my sister and her husband. This is Annie and Mano Oana."

"I've heard a lot about you," Ben said. "Lani has bugged us all to death with wanting to see you."

Annie's voice held a smile. "Lani and I are close. Thank you for taking such good care of her."

"Yoshi has been watching out for her too," Fawn said.

"Where is Yoshi?" Mano asked.

"In the house. Go ahead, and I'll get Meg out of the car."

Lani heard Ben unsnap the buckle of the car seat. "I'll show you." She gripped the harness and turned in the direction of the babble of voices. "Forward," she told Fisher. It felt good to be able to show off her new skills with the dog, to demonstrate she wasn't totally helpless and dependent. Maybe Annie was right—she could have a full life even if her sight never came back.

Once all the mourners had arrived for the funeral dinner, Ben carried Meg outside behind Lani and her sister. His church had brought in the meal, and the tables set up outside Rina's house groaned with the weight of the food. Meg slept soundly, her head on his shoulder.

He glanced at the two sisters talking eagerly together. They didn't look much alike. Annie was even tinier than Lani, and while she wasn't as drop-dead gorgeous as Lani, Annie had a quiet beauty that caught the eye. Her sweet smile would be enough to light up the room. Mano was a lucky guy.

His gaze went to Lani as she stood with her head tipped to one side listening to Annie greet their aunt. Her perfect cheekbones and rich brown eyes caught the eye and kept it. The more time he spent with her, the more he craved her company.

Meg stirred. "Gum," she said sleepily.

"Later," he told her. She felt wet. She closed her eyes again, and he carried her into the house and down the hall to her room. When he stepped into the room, he smelled something unpleasant, like stale perspiration. Maybe he'd left a dirty diaper in here, but a quick glance around showed the room in perfect order.

His gaze went to the dresser with Meg's things. A white piece of cloth stuck out of one drawer. He laid her on the bed and opened the drawer. Her tiny clothes were no longer in neat stacks but had been jumbled around. Ethan's house had been searched. Could someone have come here when they didn't find what they were looking for at Ethan's?

He quickly changed Meg's diaper, then slipped his arms under her and lifted her. Grabbing a blanket, he walked back outside and made his way through the crowd to a tree just past the food table. He dropped the blanket on the ground, kicked it around until it lay halfway flat on the ground, then placed Meg on top of it. He could stand guard here while she slept and still mingle with the mourners who wanted to offer their condolences.

"Hey, buddy." Yoshi hailed him from the food table. He approached with a plate loaded with kalua pork and macaroni salad. "Did you get some *pupus*?"

"Not yet. I will. Did you see Annie? She's here."

"Yep. She looks a little tired. That trip was grueling. One of us needs to talk to her and have her get Lani to confide in her. If Lani will tell anyone what really happened that day, it would be Annie. You get anything out of her yet?"

"You need to give this up, Yoshi. I don't think she remembers anything. In fact, I'm sure of it."

"I'm thinking about asking her if she'd undergo hypnosis."

"I don't know that I believe in that stuff. I've heard too much about people who recover childhood memories that end up being false. Any clue on who trashed my brother's house?"

"Detectives are over there now."

"I think someone searched Meg's things here."

Yoshi's eyes widened. "Here? Ethan must have had something someone wanted."

Something valuable enough to kill for? Thankfully, Meg could pose no real danger to anyone. "What about the orchid smuggling?"

Yoshi shook his head. "I've had a surveillance team keeping an eye on them, but no luck so far. I don't know, Ben. Maybe there's nothing to that theory of yours. You see anything suspicious going on down there?"

"I haven't been back down," Ben said. "We've been involved in the coffee harvest here, and Ethan's funeral, and there's been no time."

"I'd better check out the room. Which one?"

"Down the hall, last room on the left."

Yoshi nodded and went inside. Ben filled a plate and ate while he kept watch over his niece.

Soon Yoshi came back, his lips pressed together and a scowl wrinkling his forehead. "I called for a fingerprinting team, but I'm betting he was too smart to leave any prints."

While Yoshi talked, Ben's gaze went over Yoshi's shoulder. Arlo came into view. He started toward Rina and broke into a run. His expression was sober. He said something to Rina, and her mouth gaped.

"No!" she said, loudly enough for it to carry over the crowd. She put down her plate and ran in the direction of the milling barn. Arlo and Jerry followed.

"Something's wrong," Ben said. He glanced at Meg. He couldn't leave her alone. His gaze scanned the crowd. Lani stood talking with her sister and Fawn at the other end of the table. He called to her, and she grabbed Fisher's harness and hurried to him. "Can you girls stay with Meg a few minutes?"

"What's wrong?"

"I don't know. Just stay with her. I'll be right back."

Insects buzzed a lazy melody where they sat under the tree. Lani's fingers trailed through the softness of Meg's hair, then lingered on the curved cheeks of the sleeping child. Lani knew the picture she carried in her head of Meg might not even be accurate. "I wish I could see her."

"She's so pretty," Annie said. "And her uncle seems caring. He's very good looking."

Lani felt an idiotic smile curving her lips. "Oh no, you don't. I hear that matchmaking tone. We're just friends."

"I didn't say a word."

"It's the way you didn't say anything," Lani said, laughing. "Um, so what does he look like?"

"I already told you," Fawn said. "You don't believe he's as yummy as I said?" Her voice was teasing.

Annie chuckled. "I'll give you a second opinion. He's about six three. His hair is a rich chestnut, nearly the same color as Fisher's and just as thick and curly. His eyes are kind of a golden brown and kind. Broad shoulders. And big feet. I bet he wears a thirteen or fourteen shoe."

"I wish I could see." Lani took Annie's hand. "It's so good to have you here."

"It sure is," Fawn said. "I have to go back to work tomorrow, but I'll come by every day."

Lani twisted a lock of hair around her finger. "Um, how do I look, Annie? I've wanted to know, but I didn't feel comfortable asking anyone else. I thought they might lie."

"Hey!" Fawn protested.

Lani chuckled. "You're all trying to spare my feelings. Do my eyes seem strange? Is my hair in order? Aunt Rina says I look fine, but she's not exactly the fashion queen. I know you'll be honest."

"I wouldn't know you can't see if you didn't tell me." Annie squeezed her fingers. "Your hair looks a little wind tossed, but you haven't left soap in it or anything. It's still shiny and beautiful. You're not wearing makeup, but then I always thought all that goop you wore just covered up your natural beauty."

"So my appearance isn't so bad that someone would run screaming in the other direction?" Lani began to smile.

"You still turn heads," Fawn said. "Especially Ben's. There's a good energy between the two of you."

"Tell Annie the news, Fawn," Lani said with a grin.

"What news?" Annie asked.

"I've been dating Yoshi," Fawn said. Her voice held a joyous lilt.

"Fawn! I'm so glad."

"Me too," Fawn said. "I don't know if it will go anywhere, but it's fun while it lasts."

"He'll realize the treasure right under his nose," Annie said. She leaned over and squeezed Lani's hand. "Now more about you. What do you remember?"

"Not you too," Lani said. "That's all everyone wants to know. They all think I remember more than I'm saying, but I don't. I wouldn't lie to you, Annie. I can't remember anything."

"I believe you." Annie fell silent for a few moments. "If we could convince the murderer of that, you might be safe."

"Ben thinks the culprit wants me dead before I regain my memory and ID him."

"Are you seeing anything, Lani?"

"Not now. Before I hit my head again, I saw a blurry image, a sensation of movement. When I woke up, the darkness had come back." The glimpse of vision had been entrancing, something she remembered over and over again. And longed for. "And last night I saw yellow light, but Jerry couldn't see any change in my vision when he examined me."

"Do you have any idea why they would target the coffee farm and kill an employee?"

"No."

"Ben's brother and his wife were killed too. Any connection?"

"Maybe. I haven't heard for sure if the coffee used for the smuggling came from here." Lani chewed on her lip. "I think Aunt Rina's neighbor is smuggling orchids."

Annie gasped. "Then maybe they're all connected. That seems a big coincidence."

"That's what Ben thought, but we have no proof. The Asian slipper orchid was gone when we went down to investigate."

"Smuggling," Annie said in a pensive tone. "Coral and orchids. Very different commodities."

"But both very valuable."

"Do you think Aunt Rina's involved?"

"No!" Lani told Annie about their aunt's confession.

"I'm going to mingle and see what I can find out," Annie said. "Will you be okay by yourself?"

"I might take a nap with Meg," Lani said. Her eyes felt heavy. So much had happened lately, she felt as though some new problem bombarded her on every side.

"I'm going to get a fruit smoothie," Fawn said. "You want one, Lani?"

"Sure." The two women moved off through the grass. Lani lay

back on the blanket with the leaves rustling overhead and the sweet scent of plumeria on the breeze.

"Psst, missy." The hushed voice came from her left.

Lani sat up. "Who's there?" She strained to see, but there was only darkness.

"Me Simi. I watch orchids."

The young boy who'd warned them away from the orchid farm. "Where are you?"

"In bushes. I afraid, missy. Man say he sell me to woman in California. She bad woman. Beat Simi last time. I no go there."

"Sell you? He can't sell you. It's illegal to sell someone."

"Is to pay for cost to bring me here. Send back money to my family in Tonga. If I no go, I send no money."

"Come here, Simi. I'll help you."

"No, no, missy. He see me."

"Who are you afraid of?"

"Big man."

The man who had attacked Ben. Lani put her hand to her mouth. "He can't hurt you," she said, more to reassure herself than the boy.

"He say if I tell policeman, they send me back. My family need money to live."

Lani had heard of the illegal immigrant trafficking, the taking of children and working them like slaves. She'd never expected to meet anyone enslaved like that. "Let me help you, Simi."

"No, must go back." His voice rose.

"Why did you come if you won't take my help?"

"Must warn missy. Big man watch little one. You watch. Tell friends. Show this." He thrust something hard into Lani's hand. The bushes rustled.

"Simi?" When he didn't answer, she realized he'd left. Little one. Did he mean Meg? Lani's fingers brushed the sleeping child. The baby had no part in this. And what had he given her? Her touch couldn't make out what it was.

seventeen

The stench of rotting coffee cherries nearly made Ben gag. He stood beside Rina and looked at the ruin of her coffee crop. An odorous sludge filled the top of the tank. It made his stomach turn.

"It's all ruined," Rina said in a choked voice. She passed her hand over her eyes, then straightened her shoulders. Jerry put a comforting arm around her, and Arlo frowned.

"What's happened?" Ben asked.

"The beans were only supposed to ferment twenty-four hours, just long enough to break down the parchment." She plucked a messy bean from the mixture. "See, this is the parchment. It's a thin layer of fiber that's hard to remove, and we ferment it a few hours so we can get it off easily. The fermentation adds to the coffee flavor. But it can't ferment too long." She dropped it back in the sludge and wiped her hand on her shorts.

"Who do you think did this?" Yoshi asked.

"Willie?" Ben asked.

She put her face in her hands. "I don't know what to think. I don't think it would be Willie. But who else could it be?"

Ben had no answer for her. He looked back at the stinking mess.

"How did the perp manage this?" Yoshi asked.

"Honi was supposed to move these beans to the patio to dry. She's gone. Just left a note saying she quit."

"Coincidence?" Yoshi asked.

"Not a chance. Honi wouldn't just leave like that for no reason. Something's happened."

"I'll try to track her down," Yoshi said.

"Can anything be saved?" Jerry asked.

She shook her head. "The rotting meat of the cherries will make the seeds inside bitter. There's no way to get out the taste."

"What if you decaffeinated all of them? Would the chemical take it out?" Yoshi asked.

"Nothing will take it out," she answered, her voice taking on a slight edge. "The entire batch is ruined."

"You've got more cherries to pick, don't you?" Ben put in.

"Yes, but this was the bulk of the crop. We'll have three more pickings. All I can do is hope and pray it's enough to see us through until the second, smaller harvest in the spring." She sounded weary. "I'd better clean this out. You can go back to your guests."

"I'll stay and help," Yoshi said.

"I'd rather do it alone," Rina said. "If I want to cry, I can."

Yoshi studied her face. "Okay."

He and Ben walked back toward the house. Ben could hear his mother's laughter as they approached. She stood talking with Arlo and Josie. Batting her eyes at Arlo, she stood closer to him than she needed to. Ben sighed.

"What?" Yoshi asked.

"My mom. Looks like she has her claws out for Arlo. He'd better be careful."

"Doesn't seem like he's trying any too hard to get away. I thought he was stuck on my aunt."

"Maybe he's trying to make her jealous." Ben hoped that was all. Arlo had his arm slung around Nancy. He threw back his head and laughed at something she said. Ben had noticed a wedding ring on his mother's hand. Whoever his new stepfather was, Ben wouldn't be surprised to see him get the heave-ho pretty quickly.

"Wonder why they've been out of touch all this time." Yoshi said.

"Josie told me that they'd tried to find her, but she didn't show up in any online searches. Probably because she's had so many last names." As far as he knew, there had been six stepfathers. His mother went through men like he went through disposable razors.

"What about your dad? Was he at the camp too?"

"She always told me I looked like my dad. He died before I was born."

"I'd like to take a look at that orchid farm," Yoshi said, changing the subject.

"Now?"

"Later tonight. You go ahead and talk to your guests. You need to grieve your brother. I'm trying to get a search warrant but not having much luck with no evidence."

Annie waved to them from the trees. "Get over here now!" she shouted.

Ben and Yoshi jogged over to where she stood. "What's wrong?" Ben asked.

"This." Annie pushed a jack-in-the-box into his hands. "Recognize it?"

"It looks like Meg's. She had one just like it." Ben turned it over and saw Meg's name on the back. "It is hers. Where'd you get it?"

"Simi brought it to Meg."

Ben looked at Yoshi. "The last time I saw this was in Meg's toy chest. How could Simi get hold of it?"

"The only way was if it was at the orchid farm. I can get a warrant now." Yoshi took out his phone and dialed. After talking a few moments, he hung up. "Johnson is going to meet us at the orchid farm with the search warrant. It will be a few minutes, but we'll wait for him."

"Let's take the back way. Rina showed me a path through the *'ohi'a* trees." Ben didn't wait for another protest. Leading the way along the narrow path, he brushed through a thick forest of *manele* and *'ohi'a* until they came to the hillside where he'd seen the orchid the first time.

The house looked empty of everything but secrets. Ben went to the flower bed where he'd seen the Asian slipper orchid. An ordinary variety had been planted in the hole he'd found empty the last time.

"Let's sneak around the back of the house and see if anyone's there," Ben said.

"Not yet, buddy. We need to wait for that warrant. He should be here any minute."

Ben paced while they waited. The house had a closed-up look to it, as if no one had lived there for a while. But he'd seen people here. A squad car rolled to a stop beside them. Officer Johnson handed the warrant out through the window. Yoshi thanked him and told him to return to the station, then started toward the house.

Ben followed Yoshi. They walked along the edge of the woods with the wind blowing the strong fragrance of orchids against his face. His slippers sank into the soft ground. Yoshi bounded up to the front door, past the stone pillars shaped like dolphins. No one answered his pounding on the door. He looked at Ben and shrugged.

They circled around the side of the house to the backyard, where they found a goldfish pond filled with brightly colored koi that were a foot long. The back of the house had a deck that spanned its length. Vertical blinds blocked the view through the sliding glass door.

"I don't think anyone is here," Ben said. He stepped past the gas grill.

Yoshi strode up the deck steps and tried the door. "Locked," he said. He pounded on it, but again there was no answer.

Ben glanced around the backyard at the masses of orchids. These all seemed ordinary to him too, though he was no expert. A chest sat outside the sliding glass door. Made of cedar, it seemed familiar. He touched it, and a memory flooded back. His brother had spent hours bending over that chest.

"It's Meg's toy box. Ethan made it." He knelt and lifted the lid. On the underside an inscription read, "To my baby girl, Meg. Daddy loves you."

A lump formed in his throat, and his eyes burned. A hoarse cry tried to force itself past his lips, but he managed to stave it off. Ethan would never see his baby girl grow up, never give her away in marriage, never hold her children. Ben wouldn't cry. Men didn't cry.

"Ben?" Yoshi touched his shoulder.

"I'm fine." But he wasn't.

"I'm going to go around front again," Yoshi said.

Ben nodded. "I'm going to look in the woods." He didn't wait for an answer but jogged to the trees. He plunged into the cool recesses of the dark woods. For the first time he found himself questioning God. "Why!" he screamed to the treetops, and his shout caused a flock of Hawai'i creepers to take wing. "How could you do this? I thought you loved me." Lani had questioned her situation, and his words had been glib and sure. Now he slumped to the ground and put his head in his hands.

Thresh watched Ben with a smile. Ethan had been a weakling—unworthy of such grief. It had been a favor to get rid of him, really. He and his family were on a sure road to destruction. He went still. What a perfect chance to be rid of the reincarnate Ash. He'd been rising up, his face mocking at every turn. He'd been a jinx, the reason the girl was still alive.

No one was around, and it might take days to find his body in this jungle. With luck, maybe it would never be found. Thresh reached into his backpack and pulled out a gun. Firearms were so messy, but they were effective.

Ben raised his head and stood. He'd been numb before this moment, blocking out the way he really felt. What a hypocrite. Birds chattered in the trees over his head, and some small animal skittered through the underbrush. Then he heard something else. A furtive sort of sound that made him cock his head and listen. *Crack!* At the sharp report, he threw himself onto the ground. A burning pain struck his shoulder. When he touched it, his fingers came away bloody.

The gun sounded again, and Ben rolled toward a ditch on the other side of a tree. Tumbling into it, he glanced around for some kind of weapon. Leaves crunched under someone's feet, but he didn't dare raise his head. It would be a perfect target. He crawled along the ravine to where the forest thickened, and the canopy of *kuku'i* trees blotted out the spotty sunshine.

The trees had shed their nuts, and the leathery, walnutlike orbs lay everywhere. Ben scooped up a handful. Ducking behind a big tree trunk, he watched for an opportunity to drive off his attacker. A shadow moved quickly through the underbrush. He stood and began to pelt the figure with the nuts.

Then the shadowy figure vanished. Retreating steps ran through the leaves. He glanced down at his left shoulder. It burned like the dickens, and blood soaked the front of his shirt. His head spun, and he doubted he could make it back to the house. He was going to have to call for help. He pulled out his cell phone, but no bars showed. The thick jungle foliage blocked the signal.

He took a handkerchief from his pocket and jammed it against the wound, then plodded in the direction of the house. Spots danced in his eyes, and he began to stagger. Trying to focus, he looked at his cell phone again. Only one bar, but it might be enough. He dialed 911, but his vision darkened, and he fell to the ground.

The rest of the mourners had left. Arlo took Nancy to Ethan's place after an hour of her complaining that Ben didn't care enough to get her there himself. Lani heard the low voices of her aunt Rina and her friends. The night air coming through the open window held a taste of freshness from the gentle rain that had driven them all indoors. Lani sat on the sofa and listened to the conversation. She didn't know if she would ever get used to the isolation she felt with this blackness all around her.

"Is there enough harvest left to cover expenses for the rest of the year?" Jerry's gravelly voice held a touch of concern.

"I doubt it. I may need a little money from all of you to keep our heads above water. Would any of you be willing to invest more?"

Lani heard the near panic in her aunt's voice and wished she could help. She'd been the one who was supposed to oversee the milling process. If only she'd been able to be out there to make sure nothing like this could happen.

"I know I'm asking a lot," Rina said. "But the farm's good reputation is really getting around. I'm confident the profits next year will be good. We just have to hang on."

The coffee farm meant the world to Rina. If only there was something she could do to help. "Could you get an extension on the loan from the bank?" she asked.

"Maybe. I'll try. But even with that, I'm going to need some more capital." Rina sounded weary. "I'll repay you, every last cent, guys."

"I'll help," Jerry said. "How much?"

"I'll need to think about it. Go over the books," Arlo said.

"I'll show you now if you want," Rina said. "I have nothing to hide from any of you." The room rustled with noise, and footsteps moved off down the hall.

Annie sat beside Lani on the sofa. Lani leaned over and whispered in her ear. "Is Ben back yet?"

"I haven't seen him come in." The back of the sofa moved as Annie leaned back.

She moved her hand across the cushion until she found Annie's fingers. "Can we go talk?" she whispered.

"Sure, what's up?"

"Who all is still in here?"

"Yoshi and Fawn are on the loveseat. Mano is here too."

"No one else?" Lani could trust her family, but she wasn't so sure about the investors. And she was even beginning to wonder about her aunt.

"No, just us. Is something wrong?"

"I need to talk to you guys," she said. "But I don't want to be overheard."

"Everyone else is in the office. They'll probably be back there awhile," Yoshi said.

"I think they can hear down the hall," Lani said.

"We can step outside so no one overhears," Mano said. "The back door is this way."

Lani stood and found Fisher's harness. She followed Annie down the hall to the back porch.

"I'll get the door," Annie said, moving to open it.

Lani stepped into the cool night air. "We can sit out here," she said. Her hand touched the back of a wicker chair to her right, and she slipped onto the cushion.

"It looks clear," Yoshi said. "The outside light is on, and I don't think anyone could be hiding out here." The chair beside Lani protested as his bulk settled into it.

A chair dragged on the floor, and Annie's voice drew closer. "Let's sit close so you don't have to talk loud."

Lani turned her face in the direction of Annie's chair. "You remember that boy at the orchid farm?"

"Yeah."

"He came here tonight. His name is Simi."

"When?" Yoshi asked, his voice sharp.

"When I was watching Meg." Lani wet her lips. "He came to warn me. He says 'the big man' has been watching Meg. I think she should go somewhere else." Lani gripped her hands together in her lap. It had been all she could do to hang on to her composure tonight until she could share her fear.

"He can't do anything with all of us here now that we know," Mano said. "Let's move Meg into your room so we can protect you both together. That's better than splitting our defenses. We'll take turns standing guard outside your door."

Lani began shaking her head before he finished speaking. "She can't stay here. It's too close to the danger."

"Did the kid say what the guy wanted?" Yoshi asked.

"No. But it can't be good."

"The housekeeper at the orchid farm claims she's never seen him. And there was no one around tonight when Ben and I went over," Yoshi said.

"What about Honi?" Lani asked. "Is she involved in anything? It's not like her to just leave work."

"One of my men went to her apartment to talk to her, but she claimed she had food poisoning and was so sick all she could do was stagger home. He said she looked pretty green."

"You think someone made her sick?" Annie asked.

"The thought crossed my mind," Yoshi said.

"Did the kid really think Meg is in danger?" Fawn asked. "I can't imagine what they'd want with her. She's just a baby."

"We'll protect her," Mano said. "We'll find who's behind this."

Lani rose. "I wish I knew where Ben is. He's been gone for hours."

Yoshi cleared his throat. "We found Meg's toy chest at the orchid farm, and it upset him. He said he was going to search the woods, but I could tell it got to him. I yelled for him when I was ready to go back, but he never answered. I decided to give him some space."

"What? Why would the toy chest be there?" Lani put her hand on her throat. The danger to Meg must be real.

"I don't know."

"Do you think he's okay? Maybe you should look for him," Lani said.

"Maybe you're right. It's been hours. I wanted to give him some time, but he probably wouldn't leave Meg that long."

Lani heard Yoshi's cell phone beep as he dialed. He asked for some men to come out.

"Maybe Fisher could help you," Lani said. She groped for the dog. "Can you find Ben, Fisher? Find Ben." The dog barked, and his nails clicked off toward the door. "Follow him, Yoshi. Maybe he can find him."

"How? He's not a search dog."

"He smart. He knows I want him to find Ben. He went and got him when I fell into the ravine. Any dog has a good nose." Lani trusted Fisher. And right now, the dog was all they had.

eighteen

Ben floated in a sea of pain. His shoulder throbbed and burned, and he tossed on the ground. A gentle rain fell on his face, and he shuddered with cold. Shock, probably. Help wasn't going to come by itself. He had to get back to the house. His head swimming, he got to his knees and crawled through the wet grass. The moon illuminated the trees and shrubs, but his head felt so fuzzy he wasn't sure where he was.

He fell forward into the grass. The smell of the wet leaves filled his head, and he fought the suffocating sense that tried to carry him down. Had to stay awake, get help, or he would bleed to death. The sticky wetness on his shoulder told him he'd already soaked through the handkerchief. But the blackness came to carry him off again. Just before he blacked out, he thought he heard a dog bark.

When he came to, a bright light glared down into his eyes. He put up his hand to block it out. "Where am I?"

"You're okay, Ben. You're in the hospital," Lani said.

He focused his eyes on her face. Worry drooped her mouth, and a frown creased her forehead. "Lani? Someone shot me."

"I know. You're all patched up, though. The doctor said it was a clean wound, no bullet left in you." She squeezed his fingers. "He says you'll be okay. You've lost a lot of blood, but they gave you some, and you should be much better after some rest. You can come home in the morning."

A bigger figure moved into the light. Yoshi touched his shoulder. "Do you remember what happened?"

Ben tried to think. "Someone shot me," he said again.

"Right. Who was it?"

"Don't know. Too dark and far away. Threw *kuku'i* nuts." Ben closed his eyes and slept. When he awakened again, sunlight streamed through the hospital window, and he felt almost human. His shoulder complained when he sat up and looked around. Lani slept in a chair against the wall. Meg. Where was Meg? He glanced to the other side of the room and saw a crib set up. Meg slept on her stomach with her rump in the air. He breathed a sigh of relief.

Lani looked as though she would have a crick in her neck when she awoke. Her head lolled to one side, and she had a hospital blanket pulled up under chin. Her straight dark hair looked rumpled, and her face glowed with a rosy color. He allowed himself to feast on the sight for a minute. His first thoughts now seemed to be about Lani.

As if she sensed his eyes on her, she stirred and opened her eyes, seeming to look right at him. If only she could really see. "Good morning," he told her.

She bolted upright. "Are you okay?"

"Sore, but I'll live. Thanks for bringing Meg in."

"I couldn't leave her. Simi came to the house after you left. He said some big guy was watching her."

Ben struggled to maintain his calm. "I'm not surprised." He told her about finding the toy chest at the orchid farm. His head began to thump, and he felt a little queasy. Probably the drugs. "Where's Yoshi?"

"He took a chair out to the hall to guard the door."

"Tell him I need some help getting dressed. We're getting out of here."

The door whooshed, and his mother burst through the opening. "You could have been killed!" Nancy exclaimed with dramatic flair. Her steps hurried toward the bed.

"I'm fine, Nancy," Ben said. "I'm about to get out."

"What a relief. I came as soon as I heard."

"Who told you?" Ben asked.

"A police officer came to Ethan's house."

"You stayed at Ethan's last night?" Ben frowned at the idea of a woman there alone. "I'm not sure it's safe. Someone murdered Ethan and Natalie. It was no accident."

His mother gasped and put her hand to her mouth. "No one told me that!" Her eyes welled with tears. "Who would do such a thing?"

"Yoshi is trying to find out. But staying at the house alone probably isn't a good idea."

"But where am I going to stay? Hotels are too expensive."

The look she sent him was innocent, but he knew the intent behind it. Besides, what else could he do? "You can stay at my condo. I've been staying at Kona Kai anyway."

"Where's the key?"

No thank you, just a demand for the key. He bit back a sharp retort. "In my pocket." He got up and shuffled to the cabinet, where he found his clothing and fished out the key. "Just keep it clean, please." He handed her the key.

She shot him an affronted glare. "Of course I will." She sniffed. "Have you seen that place of Ethan's? His wife was no housekeeper."

He wanted to mention her own lack of homemaking skills but thought better of it. Growing up in a mess was probably the reason he was such a neat freak.

His mother took the key. "Thanks."

Lani had been quietly taking in the conversation. "How was your reunion with your friends?" she asked.

His mother swung toward her. "I had the most marvelous time!" She practically skipped to Lani's side, where she dropped into the chair beside her. "I'd always wanted to look up Arlo but didn't know how. He's loved me for years, you know." Her voice held self-satisfaction.

"He's not married?" Lani asked.

"He's getting a divorce." Nancy brushed away the problem like a gnat.

"Aren't you married, Nancy?" Ben asked. It felt stupid to be asking his own mother something he should know, but he had no idea.

"Well, yes, but we haven't been getting along. He doesn't like me to go out with my friends. I won't stand for chains like that."

Now was as good a time as any to question her. "How well did you know the woman who died at Taylor Camp? She went by Madonna Mary."

His mother blanched, and her eyes went wide. All the excitement drained from her face. "Why on earth would you bring up something so unpleasant?" She stood and started toward the door.

"Hold it, Nancy. If you won't answer my questions, the police will be glad to ask them instead."

She stopped and turned slowly. "It was a bad time in my life. I don't like to think about it." She shuddered.

"So you knew her?"

"Yes, of course. I didn't like her, but I knew her."

"There's been talk that you might have had something to do with her death, that maybe you let Rina take the fall for something you did."

The muscles in her face sagged. "I can't believe my own son would accuse me of something like that."

"I'm not accusing, just asking." He watched her closely for signs of guilt, but she was such a practiced liar, it was hard to tell.

"Well, I didn't have anything to do with it." She turned stiffly to the door and stalked out.

"I hope so," Ben muttered. "But I wouldn't stake my life on it."

They have to be dead. Ash's voice whispered in Thresh's head. The plan had come together perfectly. At the idea's conception, there was no guarantee it would work, but all the players had arrived, every detail was in place. If only ruining Blossom's coffee beans hadn't been necessary. He hated to cause her pain, but it would work out in the end.

Kato rapped on the door and stepped into the room. "Do you just enjoy failure?" Thresh asked.

Kato's face flushed, the color moving even to his bald head. "It's been the luck of the draw. I'll handle it."

"She could regain her memory anytime. We're boating in stormy waters here. Dig?"

Kato nodded. "The kid slipped away yesterday. I saw him coming from Rina's property."

"Did anyone see him?" Thresh didn't think the kid could finger them. He didn't know enough English. Or any real names.

"I don't know. He said he got lost."

An obvious lie. The kid knew the area well. "Don't sweat it. Just get rid of him."

"Kill him?"

"Get real. Just sell him to someone. We were going to do that anyway. Just do it now."

"Okay, boss."

"I want Lani dead by morning. Capisce?"

Kato nodded. "It's a done deal."

Thresh would take care of Ben/Ash and his mother personally.

Moonlight streamed through the window of the room. Ben sat up on the edge of the sofa they'd dragged in for him. His shoulder ached, but after spending the day lying around, he was going to go nuts if he didn't get outside and breathe the fresh night air.

He could hear Tyrone moving through the dark house. He hadn't asked questions when Ben had shown up on his doorstep with Lani, Meg, and the rest in tow. He'd thrown open the door and found them blankets and pillows.

Outside the door to the master bedroom, he heard someone cough, then realized it was Fawn. He made his way through the kitchen to the back door. The sliding screen squeaked a bit when he opened it and stepped out onto the patio. Inhaling the moist night air, he felt the tension in his neck and shoulders ease.

The stars were out in force. Ben sat on the patio and stretched his legs over the edge. Dew drenched the grass, and the moon lit the backyard in a ghostly glow. Yoshi prowled the front, but Ben didn't think anyone was likely to show tonight.

The screen door creaked behind him, and he turned to see Lani moving cautiously through the door with Fisher.

"I can't sleep," she said. "Annie is snoring, probably because she's so exhausted."

"Sit here." He stood and helped her sit on the edge of the deck. She was dressed in her shorts and a sleeveless top. "Are you cold?"

"I should have grabbed a jacket."

"Here, take mine." He shrugged out of his jacket and wrapped it around her shoulders.

"Thanks." She tugged the edges closed at her neck.

He stared at her. Fisher settled at her side and laid his head on her lap. He wished he could do the same. The moonlight gilded her black hair and glistened in her eyes. He couldn't tear his eyes away. She looked magical, but it wasn't just her beauty that drew him. There was something so compelling about Lani, so vulnerable and appealing. He'd never met anyone like her, strong and fragile at the same time. Before he realized what he was doing, he cupped her cheek in his hand.

She drew in a sharp breath, then tipped her head to more fully rest in his palm. She turned wide eyes up to him. What would she think of him if she could see him? He was just an ordinary guy, and she was so beautiful. Any man would be proud to have her on his arm. She deserved better, but his hand stayed put, and his thumb moved across the fullness of her lower lip. Heat moved along his arm and straight to his heart. Poor sap that he was, he'd fallen for her sometime when he wasn't looking.

He knew he should take away his hand, but instead he moved closer, slipping his other arm around her. If the way she nestled closer was any indication, she didn't seem to mind. Her face was still tipped up to him, her eyes soft and inviting. He dipped his head and kissed her. The touch of her lips and the fragrance of her breath across his face made all his reservations melt.

He kissed her thoroughly, and she responded with a soft sigh. Wrapping her arms around his neck, she pressed close to him. It felt like something he'd waited for all his life. Total acceptance and giving.

His mother might think he was worthless, but Lani's tender lips made it clear she thought he was rather wonderful. At least that's the way he took it.

He finally drew back and brushed the back of his hand over her cheek. "I probably shouldn't have done that." Was this the way Ethan felt when he was with her? The thought chilled Ben.

"You make me feel safe, Ben," she whispered.

"I want to protect you." He smoothed her hair and studied the lines and planes of her face. Their friendship might lead them to a scary place.

Lani fumbled her way back inside the house. Her cheeks felt hot. She rubbed her lips with her fingertips. Being around Ben was like standing on the edge of a lava flow—she might die or she just might bask in the heat. Their friendship had exploded into a curtain of fire, and she didn't know if she dared step through it.

Something creaked—the rocker?—when she stepped around the corner. "Who's there?"

Tyrone's voice answered. "It's me." The rocker quit its rhythmic sound. "You should be in bed."

"I was just heading there." The awkwardness between them stretched like a taut rope. "Thanks for letting us stay." He didn't answer, and the silence made her nerves scream.

He cleared his throat. "I wanted to let you know that I was more at fault than you. I hope you can forgive me for taking advantage of you."

She laughed, a hard sound that made her wince. "I was more than willing, Tyrone. Don't pretend."

"I knew better. You didn't. But Ben helped me come to terms with it. I hope you can do the same."

Tears burned her eyes. "I'm trying. Ben is really wise."

"He's the best. You're in love with him, aren't you?"

"Yes." There was no use denying it. Tyrone might have been blind, but Lani knew he was perceptive.

"Have you told him?"

"No. I don't know how he feels."

Tyrone chuckled, a deep sound of sorrow and joy mingled. "The dude is nuts about you."

Lani's heart leapt. "I'd sure like to hear it from him."

"Give him time and you will."

"Good night." Lani fled to her room with her face afire. Oh, to hear those words from Ben.

Two days they'd been here so far, and still no new leads on Yoshi's case. But Ben insisted they stay put until the killer was behind bars. They were running out of things to do, so Lani decided to go to bed early. The mattress's hardness and the sounds of an unfamiliar house kept her from resting. Ben hadn't approached her since Thursday night.

She could hear the clock on the bedside table. CeCe's party was tonight. CeCe had probably called Rina's house to arrange what time to pick Lani up and found her gone, but her friend would come get her in a minute if she called.

Footsteps crunched in the grass outside her open window, and she half rose in the bed. Tensing, she listened again, but the sound of Yoshi's and Mano's low voices reached her ears, and she realized there was nothing to fear. With her arm over her eyes, she lay back and tried to relax. Annie slept peacefully in the bed beside her, and Lani wished she could follow her sister's example. Fawn was on the other side of Annie in the huge king bed.

Lani eased her feet from under the sheet and sat up. All she had to do was take her clothes with her to the bathroom, call CeCe, and forget all about these problems for a little while. The bed springs squealed when she stood. She felt for the shorts and top she'd removed when she got ready for bed. There they were. She gathered them up and patted her leg for Fisher to come with her.

Annie stirred. "Lani, you okay?"

Busted. Lani grimaced. "Go back to sleep."

The bed rustled. "Why do you have your clothes?"

"I was thinking about going to CeCe's party tonight. I'm restless."

"Oh."

"Do you think I shouldn't go?"

Annie sighed. "What do you think? What does God say about it? You don't have to please me."

Lani examined the feelings she'd been having every time she thought of her old life. "I miss the fun I used to have. Now it attracts me and repels me at the same time."

"Do you know why?"

"I guess because I know that old life of guys and alcohol and no thought in my head beyond the next party is wrong for me. God expects more of my life than a never-ending party. I wish it didn't draw me."

"It doesn't have to, Lani. You're free to resist sin now. Before you were a Christian, you didn't have the power to break free of that life. Now you do. You've done it. Sin is always attractive, but we can see beyond the surface now."

Lani felt for the edge of the bed, found it, and eased down. Her restlessness faded. "You're right. I'm not going to go tonight." Strength flowed into her as she said the words. She could be free of the old life. She just had to take the freedom God had given her and remember she had it. For some reason, that knowledge kept slipping away.

She took Annie's hand. "Go back to sleep, Obi-Wan."

Annie laughed. "I'm glad I could help."

Fluffing her pillow, Lani climbed back into bed and turned her back to her sister. Her new life was so much better. Her fingers crept to her lips. No! She wouldn't think about Ben's kiss. She didn't want to read more into it than she should. Tyrone said Ben loved her, but Ben needed to speak for himself.

Lani touched her lips again. Was Annie still awake? "How do you know when you're in love?" she whispered.

Her sister's breathing evened out, and a slight snore came from that side of the bed. Lani should have asked sooner. She thumped her pillow again. Sleep still hovered far away. Maybe some warm milk would help. She slipped out of bed. Fisher didn't have his harness on, but he bumped her hand with his nose. "I think I can do this alone, boy," she whispered. Feeling for the wall, she moved toward the door. The tile felt cool on her bare feet. The air grew warmer in the hall-way, and she trailed her fingers on the painted surface of the wall and inched forward.

The wall made a ninety-degree turn toward the kitchen. Fisher kept pace with her, his thick fur brushing her bare calf. She negoti-ated the turn and stepped into the kitchen. Her hand moved along the top of the stove to the countertop, then continued around the room until she found the refrigerator. When she opened the refrig-erator door, the cool air rushed into her face. She wasn't as helpless as everyone thought.

Groping the top shelf, she found small, round glass containers that could have been jelly or maybe pickles. But no milk carton. That was a wasted trip through the house. Sighing, she shut the door and cut off the rush of cold air. She began to retrace her steps back to the bedroom when she heard voices outside the open window.

She was moving on past when she heard her name mentioned. Yoshi and Ben were talking about her.

"I guess your job is done anytime you want to leave," Yoshi said. "Lani seems to be doing okay with the dog. I appreciate you trying to figure out what she knows, but I think you're right. I thought for sure she was protecting Aunt Rina, but Lani's clueless."

"I'm not leaving while some madman is still running around. You need me to help protect her," Ben said.

Lani began to frown. It sounded as if Yoshi had contacted Ben before he came. Were they friends? She thought back to the first time she talked to Yoshi after Ben came. It was when that man had attacked Ben, and she'd rushed for help. Yoshi had known his name. She clenched her fists.

Yoshi spoke again. "You've got your hands full with Meg. Now that Mano is here, we can handle Lani if you want to pick up your own life. I know you have to finish that thesis. Watching Lani learn to cope with her blindness should give you plenty of material."

Lani stifled a gasp and put her hand over her mouth. He was using her for a thesis? Anger flared and began to simmer.

"I've never seen you so quick to get rid of me. I'll hang around," Ben said.

It had all been a setup. Lani brushed her fingers across her wet lashes. He wasn't worth her tears. Yoshi and Ben had lied to her. Maybe not in words, but in actions. They'd layered Ben's appearance with concern for her blindness, when all along they just wanted to find out what she knew. And Ben wanted to use her tragedy. The betrayal shouldn't have hurt so much. Ben was nothing to her. Nothing.

She knew she should go on back to bed, but she couldn't let this slide. Her hand found the screen door, and she slid it open with an angry jerk and stepped onto the deck. The wood beneath her shuddered with the force of her angry feet.

"Lani?" Ben's voice was cautious.

"I heard every word," she said, swiping again at her wet face. "So my doctor didn't refer you to me. And my dear cousin doubted my word and had to call in reinforcements. Men! Did you think I was a liar or what?"

Fisher whined and licked her hand. She could feel him trembling, and she patted him, but even that didn't drain her ire. "I don't need your help or your protection. I'm not a child anymore, Yoshi." Someone's hand touched her arm, and she jerked away. She didn't care if it was Yoshi or Ben who touched her. Neither hand was welcome.

"Why are you so mad?" Yoshi asked. "You've not exactly been the most open person in the past, Lani. I had to know the truth. This has been the must frustrating case of my career. Witnesses vanishing, empty houses. I've got nothing. You're the key, Lani. Tell me the truth."

"I told you the truth!" She backed away, her hand searching for the door. "I'm going back to Aunt Rina's in the morning, and I want both of you to leave me alone." She started back to the door and turned. "And don't even try to take Fisher from me! Possession is nine-tenths of the law, and I'm not giving him up."

She stumbled back through the kitchen, banging her shin against a chair. Fisher's nails clicked on the tile as he loped along beside her. Gaining the sanctuary of the bedroom, she shut the door to discourage either of them from trying to talk to her and climbed back into bed. Hot tears leaked from the corners of her eyes and trickled into her hair and onto the pillow.

Why had Ben kissed her? Was it to gain her trust and ferret out information? She didn't want to believe that, but it made sense. Stupid, she was so stupid. She sniffed and rubbed her eyes.

As she brushed her fingers across her eyes, she felt a strange sensation in her head. She blinked. Was it light she was seeing? Opening her eyes wider, she strained to see something. But it was gone. Probably her imagination again. Closing her eyes, she decided not to think anymore. She'd just sleep, and it would be better in the morning.

A face swam in her memory behind her closed lids. It seemed so familiar, not scary like she remembered. If only she could drag that memory from the cellar. She was at the mercy of the murderer as long as the memory of that day eluded her.

THRESH SAT OUTSIDE and watched the condo. Peekaboo had no idea of the danger she was in. The lights flickered and hummed. Did she have company? It wasn't like her to be without a man. She hadn't changed a bit, which made his job easier.

The darkened leaves crunched underfoot. A streetlight was out, which helped. It wouldn't take long to dispose of her and escape. He looked forward to seeing her expression change when she understood what was going to happen.

Ben's condo faced the water, and the smell of the sea was strong. He took the tiled steps up to the fourth floor. A Harley sign was on the door with the name Mahoney under it. This was where the party would happen.

He felt a pleasant buzz of anticipation. Peekaboo had arranged for Mary to die and for Blossom to take the fall. Now she would pay.

This day had been coming for a long time. Peekaboo opened the door. "Thresh, what are you doing here? Do you have any idea what time it is?"

"Your light was on." Thresh said. He stepped into the entry, shoving her back.

"Hey," she said, her voice rising on an indignant note.

He shut the door and turned to face her. This night would be treasured for a long time to come. Her gaze went to the gun in his hand, and fear crept into her eyes.

nineteen

Ben knew he shouldn't be mad at Yoshi. It was no one's fault Lani had overheard their conversation. The time for truth had come and gone, and he'd let the opportunity slip away days earlier. Before he kissed her, he should have confessed how he came to appear in her life. Even when Yoshi had talked him into helping her, Ben knew he should be aboveboard and honest.

He'd been the victim of half-truths himself too many times to enjoy making Lani one too. There had to be some way he could make it up to her. The memory of the anguish in her voice made him pace the deck. Would she accept an apology?

"You're making me nervous, prowling around like a cat. Sit down. She'll get over it."

"I don't think so, Yoshi." Ben dropped onto the step beside his friend. "We really hurt her." He winced inwardly at the remembrance of the way the moonlight had illuminated the pain in her face.

Yoshi didn't answer right away, and Ben turned to look at him. Yoshi stared at him. "What?" Ben asked.

"You've fallen for my cousin, dude." There was surprise in his voice. "Don't go there. She eats hearts for breakfast."

220

Ben had always known Lani attracted men. He'd watched her in action with Ethan and Tyrone. Someone that gorgeous didn't get to be twenty-five without having any boyfriends, but she was different now. "I know I don't have a chance," he admitted. "You don't have to tell me."

Yoshi appraised him. "You're not ugly. I didn't mean you'd scare little children. But Lani has been used to men swarming around her from the time she was twelve. She never stays with one long. Mano was nuts about her once too."

Ben raised his brows. "Mano doesn't seem to notice anyone but Annie."

Yoshi nodded. "It just took him awhile to see Annie's goodness. But Lani tires of men easily. I love her, but sometimes you gotta face the truth about someone." He shrugged. "Though I will say she seems different lately. Not so restless and eager for a good time."

"I don't think she's like that anymore at all," Ben said. "A friend called last week and offered to come get her for a night out, and she put her off."

"That surprises me. Lani's always been a party waiting to happen."

Ben shook his head. "I can't see it, man. I know what you're saying, and I've seen her in action in the past. She's not like that now."

"Maybe you're right. I keep waiting for the old Lani to reappear. Still, watch yourself. I'd hate to see you get hurt."

"Not a chance. I know enough to realize I don't have a shot."

Yoshi's smile flashed, and he studied Ben's face. "You've still got your hair. And you brought her the dog. That ought to count for something."

"I'd say you'll be the one to go to the altar first, buddy." Ben jabbed him with his elbow. "I've seen you making eyes at Fawn. She's a sweetheart."

"I've known her for years," Yoshi said in a pensive tone. "But I feel like I've just met her. She's pretty special."

"I don't know what she sees in a slime ball like you." Ben smacked him on the shoulder and wished Lani would show her feelings as clearly as Fawn showed hers.

"She's had a crush on me for years. I always knew it, but I just thought of her as Annie's best friend."

"Kind of like the way you don't see Lani clearly either?"

Yoshi grinned. "You're grasping at straws, man. Just be careful."

"I will." But he was afraid it was already too late.

The sun beat warm on her arm and face. Lani smelled the spicy aroma of Spam and eggs. She opened her eyes and blinked. Light flooded the room, brilliant, golden light. Bolting upright, she widened her eyes and looked around. It wasn't as bright as she first thought, but she could see shadow and light.

"Annie!" She groped for her sister's arm, but the bed was empty. Fawn was gone too. Lani's feet hit the floor, and she stumbled toward the door, blinking at the brightness. "Annie, Annie!"

She ran into the closed door and bounced back. An idiotic smile stretched her lips. Twisting the knob, she flung open the door and padded down the hall with her hand on the wall to steady herself. "Annie!" she shouted again.

"What's wrong?" Annie asked. A vague form cut off the light as her sister's voice grew nearer.

"I can see light." Lani reached toward the shadow and grasped Annie's hands. "I can see your shadow!"

"Oh, Lani!" Annie embraced her. "We need to call the doctor right away. Maybe your sight is coming back." Her wet hair smelled of something herbal.

A bigger shadow moved through Lani's vision. "What's going on?" Ben asked.

"I can see light!" Lani squinted and tried to make out his face, but he was just a blur. She moved closer, but his face refused to come into focus. "I still can't see you, though," she said.

"You can see?" Fawn's voice came from the kitchen door.

Lani turned. "Not yet, but it's coming back—it's coming back." She whirled in a circle, colliding with a hard chest. The spicy after-shave told her it was Ben's firm hands that steadied her. She pulled away, but realized her initial anger had evaporated some with the lifting of the oppressive darkness. She could deal with him now, and with her emotions. He'd never know how much he hurt her.

Lifting her chin, she stepped away. "Where's Yoshi?"

"He went after some milk. Meg wanted cereal," Tyrone said. "Congratulations, Lani."

His tone told her he didn't begrudge her her good fortune. "Thanks." She heard Annie talking to the doctor on the phone. Stepping to the window, she basked in the light piercing her darkness. "I want to go to Honaunau," she said.

"I'll take you," Ben said.

The last thing she wanted was to be with him. "Annie will take me."

Annie hung up the phone. "The doctor wants you to go to his office immediately. I'll take you, and the guys can take care of Meg."

Lani wanted to see faces now. The doctor should be able to tell her how long it would be before she could see clearly again. She was still basically blind, except for shadow and light. At least she didn't feel so walled off from everyone. "Let's go," she said.

"I'm coming too," Fawn said.

Dr. Cooper's office bustled with shadows and noise. The nurse ushered Lani, Fawn, and Annie to an examining room, and the doctor rushed in moments later. "Let's check your pupil reflexes," he said. He examined her eyes, shining the light into them, then stepped back. "How many fingers am I holding up?" he asked.

Lani could see only his shadow. "I can't tell."

"Hmm," the doctor murmered.

Was that good or bad? Lani clutched the edge of the examining table and waited for the verdict. "So when will I get back all my vision?"

"There's no guarantee you will. This may be as much as you get. Or it may all come back. Only time will tell." Dr. Cooper's shadow moved, and his little light went out.

"That can't be! If it's come this far, it has to come back. I can't even make out faces." Lani's voice rose, and Annie put a warning hand on her arm. Lani didn't slow down. "There has to be something you can do now."

"I'm afraid not, Lani." Dr. Cooper patted her shoulder. "It's going to take time before we know. I could give you another IV of mannitol, but I don't think it will do any good this late in the healing." His pen scratched on paper. "Come back in a couple of weeks unless there's a dramatic change again." He nodded to Annie and Fawn and exited the room.

The crash at the bottom of her euphoric morning brought a knot to her throat. "I was so hopeful," she murmured. She hugged herself and fought the sting in her eyes.

A shadow moved, and Annie touched her arm. "I'll pray, Lani. God's brought us this far."

Lani squinted up at her sister. "He has, hasn't he?" She'd been spiritually blind, and he had brought her light. Maybe he'd do the same with her eyes.

Meg played on the floor with her doll. Her wet hair curled around her round cheeks. With difficulty because of his bandaged shoulder, Ben had dressed her in lime-green shorts and a top and left her small feet bare. She talked to her doll and ignored the adults in the room. Ben hadn't seen her so content since her parents died. Maybe she was beginning to trust his care.

Tyrone had gone off to work, and Mano prowled the exterior of the house. Ben felt restless. His cell phone rang. "This is Ben."

His lawyer's voice sounded happy. "Hey, guy, things are looking up for your custody fight. I found a more recent charge against Steve. Burglary. Just some petty stuff, but enough I think we can get a judge to listen."

"That's terrific!"

"Yeah, but listen, Jessica called and they want to see Meg. We can't deny them access yet. Just go along with them today and we'll get it behind us soon. Where are you?" Ben told him the address. "I'll tell them where to come. Expect them in half an hour."

Ben closed his phone and looked at Meg. "Grandma and Grandpa are coming to see you."

She ignored him and began to build a block tower. Ben glanced around the living room. It was a mess, with blankets and pillows everywhere. He picked them up with one arm and threw them on the sofa. By the time the room looked presentable, sun flashed on metal outside, and he saw a car pull up and Natalie's parents get out. He went to the door and opened it before they knocked.

"Good morning." Steve Walden tried for a smile, but it fell short and made him look like an otter with bared teeth.

Ben nodded and stepped aside.

"We'd like to take Meg out for the day," Jessica said.

"What did you have in mind?"

"Natalie told us that Meg loved to splash in the tidepools out at Honaunau. We thought we might go there."

"I guess we could."

Jessica's eyes widened. "We meant just Meg."

Her reaction sent warning bells clamoring. "I'm afraid I can't do that. If we weren't fighting over custody, I might be able to trust you, but I can't be sure you wouldn't try to just take her. She's been through too much. Besides, I doubt she'd go with you willingly unless I came along."

Red stained Jessica's cheeks. "We wouldn't do that," she sputtered.

"Fine. I'm still going along. Take it or leave it."

Jessica glanced at her husband. Steve shrugged. "Guess we don't have a choice."

"Meg is in the living room." Ben led the way to where the toddler sat playing.

She looked up. Her face puckered when she saw her grandparents. Clutching her doll to her chest, she scrambled to her feet and ran to Ben. With one hand gripping his leg, she stared up at the Waldens.

Jessica squatted in front of her. "Can I see your dolly?" she asked, smiling.

Meg shook her head and reached her arms up to Ben. "Up," she said.

Ben lifted her in his arms. "You want to go to the tidepools?" he asked.

"Pools," Meg said. She bounced a little in his arms, and her smile finally came.

"I guess that's a yes," Steve said in a hearty voice.

Ben walked to the front door. "I've only got a couple of hours." He started to lock the house behind him, then saw Yoshi arriving. He told his friend where they were headed. Yoshi planned to join Mano in guarding the place.

"We can take our car," Steve said.

"Fine." He set Meg down, installed her car seat with his good arm, then buckled her in and got in beside her.

Steve and Jessica didn't have anything to say on the drive to Honaunau. Ben shifted his feet away from the briefcase on the floor. He stared down at it. Watching the rearview mirror in case Steve looked back, Ben reached down and unlatched the clasp on the case. It opened without a sound. He nudged it wider and glanced inside. Maybe their plane reservations were in here. His fingers flipped through the pages quickly. There it was—a Hawaiian Airlines e-ticket reservation.

Ben glanced into the front seat. The Waldens both had their eyes straight ahead. He pretended to be adjusting Meg's seat belt, then reached down and tugged the paper out a bit farther so he could read it. His suspicions refused to die. He finally got the sheet far enough out of the briefcase to read the passenger names. It was a reservation for Meg, leaving this afternoon for Chicago. Just as he suspected. No wonder Jessica wanted Meg to bring her doll. What should he do?

The car stopped in the lot at Pu'uhomua o Honaunau. The picnic area was deserted this early in the day. He released his niece from the car seat, then unbelted the seat itself as well. Swinging open the door, he got out with Meg, put her down, then reached back in and lifted out the car seat. Meg plopped down on the sand and began to scoop it onto her leg.

Jessica glanced at her granddaughter, then to the car seat. "Why are you taking out her car seat?"

Ben set down the seat. He reached inside the car and pulled out the reservation. "This is why. We part company here."

Her gaze went to the paper, then to her husband. "If you'd be reasonable, we wouldn't have had to resort to taking her."

"You've lost your money on this trip." He stuffed the reservation in his pocket. Didn't they care about Meg at all? If they did, they wouldn't have attempted to just uproot her and drag her off to the mainland.

Steve doubled his fists. "Hey, you can't take that!"

Ben stepped away. "You just shot yourself in the foot. No judge in the state will grant you custody when I show him you tried to kidnap her. On top of your record, you're done."

Steve glanced at his wife with a confused expression. Jessica grabbed the doll out of Meg's arms and whirled to run to the car. Ben leaped after her. He grabbed her arm and whirled her around, then snagged the doll from her hand.

"I just wanted a memento of my granddaughter," she panted.

Ben shot her a disbelieving look, handed the doll to Meg, then scooped her up and headed toward the picnic area. What a bunch of weirdos. He glanced back over his shoulder and saw the Waldens conferring by the car. Though he shouldn't feel sorry for them, he couldn't help a twinge of pity. They'd lost out. He held all the evidence he needed in his pocket.

An engine rumbled, and he glanced back again. They were pulling out of the lot. He and Meg were stuck here for now. Yoshi would come get them, but he decided to let Meg splash in the tide-pools for a while first.

She pointed to the water. "Bug."

He squatted beside her and peered into the water. "That's not a bug. It's a hermit crab." A stick lay nearby, and he picked it up and poked at the crab.

Meg giggled when it scuttled away. "Me."

Ben handed her the stick, and she poked awkwardly at the crab. It scuttled sideways. Meg giggled again. He settled onto the warm black rock and watched her play. She kicked off her slippers and splashed the water with her bare feet. How was he going to raise her by himself? A child's ways were a mystery to him.

He was getting the hang of baths and diapers and food, but her hair looked like a nest of seaweed. Her shorts and top were wrinkled too. He was used to throwing stuff in the dryer and grabbing items from it when he needed them. That look wasn't too appealing on a kid.

Lani's face flashed through his mind—the way she bent her head to listen to Meg, the tender stroke of her fingers across Meg's cheek. She'd make a great mother. But not for his kids. She was used to flashy men with flowery compliments. He had no skills to woo someone like her. She thought of him as a friend, not a potential husband. And maybe not even that, after last night.

The sound of a car engine broke his concentration. He turned to see Fawn at the wheel of Annie's rental car. Annie was in the passenger seat, and Lani rode in the back. He scooped up a protesting Meg and walked to meet them. Meg wiggled and kicked sand on his shorts. Her wet shorts soaked through his shirt. "You can go back in a minute," he told her.

Fawn parked, and three car doors opened. Fisher jumped out of the back, and Lani followed him. "How did you know I was stranded out here?" Ben asked.

Fawn looked up with reddened eyes. "We didn't." She nodded toward the two women talking in low tones by the car's trunk. "The doctor told Lani this might be all the vision she gets back—dark and light."

Ben winced. His gaze went to Lani's tear-stained face. He still didn't quite get why they were here. Annie and Lani joined them. "I'm sorry," he told Lani.

"I'll survive it." She managed a wobbly smile. "At least you can't take Fisher away from me."

He squeezed her fingers. "You can handle this, Lani. You have the skills."

"What'd you mean about being stranded?" Fawn asked.

"I came out with the Waldens. On the way here, I found a plane reservation. They'd planned to take Meg to the mainland. If I'd agreed to let her spend the day with them, she would have been gone."

"That's horrible!" Annie put in.

Meg lurched in his arms for Lani. "She wants you, Lani," he said. "How about the two of you dangle your feet in the tidepool?"

"That's why I came," she said. A tear trickled from her left eye, and she tipped her face to the sun before grabbing the dog's halter and moving toward the water.

"This way." He walked in front of her to the tidepool. "Here we are." He set Meg down at the edge. She squealed and jumped into the water, causing the small fish to dart away in a frantic effort to escape her dancing feet. "I'm going to let Fisher loose. It'd be cruel to take him this close to a pool and not let him play."

"That's fine."

Ben removed the harness. "You're free. Run, Fisher." The dog gave him a happy smile and leaped into the water. Meg squealed and splashed water at him.

Lani kicked off her slippers and edged down to the ground. She dropped her tiny feet into the water. "I'd like to be alone, if you don't mind."

"Okay." He resisted the impulse to touch her, to comfort her. Some things only God could make better.

twenty

The sun warmed Lani's arms but did little to penetrate the chill she felt inside. Meg squealed and splashed by her feet, but the happy sound didn't warm Lani's soul any more than the sunshine did. *Blind, maybe forever.* What good was the warm glow of light when she couldn't make out Meg's face, couldn't see the trees and grass?

Honaunau usually brought her peace, but today the turmoil still raged in spite of the gentle sound of the surf. She longed to see the cliffs rising to the blue sky, to scan the whitecaps as they rolled toward the land. She wanted to point out the tidepool creatures to Meg—the sea cucumbers and *'ophihi*. When she strolled through the reconstructed buildings, she sometimes thought she saw her mother from the corner of her eye. Now she might never see that again. She'd clung to hope with the tenacity of the *pipipi*, the little black marine snails that clung to the tidepool rocks. But the doctor's words had scraped loose the fragment of optimism.

Her heart slammed into her ribs. The garden design was due tomorrow. She'd go in there with a Seeing Eye dog and they would know. She had to do it, though. Her future depended on it. If this was the way it was going to be, okay. Everyone said God had given her the tools for this moment. She'd prove them right.

The grass rustled beside her, and she squinted at the shadow that crossed her face. "Who's there?"

"It's me." Ben's shadow came nearer, then moved down beside her.

"Go away."

"You've had a long enough pity party. Snap out of it, Lani. It's not the end of the world."

Her fingers dug into the sand, and she wished she had the courage to throw a handful into his face. If she could see enough to find his face. "You're not the one who's blind," she said. He didn't need to know she'd already come to grips with it.

"Hey, it's better than it was yesterday," he pointed out. "You can see light and shadow. Count your blessings. Some people are totally blind like you were. Some people deal with cancer or the loss of a loved one. You're healthy, young, and beautiful. There's no need to drop out of life."

She wiped her eyes and nodded. His hand touched her shoulder, then dropped away. The touch had been so light she wasn't sure it was real. If only she had the nerve to turn and throw herself in his arms. "You've got a lot of room to talk," she flashed back. "You lied to me. You didn't come to help me but to use me." She folded her arms and turned her back to him.

"I know it seems that way," Ben said. "I'm sorry. I care about you."

"Then act like it," she snapped. She folded her arms over her chest. "I wish God would tell me why he's done this. I'm going to handle it, but I just wish I knew *why*."

"I thought I had all the answers, but now I find I don't even know all the questions. I don't know why God let Ethan die. I don't know why he let you go blind, or why Tyrone was injured in the accident instead of me. Maybe I'll never know. But I have to trust God for the results. I have to keep my hands off the wheel. That's freeing when you think about it. I'm free to enjoy what God gives me and let him worry about making it all work out."

Lani let the words sink in. Maybe she'd been trying to take back the wheel all the time. Maybe she'd never turned it over in the first place. She heard him laugh softly. "What?"

"I just realized as I said the words that I really believed them. Two seconds ago I wasn't so sure. But God is holding us through this. I think you know it too."

Yes, she did. At least she wanted to. Maybe that was half the battle.

By Monday morning, Lani thought they'd overreacted about the danger Meg was in, but no one was willing to take any chances. Maybe Simi had mistaken his master's intentions. At least they all prayed so.

Her hands shook as she dressed for the meeting with the garden show board. "Do I look all right?" she asked Fawn and Annie.

"You'll knock 'em dead," Fawn said. "You want me to go with you?"

"Would you? It might help if they ask what something is. I can't see it, and you'll know."

"Should I change so I look like a professional designer? You know, wear wild colors that don't go together?" Fawn giggled, and her shadow moved to the door.

"You're terrible," Annie scolded. "You look lovely, Lani. You're going to do just great. Call me when you're finished. I'll be praying."

"I will." Lani took Fisher's lead and headed out. She prayed she would be calm and professional. "Should I wear sunglasses?" she asked Fawn when they got in the car. "Do people stare at my eyes when they realize I have a sight problem?"

"I haven't noticed it. You look perfectly fine. Just sail in there with your head held high."

Lani nodded. She clasped her hands together in her lap as Fawn drove her to the meeting. Her future hinged on how well she did her presentation today. Fisher pressed over the top of the seat and nuzzled her neck. "I'm okay, boy," she said.

"Here we are," Fawn said, putting the car into park with a clunk. "You ready to kick butt and take names?"

Lani smiled. "I just hope to still be standing when the dust settles."

"It's a great design, Lani. They're going to love it. Let's go."

Lani opened the door and stepped into the golden wash of sunlight. It was a glorious sensation after the darkness. Fisher jumped out when she opened the back door. She took his lead, and they headed toward the stone building. They stepped into the cool recesses of the lobby. "It's down the hall to the right," Lani said. She and Fisher followed Fawn's shadow. Her hands still shook. God had equipped her, she reminded herself.

Pasting on a smile, she followed Fisher into the room. "Good morning," she said brightly. She traced her fingers around the table's edge and placed her portfolio on the surface. "This is Fisher, my service dog. I hope you'll forgive the necessity of bringing him along, but I can't see, and he's necessary for me to get around."

"Lani, what happened?" Michelle's shadow moved toward her.

"I had an accident and lost my sight about a month ago. I've got Fisher, though, and I'm coping. In fact, I'm more than coping. He's a wonder." She patted the dog's head, and he gave his happy whine. "Shall we get started?"

"How can you design if you can't see?" a man asked.

Lani smiled. "I can still see the designs in my head. I think I've managed to translate them pretty well to the page. Let me show you."

For the next hour she went through her ideas for the garden. The exclamations of wonder and admiration from the committee warmed her soul. When the meeting concluded, she still had the job.

"I did it!" she shouted to Fawn as soon as her feet hit the parking lot. "I can't believe it."

"Congratulations! I knew you could do it." Fawn hugged her, and Fisher stood on his back paws and gently placed a paw on each of them.

"I couldn't have done it without you," Lani said.

"It was God," Fawn said gently. "Now you know that nothing is too hard for you with God's help. You're free to follow your dream."

Free. What a totally outrageous thought. She was seeing the light like never before.

Lani rubbed her forehead between her eyes. The constant squinting was going to give her wrinkles if she wasn't careful. It had almost been better when she couldn't see anything. The blurring of shadow and light made her head ache. The coming of night relieved the pain radiating around her skull. The quieting of the flickering light had eased her headache.

She sat on the porch with Fisher at her feet. Through the open window, she could hear Yoshi talking in low tones to Ben. She heard him mention Fawn. A smile lifted Lani's lips. That romance seemed to be progressing. She'd gladly welcome Fawn as a cousin.

She leaned down and found Fisher's harness. "Let's go for a walk, boy." He stood up, and she heaved herself out of the chair, every muscle protesting. Meg lay sleeping, and Annie and Mano had gone out to dinner with Fawn and their boss from the volcano center. Ben's low voice got her emotions in a whirl. No other man had ever made her feel so off center.

"Forward, Fisher," she said. The dog led her down the steps, which she negotiated carefully with her hand on the railing. Pausing when her slippers landed in the wet grass, she moved to her left toward the flower garden between the back of the property and the forest. The sweet fragrance of coral hibiscus lifted her spirits.

When her feet sank into the cultivated dirt of the flower bed, she sank to her knees and caressed the blossoms. Her sensitive fingertips plucked dead buds and dried fronds. Weeds choked the flowers, and she pulled them, dropping the debris behind her in the grass. When her fingers found no more work, she sat back. It wasn't necessary to see in order to tend the flower bed. She'd chosen her profession well, though she would need help for some things. Even so, she could find the help she needed.

The night felt alive around her. Crickets chirped, and tree frogs sounded off in the woods. Something thrashed in the underbrush, maybe a deer. Then she heard a cry. That was no deer. She sprang to her feet. "Who's there?" she called.

Fisher was instantly at her side. A low growl came from his throat. She never should have come out here by herself. The tranquility of the last few days had lulled her into forgetting that danger still lurked about somewhere. She listened past the pounding of her pulse.

"Fire!"

Lani whirled at Yoshi's voice. A bright yellow flame shot through a darker shadow. She couldn't see more than that, just shadow and light, but enough to know it was real. She ran toward the blaze with Fisher.

"Get back," Yoshi shouted. "There's a fire extinguisher in the house. I'll get it."

"I've got the hose!" Ben yelled.

A dark figure blocked the glimmer of light, and she heard water sizzling as it hit the flames.

"I've got the extinguisher." Yoshi's voice came from the porch.

Lani backed away. She should go check on Meg in case the ruckus awakened her and she became frightened. Starting toward the house, she heard a whimper. Frowning, she stopped and listened. The cry came again.

It sounded like a child. A familiar child. "Meg?" It couldn't be Meg. She was safely asleep in her bed. Lani stumbled forward, her hands outstretched. Fisher whined, then began to bark. "Find Meg, Fisher. Meg."

He tugged her across the flower bed. The cool rush of shadowed forest chilled her. She halted by the dark blur of a tree. What was she thinking? She'd never be able to find the child by herself. It might not even be Meg. The murderer had fooled her before—it could be another tape recording. Yoshi and Ben were a few yards away. As she retraced her steps, she listened but heard nothing except her own panting.

"Ben, Yoshi!" She staggered when her slipper flew off her foot. Her bare foot slid on wet grass, and she went down on one knee. The slipper would have to wait. Her right knee throbbed where she'd twisted it. Fisher pushed his wet nose against her neck and whined. She needed to be using him. Her hand on his neck, she got to her feet and grabbed the harness. "Home, Fisher." He led her to the right of where she'd been heading. "Ben!" she screamed again.

"What's wrong?" Ben's voice came from her left. "We've got the fire out."

Lani jerked toward him. "I heard something. In the woods. Is Meg okay?"

"She's fine. I checked on her about fifteen minutes ago."

"Check again. I heard a child cry out. I called to her, but no one answered."

"Stay here."

His footsteps moved away from her, then she heard the door open and close. She petted Fisher while she waited. The warmth of his coat soothed her. More than likely she was overreacting. What could the sound have been? A bird? But no, birds were sleeping by now, other than night prey birds. It had been a child—she was sure of it.

The door banged, and an agitated babble of voices rushed toward her. Her hand fell away from Fisher's ears, and she faced the house. "Is she okay?"

"Meg's gone!" Ben grabbed her arm. "Her screen is torn open. Do you remember where you heard her cry?"

"In the woods just past the flower garden." She turned and stumbled back the way she'd come. Her bare foot struck her missing slipper, and she scooped it up and continued to run. Her feet slid out from under her, and she went down hard. A hand grabbed her, but she shook it off. "Run, hurry. Don't worry about me."

"Don't move," Ben said. His hand fell away.

Feet and voices rushed past her. She heard Yoshi say he'd head toward the cliff. They had to find Meg. The thought of her with some murderer made her stomach sour. The dew soaked through her shorts. Her knees ached from the impact with the ground. Fisher laid his head on her shoulder. He was shaking. She patted him. "It's okay, boy." If only she could see and help.

Getting to her feet, she grasped the harness and moved toward the garden again, this time carefully planting her feet and letting

Fisher guide her. With her head tipped, she listened to the wind and hoped to hear Meg's glad shout at the sight of her uncle. *Please, God, let them find her.*

It seemed an eternity before she heard voices. Twigs snapped and leaves crunched with the sound of bodies moving through the woods. "Did you find her?" she called.

"I called in reinforcements," Yoshi said. "Are you sure it was her you heard in the woods? It makes more sense he'd take her to a waiting car."

She wrapped her arms around herself. "Eighty percent sure," she said. "I know it was a child, and it sounded like Meg, but she didn't call my name or anything." What would the guy want with a little girl? A lump formed in her throat.

Simi trudged through the forest behind Master. "They'll pony up the goods if they want to get the kid back," Master muttered. They cut through the edge of the woods and got into the car the big man had parked along the road. Master carried the little girl easily in one arm, and he dangled a carrier to wear on his back from his other hand.

Master put the little one down and patted his pockets. After several fruitless moments, he shoved the little girl at Simi. "I must have dropped my keys in the woods. Watch her. In fact, see if you can find anything on her. I'll be back." He vanished into the trees.

Simi looked at the little girl. Her eyes were wide with shock, and she made little sounds of distress. Patting her head, he glanced to the woods. He couldn't let Master hurt this little one. His gaze touched the carrier. "A ride, missy?" He picked her up and managed to get her legs in the holes.

He slipped it on his back and grunted. The little one was heavier than she looked. He'd expected her to be as light as his little cousin Fetina. The child's cries had tapered off, and her head dropped onto his shoulder. He turned and plunged into the trees, heading in the opposite direction Master had gone. Best not to walk the road. Master would return with his keys and quickly run him down. He could circle around and get her home.

Trees crowded around them. Branches snatched at his clothing as he struggled through the dark forest. He thought he was going in the right direction. Master didn't seem to be following. Simi heard only the occasional hoot of an owl and the night sounds of crickets.

He smiled as he glanced down at the little girl. Once he returned her to her family, he would go home. His mother would welcome him with open arms. He imagined his homecoming. His father would be proud of how brave Simi had been. Simi would show his bruises and the scars on his back, injuries he'd taken willingly in order to send home money.

Only now that he'd run, there would be no more money. Maybe he wouldn't be such a hero after all. His *fa'e* might cry. There was no going back though, not now. He would be arrested, sent to prison. His cousin had been in prison for a year in Tonga. He'd come home gaunt and silent. Simi couldn't bear to be locked away from the blue sky and the sound of the sea.

The trees began to thin, and he caught glimpses of moonlight. Quickening his pace, he sniffed the air. Was that a trace of salt in the air? He must have gone the wrong way. From the smell, he knew the ocean should be at the bottom of this hill. He could find people at the Place of Refuge. It wouldn't be far.

His people had come to that place in the past. All Polynesia knew of the sacred places. He felt safe there. He would have someone summon the little one's family, then he would go. When he'd found the old canoe at the Place of Refuge, it had seemed an omen from the sea god Kanaloa. The idea to escape had popped into his head when he found the outrigger stashed in thick brush and looking as if it hadn't been used in years. There were no holes in the hull, and it looked solid enough to make the journey. He wasn't quite sure how long it would take to sail it to Tonga, but his own boat trip here had been only a few days.

Provisions might be a problem, but he'd figure out how to get enough food once he was at the Place of Refuge. While his master had been harsh, Simi had seen much kindness from other Americans. And his own slight stature might gain him enough pity to be given food.

He trudged on through the thinning brush until the hill flattened. Moonlight glimmered on whitecaps, and he saw the white monument that marked Captain Cook's appearance on the islands. He'd made it to the sea. Now to be rid of his burden, find the boat, and escape.

Searchers from all over the neighborhood joined with the police to scour the woods. Ben's mood grew bleaker the longer they floundered with no sign of Meg and her captor. Dawn's early rays had already turned the night's dew to mist that rolled down the hillside he searched.

There had been no sign of Meg, no scrap of clothing, no dropped doll. When he stepped out of the woods into the backyard of Ethan's house, he saw police officers and other people he didn't recognize standing around talking in small groups. Slumped shoulders and soft voices told him not to expect any good news. He walked through the crowd and found Yoshi standing with Fawn, Annie, Mano, and Lani.

Yoshi's gaze lingered on Ben's face. "We're coming up dry," he said.

Ben nodded and turned his attention to Lani. "Tell me again what Simi said when he warned you to be careful with Meg."

"He just said the big man was watching Meg. That has to mean the guy who attacked you. And that we should be careful." She touched his hand. "How are you holding up?"

He pulled away. How did she expect him to be? His niece was in the hands of a maniac. "The house was ransacked right after Ethan and Natalie died. He's looking for something. If only we knew what it was, I'd turn it right over."

"Any speculation at all on what it might be?" she asked.

"We know the coral was being smuggled in Aunt Rina's coffee," Yoshi said. "I tend to think Ethan had something important—and the murderer is going to use Meg as leverage to make you cough it up."

"But what? We've found nothing suspicious or valuable." Ben balled his hands into fists at his side.

"I expect we'll get a ransom call telling us what they want. I've got your cell phone and Ethan's phone tapped."

Ben allowed himself a sliver of hope. He'd gladly turn over anything the big guy wanted if it meant Meg was released unharmed. It was hard to imagine anyone being monstrous enough to hurt a child, but he read the headlines. Monsters walked around with kind, smiling faces.

Yoshi's cell phone rang. He answered it, then barked questions. "We have a lead," he said, snapping it shut. "Someone saw a kid with a toddler walking along Highway 160."

Ben frowned. "So what? Meg would be with a big guy."

"The kid looked Polynesian. What if the guy sent Simi in after her?"

"I don't think he'd do it," Lani put in. "He warned me, remember? He was worried about her."

"He might not have had a choice. It's the only lead we have. I have to check it out."

"I'll come with you," Ben said.

"Me too." Lani grasped the back of her cousin's arm.

"Someone needs to stay here in case the kidnapper calls," Yoshi said.

"I'll stay," Annie said. "Fawn and I will clean the house or something."

"Let's go," Ben said. He couldn't sit around and do nothing. Even though the sighting probably wasn't Meg, investigating was better than waiting around for the phone to ring.

twenty-one

Simi held out a bag of potato chips to the little girl. "Chips," he said. The chips had been lying by a picnic table, dropped by someone. He'd also found a slim stick of unopened gum. The chips would at least feed the girl. He'd thought there would be more people here near Cook's monument, but only one family laughed and splashed in the water. He'd approached them, but they'd spoken some language he didn't know, neither English nor Tongan.

Meg took the chips and smiled. Her fear of him seemed to be going away, which was as it should be. He wanted only to help her, not to hurt her. She didn't have a *fa'e*, but the lady who couldn't see loved her and would want her back.

"Chips," the little girl repeated. She stuck her small hand into the opened bag and put a handful in her mouth.

Simi slid her back into the carrier, then put it on and began to walk toward the cliff. A few boaters paddled toward the white monument out in the water. Simi moved at a steady clip along the trail. If only he could have stashed the outrigger somewhere closer. Sweat broke out on his back and forehead. He looked longingly at the clear water, but there was no time for a swim. His master would realize he was gone and be out looking for him.

Since there was no one here to help, he would get the boat and travel along the coast until he found people. Then he would give them the girl and make his escape. He carried Meg through a bunch of coconut palm trees, pausing to stare at the coconuts high over his head. If he had time, he could shimmy up the trunks and get something to eat. His mouth watered at the thought of coconut milk and meat.

Simi looked around. The palms were his marker. Just past them should be a patch of high weeds with the hidden boat. There it was. He smiled and began to walk faster.

Then someone moved out from under a tree. "I thought you'd be making for here," Master said.

Simi stopped, and Meg's fingers tightened in his hair. His tongue seemed stuck to the roof of his mouth.

"Did you really think you could go anywhere and I wouldn't see? I followed you one night when you came out here. When you turned up missing, I knew where you'd headed." Master's gaze went to Meg, and he smiled.

Simi shivered at the grin. His gaze darted past Master. If he could get to the top of the cliff, there was a rope down to some caves. Master would be too large to climb down.

Master started toward them. "No!" Simi picked up a large black rock and threw it at the big man's head with all his might. Master tried to dodge, but the rock struck his forehead, and he toppled to the sand.

Simi ran up the path to the top of the cliff. Meg squealed, and her small hands held on to his hair. Small rocks slid under his feet, and he had to move around larger lava rocks. Master bellowed, but Simi didn't look back. He'd known he wouldn't be fortunate enough to hurt the big man. All he'd hoped was to slow him down.

It seemed forever before they crested the hill, then darted past a rocky outcropping that would hide them and gain a few moments. Meg hadn't cried, but she puckered when they stopped. "Shh, shh," he said, patting her small hand where it rested on his shoulder. Where was the rope? He searched behind the rocks for it. A sharp pain pierced his hand, and he snatched it back. A scorpion scurried from behind the rock. Staring at his throbbing hand, he saw it was swelling rapidly. Would he swell up and die? He didn't know how deadly such insects were here.

There was no time to waste. He spied the rope under another rock and grabbed it. "Gum," he told Meg, handing her the stick of gum. Her pucker turned to a smile, and she began to unwrap the gum. No one could climb like him. He took out his carabiner, which he'd been wise to keep. Anchoring the rope around a rock, he prepared for the descent.

"Don't look down," he told her. Hanging on to the other end of the rope, he backed to the cliff edge and looked down. The blue water was far, far below. If he was wrong about how far it was, they would die. He would never see his *fa'e*. His hands shook. Maybe this wasn't such a good idea. Then he heard Master shouting. He must try.

Grasping the rope, he began to rappel. He braced his feet on the cliff wall and bounced them down a few feet at a time. The little one's hands clung to his hair, and she chomped her gum in his ear. If the rope was long enough, he could go all the way to the bottom before Master realized it. He could get them in the boat and set out before the big man could get back down.

He kicked out and braced his feet for the next bounce, but his feet met empty space. The void left them dangling in the air. Simi looked down. They were still a long way above the water. The end of the rope dangled only ten feet below them. He looked at the cliff face. A small ledge jutted from a cave. If he could swing to it, they could hide there until Master left. He would think the rope had been there a long time.

Pumping his legs back and forth, he swung them closer to the ledge. His feet touched it, then slid off. Gritting his teeth, he tried again.

Meg began to whimper. "Down," she said.

Simi concentrated. Pumping his legs again, he swung harder this time. The rope let down a few inches, and he gasped when the rope jerked. His gaze went to the water far below again. Then his feet landed on the ledge. He staggered and caught at the rock face, teetering on the edge. His arms pinwheeled, then he flung them forward and they rolled into the cave.

Meg began to shriek. "Shh, shh, little one," he said, patting her head. The gum was gone. She must have dropped it on the way down or swallowed it. Simi stood and took off the carrier. Her sobs quieted. He put her down by a rock and went to the edge. They couldn't use the rope to get on down to the bottom unless he could release it from above. He tried to see up the side of the cave, but the rock stuck out above his head and blocked the view.

Then the rope began to slither past him. He made a grab at it, but it fell so fast he nearly missed it. He snatched at it again, then his fingers caught a loop of it and he pulled it into the cave. It wasn't nearly as long now. His fingers found the clean cut on the end. Master must have cut it loose. There was no way it was long enough to get them down, and now they couldn't climb up. Simi sat on a rock with his head in his hands and wept.

The light kept getting brighter, then dimming again. Lani didn't say anything, because her vision wasn't the most important thing right now. She was also beginning to make out faces, dark spots for eyes in the people she stared at. Maybe by the time they found Meg, she'd be able to see the toddler. And they would find her.

Fisher had his head on her lap in the backseat as they rode toward Kealakekua Bay, and she rubbed his ears to keep herself calm.

"We should have a bunch of people to search," Yoshi said. "Aunt Rina and her friends are en route too. It was near the intersection of Highway 11 and Napoopoo Road."

"There's a two-mile trail to the bay near the Captain Cook monument," Lani said. "Could they be heading toward the water?"

"Why? There's nothing out there but the bay. If you go the other direction, it leads back toward Aunt Rina's coffee farm. And the orchid farm. I'm betting they're heading that way."

"Wouldn't that be the first place you'd look?" Ben put in. "And they'd be cornered. There's only one road in and out unless they try to escape on foot. They'll be tired by the time they get where they're going."

Yoshi opened his car door. "Maybe we should wait until the other searchers get here."

"I don't want to wait," Ben said. "I've got my cell phone on me. Call me if you find anything. I'm going to head toward the coffee farm."

Lani let Fisher out of the car. She could even see the color of Ben's hair, a rich russet, though his other features were still fuzzy. It was like looking at a whole new world. A smile tugged the corners of her lips, but she quickly squelched it. She nearly gasped with the realization that her sight wasn't that important now. If they could find Meg, she'd gladly give it up.

She watched Ben strike off up the hillside. Yoshi and Mano stood talking by the hood of the car. "I'm going to take Fisher and head down to the water," she called.

Yoshi looked up. "I don't think that's smart, Lani."

"I'm seeing more and more, Yoshi. I won't get lost with Fisher anyway. I can't just stand around. I want to help."

He stared at her. "Your sight is back?"

"Not totally, but it's better. I can see the color of your hair."

"Okay, just be careful."

"I will." She took Fisher's harness and headed for the path toward the water. It was a gentle slope down to the bay and the cliffs. This wasn't her favorite spot. She could never look at the cliffs without staring into the pockets of caves, layered with the bones of Hawaiian rulers. She shuddered.

Fisher was nosing through some ti leaves. "Come, Fisher," she called. She blinked her eyes. She could actually see his tail wagging. The movement, at least. Details were still fuzzy.

The path was rough and treacherous, and Lani nearly slipped and fell several times. She knew she should turn back, but something drove her on toward the water. The bay was probably only another mile.

She skidded down a steep place on the path and landed on her behind. Fisher licked her cheek and whined. He ran a few feet and pawed at the grass. "What'd you find, boy?" She stood and walked to him. His head came up, and he held something in his mouth. He pressed his muzzle against her hand and dropped his find into it.

"Meg's doll," she said softly. Fisher woofed at her voice. She picked up the doll and hugged it. Yoshi and Ben needed to know. The doll had been in bed with Meg last night. She had to have come this way. Glancing back the way she'd come, she hesitated. Going forward would put her closer to the little girl. What if she went back and the man disappeared with Meg? While she couldn't fight him, she could see where he went. Her vision was nearly normal now. She could see the golden russet of Fisher's eyes, the curl in his coat.

"Let's go," she told Fisher. People often kayaked into the bay to snorkel, and there were boats that brought in tourists as well. She could get someone to call Yoshi on his cell phone once she figured out where the man had Meg.

"Rockin' idea," *Thresh* told Kato. They stood at the top of the cliff over-looking the bay. "They're trapped until we're ready to use them."

Kato never smiled much, and his grin made Thresh shudder. The guy looked way too pleased at the thought of the two kids trapped in a cave. Thresh just wanted to do what was necessary, even though it was unpleasant.

"Did the kid have it?"

Kato shook his head. "Like I said, I think it's at the bottom of the ocean."

"I would know if it was gone. I have a connection with it. I want you to call Mahoney and tell him he gets his niece back if he turns over the goods."

Kato nodded and pulled out his phone.

Thresh grabbed his hand. "Not on your own phone, meat! The fuzz can trace it. Use a pay phone."

"The nearest one is in Kealakekua."

Thresh's lip curled. "Don't be a sissy. Just do it. I'll wait down by the water."

Kato jerked a thumb toward the cliff's edge. "What about them?"

"They're not going anywhere."

Ben walked all the way to the coffee farm but found no one around. They'd all turned out to search for Meg. Maybe they had her at the orchid farm. He walked past the sugarcane fields toward the lane. An egret scurried out of his way, and several laughing thrush sang in the trees over his head, though he took no pleasure in their chirps.

A truck turned out of the orchid farm and came barreling down the road, and he stepped behind a tree. As it flew past, he caught a glimpse of the Waldens. He stared after them. Maybe his guess that they were involved in the smuggling wasn't so far off. He stepped back onto the road and picked up his pace to a jog. When he turned into the orchid farm lane, he slowed and listened. The place was as deserted as the night he and Yoshi dropped in. The memory put him on guard.

He walked up to the house and rapped on the door. If they had Meg, he was going to break in and get her. No footsteps echoed from inside. Glancing around, Ben tried the door, but it was locked, just as he expected. Pyracantha screened the side of the house, and he couldn't get close enough to peer in the window. He went around to the back and tried the door. Locked.

Glancing around the yard, he saw the hothouse at the back of the property. Maybe something would be inside it. But it was locked too.

Ben stared at the house contemplatively. He needed to get inside, but he didn't want to end up in jail. He decided to walk the grounds. Maybe there was something else he'd missed. Neat beds of orchids covered a good two acres of land. Ben strode through the rows of flowers, but he really didn't know what he was looking for.

Passing the back of the rear bed, he walked into the woods toward a small shed. He'd never seen it before. A shiny lock barred him from entry. The place was hardly bigger than an outhouse. Not expecting it to budge, he jerked on the door. To his surprise, the lock popped open. Someone hadn't latched it properly. Simi?

Ben opened the door and peered inside, expecting to see a dank, dusty interior. Instead, it was clean and swept. A trapdoor stood open in the floor. He stepped to the edge and peered down, but it was too dark to see. A switch was on the floor, so he flipped it, and light flooded the hole. A ladder stretched down to a dirt floor.

He could only hope there were no scorpions or spiders. Using his good hand to hang on to the ladder, he tucked a flashlight he saw lying on the floor into his waistband, swung his legs onto the ladder, and started down.

Simi crouched by the front of the cave and stared down. He didn't know how long they'd been here, but his belly hurt with hunger. The little girl slept on the weathered cave floor, but she would want food when she woke up.

His mouth was dry, though he'd popped in a stone to suck on. It was so hot. He wiped his face and began to cry. He and the little one would die with no food or water. It wouldn't take long, especially for the little one. He cast a sorrowful glance at her blond hair. He'd meant to save her, but instead he had brought about her death.

He tried to bend his stung hand, but it hurt so badly he whimpered. It scared him to look at how swollen it was. He looked out toward the sea and tensed. A small dot moved along the water not far from the crashing surf. Closer than was safe, really, but maybe they could hear him. He leaned out as far as he could and screamed at the top of his lungs. The cry burst forth with such power it scraped his throat and tore at his chest. He called again. "Help!"

The kayak continued to move along the whitecaps. It never

slowed. Simi continued to scream until it was out of sight, then slumped back against the wall of the crevice. He put his hands over his face and sobbed. They were going to die, and there was nothing he could do about it.

twenty-two

*L*ight, color, and shadow danced in Lani's vision. Leaves on the trees around her blew in the breeze, and she could see them. Puffy clouds floated across a sky of wondrous blue. Her sight wasn't sharp yet, but she thought she'd be able to recognize her sister or cousin from about five feet away. With glasses, she might be able to see perfectly.

Holding the doll close, she and Fisher walked the last two hundred feet or so to the bottom of the slope. Its harsh edges softened by green vegetation, the cliff face loomed over the sea. Lani glanced around, but all she saw were snorkelers in the water. No sign of a little girl, Simi, or the man.

The waves ran up onto the beach with white foam. Lani marveled at the detail. It was a whole new world to her. She tipped her head. Was that a cry? Her hearing was so much more acute now. It sounded as though it had come from up the cliff. Taking Fisher's harness, she walked toward the cliff and found the faint impression of a path leading upward. Vegetation lashed her bare legs, and she nearly lost her slippers several times climbing over rocks in the way. Her head spun when she finally stood panting at the top of the cliff.

Pausing to catch her breath, she listened again, but this time she heard only the breeze and the faint shouts of children playing in the water. The waves crashed on the rocky black shoreline below. Still holding the doll, she wandered closer to the edge, then realized she was too close when vertigo made her sway. She stepped back quickly.

Fisher nosed at a gum wrapper that lay on the ground. Lani picked it up. Meg's? The bugs hadn't gotten into it yet, so it must not have lain here long. A rope wrapped snugly around a rock. Its cut edge stuck up at the top of the stone like an exclamation point. She sat on the rock and wondered what to do next. As she contemplated her next move, she toyed with the weighted hemline at the doll's ankles. The hem was pulling loose, and she plucked at the threads absently. A weight fell into her hand. It felt smooth and different.

Lani pulled it close to her face to examine it. She gasped at its beauty. Hesitantly, she ran her fingers over it. The surface was smooth and perfect. Could it possibly be real? She'd seen pictures of La Peregrina, the famous pearl owned by Liz Taylor, and this looked nearly as large. It was a pale gray with a hint of blue. Her pulse beat faster just touching it. If it was real, it would be worth a small fortune.

Someone had ransacked Ethan's house and searched through Meg's things. Could they be looking for this pearl? The more she touched it, the more convinced she was that it was genuine. Pearls had a special luster that was hard to duplicate.

Jerry collected pearls. Lani rejected the idea at once, but it hovered in her mind like vog. But even if Jerry was after the pearl, how did the coral and the orchids fit in? Lani rubbed her head where a heaviness pulsed. This was too much for her to figure out. She needed help from Ben and Yoshi. Maybe the smuggling had nothing to do with this pearl.

She stood to go back to find Yoshi when she heard the cry again. The back of her neck prickled; it seemed to come from nowhere. This mountain was said to be haunted with the spirits of the *Ali'i* who were buried in the caves and crevices up and down the cliff face. Fisher whined, then the sound came again, and she realized it was coming from below the ledge. She sidled as close to the edge as she could get and tried to peer down, but dizziness left her head spinning again, and she saw nothing below except the foaming waves.

"Hello?" she called. "Anyone down there?"

"Help, help!" The cry came again.

Please help me, Lord. Free me from my fear. Lani dug her fingers into the crevices of the large rock beside her and tried to get closer to the edge. She took a quick glance downward and thought she saw a face peering up at her. All she caught was a quick glimpse. She had to be brave and take a better look. Maybe if she laid down. She dropped to her knees and then onto her stomach. At least she couldn't fall this way. Inching closer to the edge, she finally got her head out over the drop-off and looked down.

Sure enough, a small face was looking up at her, and she saw a hand wave. She thought it was Simi, but her blurry vision made her uncertain. She had to get help. She scrabbled away from the edge and stood up. As she started down the path, a pair of large shoulders loomed before her. She caught her breath and stepped back, but it was too late. The man had already seen her.

Ben heard water dripping somewhere. The dank odor of dirt filled his nostrils as he walked along the narrow corridor. The tunnel walls were smooth, rammed earth. Lights had been strung up along the way, their beams casting a sickly glow over the dark space. A scorpion scurried away from his feet, and the place echoed with silence. Being this far down made him feel like he was buried alive.

The passage ended in a cavernous room filled with light. Modern and bright, the room held tables and lab equipment. An underground lab meant whatever was going on down here was probably secret. He walked to the closest table, sleek stainless steel that held beakers and an assortment of devices he couldn't even attempt to identify. Two stainless bins had covers. He lifted off the first one. Coral. The second held two-inch pieces of what looked like orchid parts.

Curiouser and curiouser. Was this some medicinal thing like coral calcium? Maybe orchids were medicinal as well. Josie might know. He looked around a bit longer, then glanced at his watch. He'd been down here way too long. If Yoshi had tried to call him, he wouldn't have been able to get through. As he started to retrace his steps, he noticed a steel ladder affixed to the wall. Peering up, he realized it led to another trapdoor. Maybe it would be faster to get out this way. He put his foot on the first rung and began to climb. His injured arm ached from the movement.

At the top of the ladder, he inspected the trapdoor. It didn't seem to be locked, so he gave it a shove with his good shoulder. It opened with a shriek, and he winced. If the bald guy was around, he'd come running. His head poked through into clean fresh air. The door had dislodged a shrub that covered it. He touched it and found it to be fake, an excellent imitation that had camouflaged the door. Looking around, he realized he was on Rina's property facing the back of her house.

He didn't want to believe she was involved, but the evidence was beginning to mount. Lani would be crushed. His cell phone rang, displaying Yoshi's number. "Mahoney," he said, answering it. "Did you find her?"

Yoshi's voice came over. "Hey, where are you?"

"Behind the coffee farm. Did you find her?"

"Not yet. I was hoping you did." Yoshi sounded discouraged.

They hadn't found Meg. "Can you come get me? I'll be at Rina's house. It'll be faster than walking." His throat closed, and he clicked off his phone.

He went to the porch to wait. Putting his head in his hands, he tried to pray. "Please, God, let us find her. Let her be okay," he whispered. His eyes and throat burned.

A car came tearing up the drive. Yoshi was laying on the horn. Ben bounced down the steps to the car. He was almost thankful he didn't have to pray anymore. If God's answer was no, he didn't want to hear it. He glanced into the backseat. "Where're Mano and Lani?"

"Mano is out searching. Lani went down toward the water to look."

"Alone?"

"She says her vision is coming back."

"Yeah, but there's a maniac out there somewhere."

"I shouldn't have let her go," Yoshi admitted. "I was distracted, and she slipped away."

"How long has she been gone?"

"As long as you."

Ben glanced at his watch. Nearly an hour had passed. "I hope she's back by the time we get there."

"I told her not to go far. And she knows the area well." In spite of his calm words, Yoshi wore a worried frown.

The car rolled to a stop. Ben jumped out and rushed to meet the other searchers. *Please, God, let Meg and Lani be all right.*

Lani's gaze darted past the big man, but she didn't see how she could get around him. Then Fisher grabbed the doll from Lani's hands, laid his ears back, and ran past the man, just out of his reach.

"Hey, come back here!" The man turned to give chase, and his feet slipped on the loose stones along the path. He went down hard.

Lani dashed around him. Her slippers threatened to lose their grip along the narrow path at any moment, but she managed to keep her balance. The man shouted behind her, but she hurried faster without looking back. Pebbles slid down the slope ahead of her, and she clutched at small shrubs along the way to steady herself.

When she reached the bottom, she found Fisher waiting for her. "Good boy," she said, taking the doll from his mouth. She tucked the doll and the pearl into her shirt. "Let's get out of here." She and the dog ran for the safety of the beach, where half a dozen people strolled beside the water. Surely the guy wouldn't attack her in the presence of witnesses. Maybe someone had a cell phone.

She fell into step beside a smiling middle-aged woman. "Excuse me, but would you happen to have a cell phone? I need to call the police."

"I'm sorry, no." The woman gave her a curious glance, then hurried away.

Did she look so alarming? Lani batted away the hair hanging in her eyes and stared around for another likely source of aid. The only other residents of the beach were teenagers dressed in swimsuits. She glanced over her shoulder and saw the man approaching with balled fists. She kicked off her slippers and dove into the water. Fisher jumped in with her. Maybe she could find a kayaker out by the monument who would agree to take her and Fisher to safety. She spared a glance behind her. The man stood on shore watching her, then he wheeled around and stalked away.

Lani dogpaddled and watched him disappear up the trail to the top. She struck out for shore and waded to land. Retrieving her slippers, she hurried for the trail up the slope to the road. About two hundred yards up the incline, Fisher's ears perked, and he ran forward a few feet. Then Lani heard the distant shouts of someone calling her name. She and the dog picked up the pace, then she saw several figures running down the path toward her.

She recognized her cousin and waved. "Yoshi!" Several other men ran with him. One had hair the color of a dark penny, and her gaze stopped. Could it be Ben? When his face came into sharper focus, she gasped. It was the man who had visited her after work and demanded she quit seeing Ethan. That Ethan? He had never identified himself, but Lani would never forget the curl of his lip when he informed her she was dating a married man.

Her legs felt like jellyfish, and she wanted to bolt the other way. He had to remember that encounter. Why had he never said anything about it? Her throat closed. She slowed her steps and waited for them to catch up.

"Did you find her?" she asked when they reached her. The answer was written in the tightness of their lips.

"No. Are you okay?"

She nodded. "I ran into the guy." She pointed. "Up there. We need to investigate more."

"Show us," her cousin said.

Lani nodded and led the way back up the mountain. Ben hadn't said anything. Did he realize she recognized him? She kept stealing glances at Ben as they trekked topside. He was a handsome guy, broad-shouldered with kind eyes. His strong jaw spoke of strength of character, and she knew he had that. Her face burned as she remembered the way she'd flirted with him the day he confronted her. He'd made no secret of his contempt, either. It was the single most humiliating moment she'd ever endured.

So why had he kissed her when he knew what she was? To test

her? The thought made tears squeeze past her resolve. They reached a vantage point where Lani could point out the cliff face. She paused for breath. "I saw someone trapped down the cliff face," she said, pointing. "I think it's Simi, but I'm not sure."

Ben finally spoke. "How well can you see?"

She felt he could look into her soul. Lani didn't dare lock gazes with him. "Almost as well as before the shooting. Things far distant are still a little blurry, though. What about the climber?"

"I'll have someone check it out. Meg is our main concern now," Yoshi said.

Lani nodded. The little girl was her main concern too. No way could Simi have gotten Meg down the cliff wall. If it was Simi she'd seen.

The muscles in Lani's legs burned as she climbed the path again. Spots danced in front of her eyes when she crested the top, and she blinked rapidly to dispel the obstacles to her vision. Surely she wasn't going blind again. She stood panting until her sight cleared.

Lani pointed. "Down there is where I saw someone."

Ben and Yoshi followed. Ben looked over the edge. "Anyone down there?" he shouted.

No answering shout echoed up the valley below. He yelled again with the same result. "You sure you saw someone?"

Lani hesitated. "My vision still wasn't fully clear, but he yelled for help. I'm sure there was someone."

"Maybe it was a rock climber fooling around, and he's gone now," Ben said.

Lani pointed to Fisher as he stood barking at the drop-off. "Fisher knows something." She moved to join the dog and looked down on the rocks.

"No!" Ben said. "She didn't fall. She's not dead!"

The rocks were hard under Simi's back and head. He was hot, so hot. He curled in a ball at the back of the rock's indentation and dreamed he was back on Tonga with the good heat of the sun baking onto his skin. Then he was plunged into a cold pool. He shivered, his teeth chattering. He thought he heard his father calling him, but the wind carried the words away.

In the twilight between dream and reality, his hand throbbed, the pain radiating up to his shoulder. Perhaps he had fallen onto the rocks by his hut. His little cousin curled at his back, her small chest heaving with silent cries. She called for water, but when he offered her a gourd of water from the spring, she turned her head.

Tears sprang to Simi's eyes when he saw her gaunt face. He should have stuck it out with Master. She needed money for food, and he would have to leave the island to get it for her. The pain in his hand intensified, and he rolled to the other side, banging his head on a rock. He came fully awake, the pain so bad he thought he might pass out. The little one stirred from her place at his back, and she whimpered. Her lips were dry. She needed water.

Simi managed to get to his feet. Death would come quickly if he took her and jumped. Wouldn't it be better than this slow wasting from lack of food and water? He turned and lifted her in his arms. Staggering toward the opening, his vision darkened, then he and the little one were falling.

twenty-three

The *whup-whup* of an approaching helicopter filled Ben's head. His stomach felt as if one of the black boulders strewn around the ground was lodged there. Meg had been gone seven hours already. What was she going through? He had to find her. *Why, God, why?* The plea echoed through his soul. He didn't understand.

Yoshi and Mano had gone down below to search the rocks. Fawn and Annie were meeting them there. Ben didn't have the heart to go. Lani sat quietly beside him on a rock as he stared out over the cliff.

"The guy was up here too," Lani reminded him. "I don't think she's dead."

He raised his head and met her gaze. The compassion in her face made him look away. "That should tell us something."

"Oh, I forgot." Lani held out Meg's doll. "This is what he was after."

"The doll?" Ben took it and glanced at its face. It looked just like Meg. In fact, he'd bought it for her from one of those places where he provided a picture and they made it to match. "Why?"

"This was in the hem." She held out something pear-shaped in her hand.

"Holy cow, is that what I think it is?" His fingers ran over the smooth surface. "It looks like a real pearl."

"I think so too. It would explain why they searched the house and Meg's things, and why they took her toy chest."

He nodded. "I found an underground lab at the back of your aunt's property. I haven't had a chance to tell Yoshi yet. It looks like they're experimenting with ground coral and orchids." His gaze went back to the pearl.

"Jerry is mad about pearls. And he's a doctor. Could he be experimenting with a drug of some kind?" Lani put her hand over her mouth. "Someone connected with the coffee farm has to be involved in the coral smuggling." She chewed on her lip. "Ben, I just thought of something. Jerry has some new concoction that's worked on Aunt Rina's lupus. Hawaiians have used orchids for medicinal purposes for years. What if he's come up with a cure for Aunt Rina's illness?"

It made sense in a twisted kind of way. "Would he have taken Meg, though? He seemed to like her." Ben's cell phone rang before he could say more. He answered it. "Mahoney."

A rough voice spoke in his ear. "Give me the doll, and we'll hand over the kid."

Ben's heart leapt. "Is she okay? Let me talk to her."

"She's sleeping. Bring the doll to Honaunau after dark. Leave it on the picnic table."

"What about Meg?"

"Do what I say and she won't be hurt. Once I've got what I want, I'll tell you where to find her. And don't bring the cops, or she's fish food."

"That's not good enough," Ben began. The phone clicked. "Hello? Hello?" The man had hung up. He dropped his phone back in his pocket. "The guy wants to exchange the doll for Meg."

Lani's face lit. "She's alive!"

"So he says, but he's not even bringing her to the drop spot. He just says he'll tell us where to find her. I don't think we can wait that long."

"What do you have in mind?"

"Let's find Jerry."

Lani longed to talk to Ben about the day he told her Ethan was married, but now wasn't the time. Still, she kept stealing glances at the strong line of his face and throat. Did he think she'd forgotten? "Did you see Jerry when you were at Aunt Rina's?"

He shook his head. "They've been out searching too. I think we have half the island looking for Meg."

Lani mopped her forehead. Her mouth felt dry, and she longed for some water as the heat beat down on her. For some reason, she didn't want to leave this area. Not until the search was completed. Meg was here somewhere—she just knew it. Dropping to her stomach again, she wiggled forward until her face hung over the edge. There were so many crevices and indentations in the cliff face below, she couldn't tell for sure where she'd seen the person wave.

The helicopter still hovered around the escarpment, but there was no indication the searchers had found anything. Far below, she could see hopeful rescuers picking their way along the rocks. Lani didn't want to believe they would find anything in the water.

Lani stood and rubbed her palms on her shorts. "I hate to leave until they figure out who I saw down there." She rubbed her head where a headache throbbed. "Do you really think it's possible Jerry is behind all this?"

A voice spoke from behind them. "I didn't think you'd figure it out," Jerry said. The big man stood beside Jerry with a gun in his hand. Jerry's head was tipped to one side. He looked so ordinary in green shorts and an aloha shirt, with his hands relaxed at his side.

Lani's gaze went to the gun's bore, and shivers rippled along her muscles. Without looking down, she backed up to the edge of the cliff and held the doll out over it. "Put the gun down or I drop the doll."

The smile on Jerry's face morphed into a thin line. "Put your gun down, Kato. I don't think we want to run that risk." The big man scowled, then stuffed the gun into his waistband.

"No, toss it away," Lani said.

Kato hesitated, but when Jerry nodded, he tugged out the gun and tossed it into the thick vegetation. "I don't need a gun to handle either of you," he said.

"You can see," Jerry said, his pale blue eyes examining her face. "I suppose you remember the day I shot Pam."

"No. We figured this out without my memory." Lani edged closer to the edge.

Jerry advanced a step. "Give me the doll."

"Not until you tell us where Meg is."

"Why, she's right below you," Jerry said. "She and Simi decided to do a little rock climbing. Feel free to go get her."

Lani's courage failed at the thought. Her pleading gaze went to Ben.

"I'm a good climber. I'll get her," he said. "I need a rope and a carabiner."

"I don't think we have time for that," Jerry said. "The searchers will be back up here soon. Give me the doll."

"Not until Meg is safe and sound." Lani stretched her arm farther out over the abyss. "Get him a rope."

"I brought one to retrieve them," Kato said when Jerry jerked his

head at him. He stepped off the path and into the knee-high vegetation, where he bent and beat around in the weeds. "Got it." He held
up a length of rope, then walked back to his boss. He tossed the rope
to Ben.

"Climb it, Tarzan." Jerry's sneer allowed dislike to show in his eyes.

"It's got a carabiner on it," Ben said, examining it. He went to
the rock that held a short length of rope. Wrapping the rope around
it, he tested the knot and nodded. "Pray for me," he whispered to
Lani. "I'll be back."

He locked gazes with Lani. The smile lifting his lips was tender.
Lani didn't dare believe the promise in his eyes, not now that she
realized he knew exactly what she was capable of. Her lips trembled,
but she smiled. "I'll be praying." She watched him go over the side.

Ben dangled in space with the jagged edges of the cliff in front of
his face. Crevices and small caves pocketed the entire escarpment, and
he despaired of finding the right one. He had to try. Fiddling with the
rope, he let himself drop down a few feet, then scanned the surround-
ing area as far as he could see before rappelling a few more feet.

It was taking forever, and he spared a glance upward but could see
nothing. Not even Lani's hand now. A jutting black rock obscured his
vision. All he could do was pray she would be okay until he got back
up there with Meg and Simi. A thought struck him. How could he
get both of them up there, even one at a time? He'd need his hands
and feet to climb, and he would need to hang on to Meg. She
wouldn't have the strength to hold on to him while he made the ardu-
ous climb back to the top. The rope wasn't long enough to get all the
way down, even if he could get them to untie it topside.

He gritted his teeth and kicked out with his feet to rappel again.
Vegetation scratched his arms and face, and he saw nothing at this level
either. Just as he was about to swing out again, he heard something. It

almost sounded like a kitten. Swinging in midair, he hung still and listened. There it was, just to his right. Peering closer, he saw that the opening went back farther than he thought.

He stuck his feet out perpendicular to his body, then, reaching into handholds, crab-crawled his way over to the cave. The rope slipped a little, and he landed hard on the ledge. Pebbles rolled away, but he didn't. He lay panting on the ledge for a moment, then got on his hands and knees and crawled past the ironwood shrubs.

It took several seconds for his eyes to adjust to the dim interior after the brilliant sunshine bouncing off the water. Then his gaze took in the huddled forms lying just inside the cave. They were entwined together as though Simi had been holding Meg and they'd fallen together. Dirt and moisture matted Meg's blond curls, but Ben had never seen a more beautiful sight than when she sat up and reached out her arms.

She began to cry. "Ben," she said.

Tears left streaks on her dirty face. She seemed okay, though. Nothing broken, he decided, running his hands over her limbs.

Meg crawled onto his lap and poked her fingers in his pocket. "Gum?" she asked, her blue eyes full of hope. They lit up when her small fingers found the pack of gum he carried.

While she unwrapped the gum, Ben checked out Simi. His right hand was swollen to nearly twice its size, and he saw the mark where something had stung him. Probably a scorpion, though their sting usually didn't cause such a severe reaction. Simi must be allergic to the venom.

Ben went to the cave opening and glanced out, hoping the helicopters were still there, but they had moved off. He saw a few people moving below, but they were so distant, and the wind so strong, he knew they'd never hear him.

Meg chomped on her gum. She looked up at him. "Eat?" she said hopefully.

"We'll get some food soon." Ben gazed around the cave. His eyes lit on the backpack carrier. Pulling it out of the crevice, he brushed it off, then lifted Meg and deposited her into it. Before he slipped his arms into the carrier, he spied another length of rope. If he tied the two ropes together, maybe he could rappel them all down to safety. It was worth a try.

He grabbed the rope and tied a secure fisherman's knot. Glancing at Simi, he realized the boy was going to be no help. Ben would have to use part of his rope to create a sling. His pocketknife made short work of the cut, then he fashioned a sling and maneuvered Simi's legs into it. With Meg on his back and Simi lashed to his front, their combined weight was probably three hundred pounds, maybe three fifty. As he stepped into space, he could only pray the rope held.

Lani's arm ached from holding it out, so she switched hands. Kato jumped toward her, but she extended the doll again before he could reach her. "Back off!" she said.

He held up his hands. His eyes thinned to a sliver. "Fine. But you're so gonna regret this."

Jerry settled on a large black rock. He leaned back as though he were watching a movie play out.

Lani ignored Kato and fixed her gaze on Jerry. "Ben found your lab. It's all over."

Jerry straightened. "Everything I do is for Blossom." A soft smile lifted his lips. "Blossom is worth every moment of trouble."

"You've found a treatment for Aunt Rina's lupus, haven't you?"

Jerry's eyes widened. "Not just a treatment, a cure. How did you figure it out?"

"I've seen the difference in her lately with the new concoction. When Ben told me about the orchids and the coral, I knew. Aunt Rina doesn't know she's taking an experimental drug, does she?" Lani guessed. "Or that you're selling the ingredients to make more in labs on the mainland."

"She just thinks it's a new supplement that's making her feel better. She'll be so grateful when she knows what I've done for her. And with all the money I'll make, we can travel. I'll buy her anything she wants."

Lani spared a glance over the side. She thought she saw something moving down there, but she didn't dare take her eyes off her adversaries to make sure. Fisher growled. When she refocused on Kato, she found he'd moved three feet closer. "Back away," she said, shaking the doll. He scowled but backed up. Lani stared at Jerry and wondered how she could have missed his obsession.

"The pearl is for Aunt Rina too, isn't it?"

"Of course. I found it in the coral cave a month ago. I'm going to have it made into a ring for her."

"You're going to ask her to marry you."

"I think she'll say yes when I tell her all that I've done for her."

Lani thought back to Jerry's hostility toward Ben's mother. "You hate Nancy, don't you? Is that why you tried to kill Ben?"

Jerry stood and folded his arms across his chest. "Thirty years hooked away from me! Peekaboo knew Blossom was innocent and let her rot in jail for thirty years. Rina and Nancy were together, and Nancy refused to provide an alibi."

"And Ben looks like Ash." Lani tried to remember all she'd heard of that time. "Rina was in love with Ash, and so was Nancy, right? That's what the fight was all about."

"Blossom was Ash's next victim. I couldn't let that happen." Jerry's lip curled. "Ash came back to taunt me. He's always whispering to me. He has to die."

"You already killed him," Lani whispered.

Jerry shrugged. "He deserved it."

"You said you couldn't find Peekaboo. Ethan's death was a godsend for you, wasn't it?" Lani's eyes widened as the truth penetrated. "You killed Ethan to get to her, didn't you?"

"It was the only way to draw her out. She's dead, you know. I doubt anyone will find her body." Jerry's smile was calm and confident.

"But your plans went awry. Ethan stole your pearl."

"He had no right to even touch it! We left him alone to check on a problem with the shipment." Jerry sent a dark glance toward Kato. "It was all his fault."

"Let us go, Jerry," Lani said quietly. "For Aunt Rina's sake. She won't be happy if you hurt me. Just walk away. I'll give you the pearl if you'll just walk away."

Jerry smiled and held out his hand. "That's all I want. Give me the pearl, and I'll let you all live."

Looking into the dark secrets lurking in Jerry's eyes, Lani finally remembered. His eyes were the ones that haunted her sleep, the ones that had promised death. "Why did you kill Pam?" she asked.

"You remember now, do you?" Jerry shrugged. "She was blackmailing me. She wanted marriage and finally figured out I was using her. She had to go."

Once Jerry got his hands on the pearl, she, Ben, and Meg were all dead. Jerry came toward her. "Stay back," Lani shouted. "I'll drop it. They'll find it at the bottom before you can get your sorry self down there." He thought the pearl was still in the doll's dress.

Jerry swore. "My patience is gone, Lani. I want the pearl, but I want my freedom more. The longer we wait here, the more likely your cousin will return with reinforcements." He nodded to Kato. "Take her."

twenty-four

The rope zipped through Ben's hands as he rappelled down the rock face. He moved faster than he liked, but he feared the rope would find their combined weight too much. The knot tied the two strands together a hundred feet above his head, so he couldn't tell if it held strong. He could only pray it did.

Meg's fists curled in his hair, and Simi sagged against him. The poor kid hadn't stirred. Once he got some medical attention, he'd be fine. Ben's hands burned, but he didn't slow. The foam-covered black rocks below grew closer, and he tasted salty spray. He could make out Annie's face as she walked along the shore. No one else wandered the craggy landscape, and Ben wondered where Yoshi had gone.

The rope stopped with a jerk, and Ben dangled six feet above the ground with the children. His wounded shoulder felt as hot as his hands. The line extended only another foot or so. He didn't want to jump the rest of the way, but he had no choice.

The tide threw sea foam over the rocks, then eddied back, leaving the stones slick and treacherous. Landing on his feet might prove to be impossible with his burden. Ben examined the possible landing spots. One rock looked flatter and drier than the others.

Even while he was trying to decide how to get down, the rope sagged, and he caught his breath and looked up. Then they were falling, hitting the rocks in an instant.

He let his knees give to absorb the impact. The soles of his slippers slithered on the wet surface, and he began to teeter on the edge with the water rolling over his feet.

The sliding stopped, and he stood firm on the rock. He breathed a prayer of thanks. Nearly groaning under the pressure on his shoulder, he inched over the slippery rocks to safety. Annie rushed to meet him. He dropped to his knees and drew in giant heaves of oxygen. Spots darkened his vision, and he dimly heard Meg crying but couldn't summon the strength to comfort her.

Annie reached him. "You found her!"

Lani. Ben unfastened Simi, then shrugged out of Meg's carrier and lifted her from it. He handed her to Annie. "Take care of her. Find Yoshi and tell him the killer is Jerry, and he has Lani at the top of the cliff. Simi's got a scorpion sting and needs a doctor."

"I'll take care of it." Annie cradled his niece. "Get going."

Ben staggered to his feet and ran back toward the trail to the top.

Kato sprang toward Lani as if he had been waiting for the signal. She wheeled away and ran toward the trail. Tucking the doll into her shirt as she sprinted for safety, she shot up a bullet prayer for help. Kato's feet pounded behind her, and she could almost feel his hot breath on her neck. Fisher barked ferociously as he ran by her side.

She reached the trail and began to descend. Kato's feet dislodged pebbles, and they rained down on her. Small stones rolled away from her slippers as well, and one flew off. The sharp rocks bit into her bare foot, but she couldn't stop to retrieve her sandal. Then the trail turned sharply, and she couldn't slow in time to navigate the curve.

Her other shoe came off. She went down on one knee, then slid off the trail into the tall vegetation. Brambles whipped her in the face and scratched her bare arms and legs. She hit a boulder, and the jar made her bite down on her tongue. She tasted blood.

There was no time to be winded. She staggered to her feet and plunged down the slope through the bushes. But her fall had slowed her enough that Kato snagged her by the hair and jerked her to a stop. Tears sprang to her eyes from the pain, and she fell backward against him.

Fisher lunged at him, and Kato kicked him. The dog yelped and went down.

"Leave my dog alone!" Lani struggled. He wound one meaty arm around her waist and half dragged, half carried her back up to the trail.

Fisher got up and shook himself, then sprang toward them. "Call off the dog or I'll kill it," Kato snarled.

"Fisher, stay!" Lani stumbled after Kato. Fisher fell back but did not stay.

Jerry stood waiting for them with the gun in his hand. "I'm an expert shot," he warned. "Bring her to the boat. Let's book."

Kato's grip hurt Lani's forearm as he propelled her down toward the bay. She could only pray Yoshi was down there somewhere. She glanced back toward the top of the cliff.

"Forget about your boyfriend. I cut the rope. He and the kids fell to the rocks." Jerry smiled and jabbed her with the gun. "Hand over the doll."

Lani's knees sagged. She shuddered at the thought of Ben and the children lying broken on the rocks. She slowly pulled the doll from her blouse and gave it to him. Fisher pressed close to her leg. "You won't get away with this. God sees, you know. Even if you escape the law, you can't escape his judgment."

Jerry's eyes darkened. "My god can take on yours any day.

Kanaloa has guided and protected me for over thirty years. You can keep your ominous warnings to yourself." He prodded her with the gun. "Bug out."

The cuts Lani had gotten from the brush began to sting and burn. She stumbled along the narrow trail with her head growing lighter and her vision blurring. Had she damaged her sight again? She blinked her eyes, and they cleared. Maybe it was just fatigue and stress.

A few feet from the bottom of the trail, she saw a broad-shouldered figure leap onto the path and start up. Her pulse leapt. Ben was alive! A glad cry sprang to her throat, but she choked it back, not wanting to give away that she'd seen him.

Kato's hold on her arm slackened, and he started toward Ben.

"Hold it, Chrome Dome, we've got control," Jerry said. "I've got the gun." He put it to Lani's head. "Hold it, Ben. I don't know how you managed to survive the fall, but no matter. Move, both of you."

His grip on Lani's arm was nearly as painful as Kato's had been. Kato grabbed Ben's arm and propelled him down the last few feet. They reached the bottom. Lani heard the sound of teenagers laughing out in the water by the monument. Instead of going that direction, Kato and Jerry marched them away toward a deserted canoe landing. A small motorboat floated in the shallow water.

"We'll take this one," Jerry said. "Get in."

His hard hand guided Lani into the boat. Fisher leaped in after her. Kato thrust Ben forward, and he stumbled in as well. Jerry stepped aboard with the gun still trained on Lani. Kato shoved them off, then clambered aboard too. He started the engine, and the little boat navigated the swells out to sea.

Lani sat beside Ben. He took her hand, and she locked her gaze with his. "Is Meg okay? And Simi?" she whispered. Fisher pressed against her leg and whined.

He nodded. "I left them with Annie. She was going to find Yoshi."

"Shut up, both of you," Jerry snapped. He stared intently out over the bow of the boat.

The small craft shuddered at the impact of the waves. Spray flew over the sides and struck Lani in the face. The salt stung her cracked lips, and she licked them and watched Jerry. Maybe they could jump him while his attention was averted. Glancing at Ben, she read the same thought on his face. He dropped her hand, and she saw him tense and lean forward slightly.

Jerry's glance swung back to them, and he brought the gun up. "Easy, meat. Don't make me shoot her."

Ben settled back. "Where are we going?"

"You're about to meet my god," Jerry said, smiling.

Kanaloa was the sea god. Lani's stomach roiled. Sharks often frequented the reef here. Her gaze scanned the waves, but no ominous fin disturbed the rolling whitecaps. Land was only a distant blur, and no other boats plied the waters other than the tiny dots of kayaks in the distance.

"Cut the engine," Jerry ordered. "You have a knife, Kato?" He nodded and pulled out a switchblade. Jerry took it, touched the button, and the blade sprang into view. His fingers caressed the blade. "Nice," he said, handing it back to Kato. "Cut them. I don't care where."

Lani shrank back against the seat as Kato approached with the knife. Ben leaped to his feet and blocked Kato's access to Lani. "You're not touching her," he said. He coiled to spring onto the other man, but Kato reacted with a fast slash at Ben's stomach.

Lani screamed. Ben looked down. A line of red leaked through his shirt. He touched the sticky blood and realized the cut wasn't deep. Kato gave him a shove, and Ben stumbled back over Lani's legs. Teetering on the edge of the boat, he grabbed at Kato's shirt. Kato flung out his arms, and the knife clattered to the deck. As Ben fell into the water, he took Kato with him.

The warm water closed over his head. Ben kicked away from Kato and swam under the boat to the other side. The salt water stung his cut, and he saw trails of red drifting out from his body. The blood would bring the sharks for sure. A hand grabbed his ankle in a hard grip. Ben surfaced, grabbed another lungful of air, then dove down to battle Kato.

Kato caught him in a bear hug that caused air to bubble out through Ben's mouth and nose. He thrashed in the water to escape Kato's grip, but the big man held on. Ben jabbed his fingers in Kato's eyes, and Kato let go. Ben kicked away from him and surfaced again. He grabbed the side of the boat and hauled himself in, where he lay gasping on the deck.

Jerry stood over him. He pointed the gun at Ben's head. "Get up," he said.

Ben staggered to his feet. Jerry raised the gun to his head, and Ben read in his eyes that he intended to pull the trigger. He coiled to jump Jerry, but before he could move, Lani sprang to the deck and grabbed the knife. She jabbed it into Jerry's calf as the gun went off.

Jerry screamed and grabbed at his leg. The bullet whined past Ben's ear. Jerry regained his balance and brought the gun up again. Before he could fire, a snarling bundle of red-gold fur launched into the air. Fisher's teeth clamped down on Jerry's arm. He dropped the gun and staggered back.

The boat rocked, and Ben turned his head to see Kato's fingers latch onto the side. The vessel tipped as Kato began to clamber aboard. The tilt threw Jerry toward the side. He teetered for a moment, then toppled over Kato's head and into the water. Kato lost his grip on the side and disappeared under a wave.

Ben sprang to the side of the boat. "I can't see them."

"Sharks!" Lani pointed at the fins cutting through the water. She leaned over the side. "Where are they? We've got to get them out of the water."

Shark fins circled the boat. Kato came up and began to thrash toward the boat.

"Here!" Ben shouted, holding out his hand.

Kato splashed faster, but he was still several feet from the boat when he was jerked under the water.

A hand slapped the side of the boat, and Jerry's face appeared above the waves. "Help me," he gasped.

Ben grabbed for his hand to haul him aboard, but Jerry's eyes widened. He gave one last gasp, then was pulled under. The water boiled with blood and bubbles. Lani cried out, and Ben put his arm around her.

She buried her face in his chest. "It was so horrible," she sobbed.

He smoothed her hair and held her close. "It's over now. We're safe. Meg and Simi are okay too."

She turned to face him fully. Both arms wound around his waist, and she burrowed closer to him. Her shoulders heaved. He rubbed her back. "Shh, it's okay."

Lani lifted her head and gazed up into his eyes. Her lips trembled, and her eyes were luminous with tears. His arms tightened around her. "I almost lost you," he whispered. He bent his head and kissed her. Her lips were cool, but they warmed quickly beneath his.

Her fingers clung to his wet shirt, and she kissed him back with a tenderness that grew in passion.

When he broke the kiss and lifted his head, her eyes were still closed. She touched her lips with the fingers of her right hand. He gathered her against his chest and listened to the roar of the approaching Coast Guard boat.

twenty-five

There hadn't been time to talk. The Coast Guard boat arrived and took them aboard while seamen cruised in small crafts for the remains of Jerry and Kato. Nothing surfaced, just as Lani expected. The "god" Jerry had served had turned on him in the end.

Lani realized she was touching her lips again. They still tingled from the passion in Ben's kiss. Loving him was useless, though. He knew her past. A man like him would never want someone like her, and he would come to his senses once the stress of this day was over. She was soiled goods. He took her hand in the back of Yoshi's squad car, but she pulled away and sat looking at the passing landscape. She would never be good enough for Ben, so it was useless to allow him to dig more deeply under her skin.

Yoshi stopped the car in front of her aunt's house. "I need to know everything," he said. "Are you up to talking about it?"

"Sure," Ben said.

"I guess," Lani said. They got out of the car, and Meg came running from the house.

"Up," she demanded, clinging to Ben's leg.

He lifted her in his arms, and she stuck her fingers in his mouth. "Gum?"

"No gum," he mumbled.

Lani's vision blurred with tears at the sight of the toddler. "Meggie, you okay?"

"'Kay," Meg said. She reached for Lani.

Lani took her in her arms and snuggled her close. Meg's breath eased over the skin of Lani's neck. Her curls were damp, and she smelled like baby shampoo and soap. "Thank God you're okay, Meggie."

"Eat?" Meg suggested.

Rina came out the door. "I just fed you, you little scamp. You can't be hungry."

"Hungry," Meg agreed. She wiggled to be let down. She ran to Rina, who lifted her and carried her back to the house.

Ben and Lani followed with Yoshi. Yoshi pointed to the sofa. "Sit and spill it," he said.

"I think I should be in on this discussion," Rina said, standing in the doorway with Meg in her arms. "Let me put her down for a nap."

Rina took Meg down the hall to her bedroom. They sat in silence until she returned. Lani was too tired to think. She hadn't gotten any sleep last night—none of them had—and the day's traumatic events had drained her even more. She supposed Ben and Yoshi were just as exhausted. Ben had a tired droop to his mouth. She found her gaze lingering there. He caught her looking, and her cheeks grew hot.

Rina rejoined them. She sank into the rocker by the window. Her eyes were shadowed with fatigue, and she looked pale.

"Where's Simi?" Lani asked.

"In the hospital," Ben said. "He was suffering from a reaction to a scorpion bite, and his dehydration made it worse. He's undernourished as well, and that didn't help. Meg handled the whole ordeal better."

"What will happen to him?" Lani asked.

"Don't know. We're checking on it." Ben sat back in a chair and blew his breath out.

Yoshi stared at Lani. "Tell me what happened out there."

Lani sighed. "It's a long story."

"It's my lupus, isn't it?" Rina asked with a calm note to her voice.

Lani nodded. "Partly. That's the reason for the coral and orchid smuggling. He developed a compound that he called a cure."

"It wasn't, not really," Rina said. "Whenever I quit taking it, I'd feel bad again."

"He was obsessed with you," Ben said.

Rina bit her lip. "He was my friend, always," she said. "I knew he was always a little jealous of the men in my life, or any of my friends for that matter. He didn't like how close Josie and I are. When I went to prison, he went to school nearby, got his medical degree, and set up his practice. He brought me money on every visit."

"You met at Taylor Camp?" Yoshi asked.

Rina nodded. "We became close from the start. Jerry was always a little odd, but I liked him."

"How did Ethan's death tie in?" Yoshi asked. "And what about the way his place was ransacked? And Meg? I still have a million questions."

"He killed Ethan to flush out Nancy," Lani said. "He'd tried to find Ben's mom for years and didn't realize Ethan was her son until he met Ben and saw the resemblance to someone from Taylor Camp named Ash. He'd killed him and thought Ben was Ash resurrected."

Rina gasped and put her hand to her mouth. "He killed Ash?"

Lani nodded. "And he wanted to punish Nancy for letting you go to prison when she could have given you an alibi."

"I saw Natalie's parents at the orchid farm. Pick them up for questioning. They're involved. I'm sure they knew about the pearl," Ben said.

"What pearl?" Rina asked.

"Jerry found a pearl in a coral cave that he intended to give to you," Lani explained. "When he realized Ethan had stolen it, he had Kato search for it." Lani remembered what Jerry had said about Nancy. Ben needed to know the truth. She took his hand where he sat beside her on the sofa. "Jerry said he killed your mother, Ben. And that her body would never be found."

His eyes widened, and he sagged back against the sofa. "No," he said. "That can't be true. I never—" He gulped and stood. He rushed to the door.

Lani remembered how she felt the day her own mother never came home. She jumped up and hurried after him. Fisher followed her. When she stepped outside, she saw him mounting his bike.

"Wait, I'm coming too," she called. She ran to join him.

He jerked when she touched his shoulder, then turned and pulled her into his arms.

"I didn't think it would hit me like this," he whispered in a choked voice. "She never loved me."

She clutched him tightly and wished she could share the hurt. "Sometimes the relationships that are the most strained are the hardest to lose. You know there's no second chance." The words *I love you* hovered on her tongue, sweet and bitter at the same time. Her love might feel cheap to him. Her past might leach any comfort out of her words.

He nodded against the top of her head. His lips trailed across her hair and down to her forehead, then lingered along her cheek and finally found her mouth. His kiss held a tenderness she craved. She wrapped her arms around his neck and plunged with him into a maelstrom of emotion far above anything she'd ever felt. While she'd thought herself in love a time or two, she knew now her heart had never been touched. Ben owned it.

His hand became tangled in her hair, and his kiss deepened with promise and passion as pure and intoxicating as the flowers over their heads. Lani drowned in his kiss, reveling in the touch of his lips, the whisper of his breath on her face. She felt bereft when he pulled away, and she tried to burrow closer.

He cupped her face in his hands. "I love you, Lani." His gaze searched hers, and he nodded finally, a slight smile curving his lips as if he'd found what he was looking for.

"It was you," she whispered. "You were the man who changed my life. I hated you for a while."

His tender smile broadened. "I'm the one who came to you and told you that Ethan was married," he said. "Is that what you're talking about?"

She nodded. "My life changed that day. I saw myself for what I really was, and I didn't like the picture. It set me on the path to find Jesus."

His eyes lit. "I didn't know. I'm glad I had a part in that." He moved to take her in his arms again, but she stepped back.

"Are you sure you can love a girl with a past like mine?"

"Your past is gone. You're free from it, Lani. It's buried in the sea. You're the woman I want to marry. I want you to help me raise Meg. I love you."

How could she believe it? "What happens when I'm home late from shopping or you don't know where I am? You'll remember what I was and wonder. Anyone would."

"I won't," he said. "I know your heart, Lani. Say it." His eyes crinkled at the corners as his smile widened.

She swallowed past the words clogging her throat. "I love you," she whispered.

He scooped her up in his arms and twirled her around. "I knew it," he crowed.

"Stop—your shoulder!"

"You don't weigh anything," he scoffed. He set her down and kissed her thoroughly.

Her bones dissolved, and her breath whispered away by the time he released her. "Are you sure you want to trust me with Meg?" she asked.

"I wouldn't trust her with any other mother," he said. "I want some of our own too."

Her cheeks warmed under his smile. "I love kids," she said.

He folded her in his arms again. "You're the only family I have now," he whispered.

Snuggled next to his chest, Lani couldn't think of a better future than one shared with Ben. "Leilani Mahoney has a nice ring to it," she said, smiling into his eyes.

His gaze sobered. "I'll do anything to make you happy, Lani."

Tears stung her eyes. A smile blossomed. "There's just one thing I really want before I promise to marry you," she said. "No, wait, two things."

His eyes crinkled with laughter. "And they would be?"

She glanced at Fisher pressing against her leg. "You have to promise I can have Fisher. He's mine."

His chuckle came quickly. "Don't you know even ex-cops have to report extortion?"

She gave a mock gasp and put her hand over her heart. "It will be my engagement gift. I won't ask for another thing."

He bent his head to brush his lips against hers. "You drive a hard bargain, sweet girl," he whispered. "But I think I can agree to that condition. What else?"

"I want to ride away from our wedding on your Harley."

He gave a shout of laughter and swept her into his arms. "I suppose that's with Fisher too?"

"Of course," she said, smiling up into his face. "Whither thou goest, I goest, and so does my dog."

"A fair deal," he agreed as his lips met hers.

epilogue

Amy Hanaiali'i Gilliom's voice sang "Aloha No Kalakaua" from the speakers strewn around the garden. Hawaiian prints covered the tables, and long leis of leaves, ferns, and flowers ran down the middle of the tables. Tantalizing aromas of chicken and pork wafted from the imu, and Lani's mouth watered. She realized she'd skipped lunch.

She lifted the train of her wedding dress and ran lightly over the sand toward where her bridesmaids stood under the arch awaiting the start of the wedding. Tiki torches enlightened the beach, and masses of orchids, ginger, and plumeria infused the air with fragrance. Sunset illuminated the water and beach with a pink and orange glow. It was a perfect night and a perfect setting for her wedding.

Lani reached her sister. "Sorry I'm late. I wanted to knock Ben sideways."

Annie squeezed her hand. "You will."

Her father cleared his throat. He'd flown in the day before, but they'd hardly spoken other than during the rehearsal. "You look very beautiful, my daughter. I'm proud of you."

She hugged her dad and forced back her tears. There was room in her heart to forgive him his failures. "Thank you, Father."

Fawn hugged her. "Let's get you guys hitched!" She and Annie were dressed in traditional *holokus*, seamed, loose-fitting dresses with yokes. The bright aloha patterns glowed in the tiki lights.

Lani's stomach fluttered as the music ended and drums took over. Mano stepped to the front and blew the conch shell three times. Lani's pulse kicked up at the melodious sound. Excitement surged through the audience as well. She smiled at her aunt, who sat with her head held high. Annie winked at Lani as she started out. Annie and Fawn proceeded down to join her brother, Tomi, and Mano under the gazebo. The men wore aloha shirts that matched the bridesmaid dresses over white pants and maile leis.

Lani had eyes for no one but Ben, looking so handsome in his white pants and loose-fitting shirt. Meg looked darling in her white dress as she dropped orchid petals along the path. She reached her uncle and grabbed his legs. "Gum!" she demanded in a loud voice. Laughter rippled through the gathering.

Ben slipped Meg a piece of gum and turned to catch Lani's eye. As her father walked her down the path that led to Ben's side, her heart felt so full she wanted to burst into song. Ben's gaze never left her face. She drank in the love in his eyes, the tender smile on his face. He took her hand when she reached his side.

The warm pressure of his fingers steadied her. With her eyes fixed on his, she barely noticed her father's words or what the minister said. She repeated her vows in a daze of love and happiness.

Then Ben lifted her veil, and they shared their first sweet kiss as man and wife. She clung to him, nearly drunk with the scent of him, the amazing devotion in his eyes. The crowd shouted when Ben finally let her go, and Lani buried her face in his chest.

"Let's party!" Ben shouted. He swept her into his arms and whirled her around. Fisher ran around them barking and giving his happy whine.

"Party!" Meg said. Her uncle swooped her up to join Lani in his arms.

By the time everyone had hugged and congratulated them, the moon was out, casting a romantic glow over the reception. The music strummed out over the water. Tyrone appeared with his dog, Ranger. He slapped Ben on the back. "I wouldn't say the best man won, but I'm happy for you, Ben. Sort of." He grinned and grabbed Ben's hand. "You take good care of her."

"You can count on it," Ben said.

Tyrone walked away, and Lani squeezed Ben's hand. "I'm ready for that bike ride," she told him.

"There's one more surprise," he whispered. He scooped up Meg, then motioned to Simi, who had been standing along the sidelines.

Simi fell into step with her. They were trying to reach his parents, but so far the red tape had been overwhelming. He smiled shyly when he reached Lani's side. Her gaze went to his hand. "Looks like it's back to normal."

He nodded and flexed it. "No hurt." His shy gaze met hers. "You very pretty, Miss Lani."

She curtseyed. "Thank you, Simi. Please dance with me later."

"Come with me," Ben said. "You too, Simi." He took her hand and led her toward the parking lot.

"What on earth?"

"You'll see," he said with a mysterious smile.

A blue Taurus pulled up as they reached the lot. Five people got out. Arlo exited the driver's side. A Polynesian man, short and stocky, helped a woman out of the backseat and held her hand solicitously. Two children came behind them. The little boy looked like a younger version of Simi, and the little girl held his hand and scurried as fast as her short, plump legs would carry her.

Lani stopped and put her hand to her mouth. Simi hadn't seen them yet. "Simi, look," she said.

Then the little girl called to him. "Simi!" Her small legs pumped, and she jerked her hand out of her brother's and ran toward Simi.

Simi turned at her voice. The look in his eyes would be a treasure Lani knew she would take out often and remember. "Go," she told him.

Tears sprang to Simi's eyes as he started forward. *"Fa'e! Tamai!"* He shouted out the Tongan words for "Mother" and "Father." *"Fetina!"* He scooped up his baby sister. She wrapped thin arms around his neck and kissed his cheek over and over.

His parents and brother reached him. They fell into one another's arms, and tears flowed. "How?" Simi asked, turning to Ben.

"Rina is giving your father a job in the coffee business. She's lost quite a bit of help. There's a small cottage on the property where you can all live."

"It is too much." Simi's tears came again. "Thank you." He turned to Lani. "And thank you, Miss Lani. I never forget you. And Meg."

"You're family now," Lani said, kissing his cheek. She, Ben, and Meg moved away to let the little family enjoy their reunion in private. Ben's fingers gripped hers tightly as they strolled the perimeter of the laughing crowd.

A wind stirred and blew through the gathering. Lani's fingers tightened on Ben's, and her eyes blurred with tears. Her heart throbbed with a painful joy. Tradition said that wind at a wedding was the loved ones who had gone on to heaven rejoicing with the family. Lani wanted to believe her mother was approving Lani's love for Ben. From the crowd, Annie glanced her way and smiled. It was affirmation to Lani that her mother's breath of love was on her life.

"Your mother?" Ben whispered.

He always seemed to know her thoughts. She nodded. God's aloha seemed to hover in the air, to whisper through her heart. Looking into Ben's smiling eyes, she felt God's blessing on their future. And she was content to leave it in his hands.

"I'm ready for that bike ride," she said.

"Me too." He led her to the bike with the sidecar attached. Annie ran to take Meg from her arms, and the guests gathered around to watch their departure. Fisher hopped into the sidecar. Lani had asked for special hooks to be added when her dress was altered so she could gather it up to ride safely. She hooked up the bustle and gathered the folds of the dress together, then hopped on the bike.

She put one arm around Ben and let go of her veil with the other as the bike sped away. She was free to love, free to laugh, free to leave her past buried in the sea. And God smiled.

acknowledgments

$\mathscr{H}$ave I mentioned I *love* my life? Who would have thought God would take a simple country gal and give her the opportunity to work with my wonderful family at WestBow? I love them and appreciate them so much. Mahalo to my priceless editor Ami McConnell. You have such a gift for story. I'm in awe of the things you pull out of my books. Mahalo to Allen Arnold, publisher of WestBow. Your vision and passion drive us all to bigger and better things. Mahalo to Jennifer Deshler. Your creativity has to be experienced to be believed, and I love your belief in my books. Mahalo to Natalie Hanemann. You are a light in my day. Mahalo to Mark Ross and Belinda Bass for my awesome covers! You are the best in the business! Mahalo to my fellow Hoosier Lisa Young, Allen's fabulous assistant. You smooth all the bumps in the road. And a big mahalo to my freelance editor Erin Healy. Girl, you make me look so good! The insight and polish you bring to my books can't be repaid with money.

Mahalo to my agent and friend, Karen Solem. I thank God every day that he put you in my life!

I'm an e-mail junkie. E-mail me at colleen@colleencoble.com and you'll likely get a response back in minutes. My fellow Girls Write Out bloggers keep me sane and make the journey worth the work. Mahalo to my buddies Kristin Billerbeck, Diann Hunt, and Denise Hunter. Love you, girls!

A special mahalo to my friend Robin Miller. Your constant encouragement and belief in me bolsters me on the days when I think I should toss everything I've written. Mahalo for reading the manuscript and pointing out where it stunk. And a big mahalo to Malia Spencer, my Hawaiian expert who has the good fortune to live in the islands. She catches the things only a Hawaii resident would know.

And always my very special mahalo to my family. To my wonderful husband, Dave: there has never been a more supportive husband than you. (Check out the T-shirt he bought with my face and the cover of *Alaska Twilight* on it at www.girlswriteout. blogspot.com). My son and daughter by marriage, Dave and Donna Coble, and my baby girl, Kara Coble, are part of everything I do. Don't you just love the way your activities make it into my books? (Scuba; Harleys; tall, curly-headed guys; strong and beautiful women!) That's what moms do. Love you guys.

And all my love and thanks to Jesus, who gives me wings.

Midnight Sea Reading Group Guide

What do you think would be the worst thing about being blind?

Ben struggled with guilt. Why is guilt such an insidious weed in our lives? How do we eradicate it? Or can we?

Did Ben do the right thing when he found Meg hungry and wet, and her parents drunk? Why or why not?

Is there anyone in your life who struggles with growing up and being responsible? Is there anything you can do to help?

Lani had a past that shamed her. Why is it so hard to live down our past mistakes?

Were you a child of the hippie era? Do you still carry some attitudes left over from the way you grew up, like Rina and her friends? If so, are they helpful or harmful?

For a time, Lani refused to accept her blindness. What have you refused to accept in your life? Should you accept it?

Ben's career path changed when his friend was blinded. Did he over-react or was it meant to be that way?

One of the themes of the book is finding freedom from our past. Discuss some ways to do that.

Ben rejected the idea of letting Meg's grandparents raise her. How did you feel about this? Should he have been more willing to turn her over? What if he hadn't known anything negative about them? Would that have changed how you feel?

How do you feel about genetically engineered plants? Was Rina over-reacting?

Thresh's obsession with Rina consumed his life. Has love ever made you do something that surprised you?

An Interview
with the Author

Q: *Midnight Sea* is a thrilling, beautiful story—a real page-turner. Can you tell us what inspired you to write it?

A: I was legally blind before LASIK—I couldn't even see the big *E* on the board. My sight has always been a precious thing, especially since I love to read. And trust can be hard for all of us. When I was thinking out this story, I wondered what event could come into my life that would rock my world the most and make me question everything. Losing my sight came to mind immediately, and I began to think about how hard it would be—how it would affect everything about my life. I just had to explore that theme in fiction. Incidentally, it's great to be able to see the clock in the night now since my LASIK surgery. I felt like Lani after her sight came back.

Q: Leilani has to wrestle with her disability over the course of the novel. Was it tough to write about a blind character?

A: It was very tough. I did things like move around my house blindfolded. One afternoon I sat in my chair with my eyes closed and just listened to what was going on outside my window—trying to see if I could tell what vehicle was rolling past and the age of the kids who were laughing as they walked home from school. The experience left me filled with admiration for those who live with a disability every day.

Q: Your protagonists often struggle with physical difficulties of one nature or another. Tell us a little about that.

A: I've often seen the way people ignore disabled people—almost as though they're nonpersons. Not only do they struggle with their disability, but they fight against preconceived ideas. Sometimes people won't even *look* at someone in a wheelchair. I like to be a little light that illuminates their struggles in some way. We have a man in our church, Terry Carpenter, who was paralyzed in a car accident. All Christians should be as sold out for God as he is! He's often the inspiration for the tenaciousness of my characters who struggle with some kind of problem.

Q: I had no idea who the killer was. I thought I had it figured out several times, but then my idea would dead-end. How do you do it?

A: I figure out who the killer is, then layer in other people who could do it too. I sprinkle red herrings in places and try to lead my reader away from guessing the real killer. I also have some great readers who point out if the killer is too obvious, and they make me fix it. And the final wall of defense against predictability comes with my fabulous editors, Ami McConnell and Erin Healy. Editors are the unsung heroes of the publishing world. A book can only be good with great editing!

Q: How does Kona coffee compare to a run-of-the-mill cup o' joe? Does it taste better when you drink it in Hawaii?

A: I'm a coffee lover. My husband calls me an addict, and I'm sad to say he's right. I love trying new coffees, the deeper and richer the better. You haven't lived until you've had pure Kona coffee. Not a blend, but 100 percent Kona. It doesn't have a hint of acidity. It's so smooth and wonderful. And *everything* is better when you're actually in Hawai'i!

Q: What impressed you most about your visits to Hawaiian coffee plantations and roasters?

A: I love learning about my passions, and coffee definitely qualifies. I visited coffee farms on the Big Island and also one on Kaua'i. I also visited several roasters. The Hawai'ian growers are totally committed to quality. All of the farms offered sample pots of different blends to try. A girl can overdose in places like that! Also, the coffee trees were beautiful. Shiny red berries decorated vibrant green leaves. I could have gawked for hours. But there was coffee to drink inside, so I managed to tear myself away.

Q: So how many cups did you drink while writing *Midnight Sea*?

A: Um, too many to count. And I tried many different varieties in an attempt to taste the different qualities you're supposed to taste.

Q: Why was it important to Rina to grow only organic beans?

A: I'm an organic nut myself. Some of my passions always spill over to my books. Rina shares some of my own beliefs about the danger of genetically engineered plants. If you read up on it, some of the facts are scary. You might check out these Web sites for more information: http://www.safe-food.org/ and http://www.holisticmed.com/ge/.

Q: How did you dream up the orchid-and-coral concoction that Jerry develops to treat Rina's lupus?

A: I did some research on medicinal qualities of both. Many of the drugs developed these days have a plant base, and orchids have been used for some time. The dried roots, for example, have been used to treat depression and as a stimulant. Coral has some amazing medicinal properties and is the base of an AIDS drug. AIDS affects the immune system, as does lupus. When I read that the tubers in the center of the orchid could be used to treat rheumatism—which is related to lupus—I was inspired to combine it with the coral for a more powerful treatment. Wouldn't it be a hoot if scientists actually found it works?

Q: How have you benefited from homeopathic approaches to your personal health habits?

A: I think everyone needs to take charge of her health. Our food is so much more processed today. Much of the nutrition has been lost, with devastating results that we try to treat with synthetic drugs. We need to go back to the basics with our health. I read everything I can on health issues that affect me. I was allergic to everything under the sun until I found a new alternative treatment called NAET that helped tremendously. And I take little homeopathic drops all the time for different things. I'm in good company—even the Queen of England uses homeopathy!

Q: What is it about Harleys that helped Ben to get through his personal crises?

A: As one who's been a scaredy-cat about bikes since an accident at sixteen, I'm clueless. But I look at my son, who adores his new Harley, and see his joy in the freedom of the road. Ben could forget his troubles and take in the fragrance of the breeze, the beauty of the day. On a bike, you feel nimble and in control of that big motor throbbing along the highway. You're not tethered to anything and can go places a car can't navigate. Hmm, it's almost enough to make me want to buy one.

Q: So if your temptation ever gives way to reality, which model would you buy?

A: My son has been trying to talk us into a touring bike. It's bigger and has lots of padding. It's supposed to be comfortable. (My son knows his mother well.) But I'm holding out for one that's been modified to be a tricycle. I'd be hard-pressed to wreck something like that.

Q: Have you ever ridden a Harley blindfolded? (As a passenger, of course!)

A: Does closing my eyes and screaming at the top of my lungs count? I closed my eyes when my son took me for a ride just to see how it felt. Terrifying! I don't know why Lani likes it.

Q: How do a blind person's senses compensate for lack of sight? How long does it take new sensitivities to fully develop?

A: A newly blind person has to learn to get in tune with his other senses. Just as Ben told Lani to reach out and listen to the way the waves hit the shore and the rocks, to feel the direction of the wind, a blind person begins to pay attention to the environment in a way he's never had to do before. It can begin right away with the person just becoming attuned to what he's hearing, smelling, and touching, but it develops with practice.

Q: After her injury, Lani must learn her limitations *and* discover new ways to pursue her dream of being a landscaper. Why did you want Lani's success to happen before she recovered her sight?

A: It was important to me to have Lani overcome her adversity. We all experience hard things in life. We can choose to let them defeat us, or we can find a way over, under, or around the challenge. Nothing can defeat us if we are determined!

Q: Lani has a terrible time forgiving herself for her past. Why do you think self-forgiveness is so hard for women, even when we know God and our loved ones have forgiven us?

A: We women think we need to be all things to the people we love— superwoman. Society holds us up to high standards too. We have to be beautiful, poised, and strong, and we have to excel at our jobs. Of course we're going to fail! We need to get past what others expect to what God expects. Inner strength and beauty are much more important in the eternal scheme of things.

Q: As I read the novel, I felt as if I were actually *in* Hawaii. You must do a great deal of research to immerse readers so in the setting.

A: I do. I could spend months on research if time would permit. And one thing many writers don't realize is how much research can help you with your plot. I love to find little tidbits of information about history or culture that I can weave into the story. I want the reader to come away feeling like they've been on a trip to that location, and even more important, I want that story to work only in that locale. I don't want to write a book where you could plop that story down somewhere else and it could function just as well. The sights, sounds, and smells of a place are so important to anchor the story.

Q: I loved Fisher, the dog Lani becomes attached to over the course of the novel. I'll bet you're a dog person—is that right?

A: Oh, I am. We had wiener dogs when I was growing up, and I love animals. My daughter got a new golden retriever this spring, and for the first time, I realized what wonderful dogs goldens are. I just had to write one into my story! Parker is amazing. Okay, I'm gushing like a grandmother so I'd better stop. But dogs bring so much to our lives. I think of them as a little bit like God in their unconditional love.

Q: Lani struggles hard to change her life. Did this have any personal significance?

A: Grace is a huge theme to me. I'm grateful every day of my life for the grace God gives me, the way he doesn't hold my past mistakes against me. People usually aren't that generous. We remember every transgression, every hurt. I wanted to show how important it is for the rest of us to remember that we are all fallen souls in need of support and forgiveness. If we could each extend even a fraction of the grace God gives us, the world would be a better place.

Abomination

Coming Summer 2007

"These six things the LORD hates, yes, seven are an abomination to Him: A proud look, a lying tongue, hands that shed innocent blood, a heart that devises wicked plans, feet that are swift in running to evil, a false witness who speaks lies, and one who sows discord among brethren" (Proverbs 6: 16-19).

Experience this ground-breaking novel by award-winning author Colleen Coble.

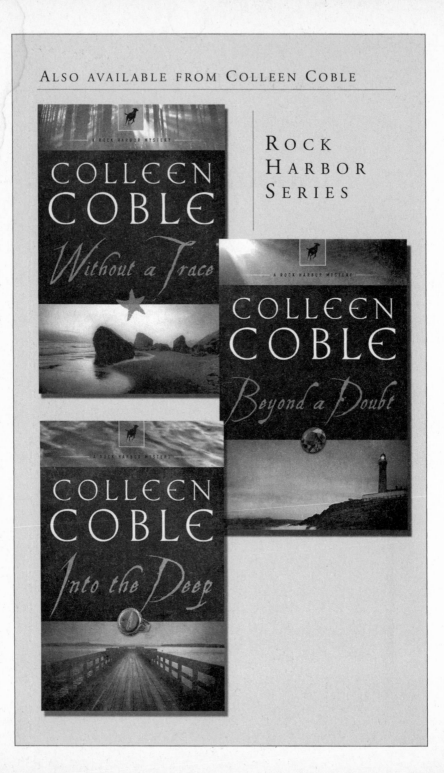

WOMEN OF FAITH

Amazing Freedom

2007

"So if the Son makes you free, you will be truly free." – John 8:36

We often catch *GLIMPSES OF FREEDOM* but what about the *promise* of being truly free? That's *AMAZING!*
Women of Faith...as always, *FRESH, FABULOUS,* and *FUN-LOVING!*

2007 Conference Schedule*

March 15 - 17 San Antonio, TX	July 13 - 14 Washington, DC	September 28 - 29 Houston, TX
April 13 - 14 Little Rock, AR	July 20 - 21 Chicago, IL	October 5 - 6 San Jose, CA
April 20 - 21 Des Moines, IA	July 27 - 28 Boston, MA	October 12 - 13 Portland, OR
April 27 - 28 Columbus, OH	August 3 - 4 Ft. Wayne, IN	October 19 - 20 St. Paul, MN
May 18 - 19 Billings, MT	August 10 - 11 Atlanta, GA	October 26 - 27 Charlotte, NC
June 1 - 2 Rochester, NY	August 17 - 18 Calgary, AB Canada	November 2 - 3 Oklahoma City, OK
June 8 - 9 Ft. Lauderdale, FL	August 24 - 25 Dallas, TX	November 9 - 10 Tampa, FL
June 15 - 16 St. Louis, MO	September 7 - 8 Anaheim, CA	November 16 - 17 Phoenix, AZ**
June 22 - 23 Cleveland, OH	September 14 - 15 Philadelphia, PA	**There will be no Pre-Conference in Phoenix.
June 29 - 30 Seattle, WA	September 21 - 22 Denver, CO	

FOR MORE INFORMATION CALL **888-49-FAITH**
OR VISIT **WOMENOFFAITH.COM**
*Dates, Time, Location and special guests are subject to change.
Women of Faith is a ministry division of Thomas Nelson Publishers.

Women of Faith Fiction

ANGELA HUNT

The Note

a story of second chances

WOMEN of FAITH
FICTION

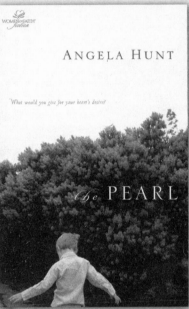

WOMEN of FAITH
fiction

ANGELA HUNT

What would you give for your heart's desire?

the PEARL

THE STORY of a PAST REDEEMED

THE DEBT

A Novel

ANGELA HUNT

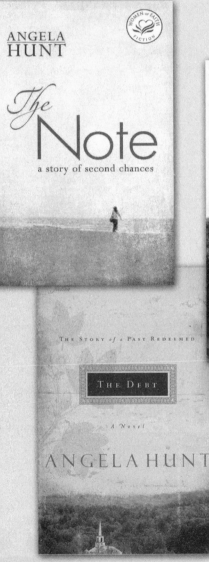

Women of Faith has shared the message of hope and grace with millions of women across the country through conferences and resources. When you see the words "Women of Faith Fiction" on a novel, you're guaranteed a reading experience that will capture your imagination and inspire your faith.

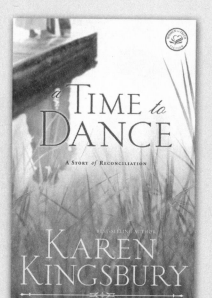

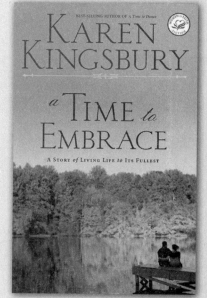